'A hard-hitting and suspenseful political/war/crime/domestic thriller/drama that had my little grey cells and my heart working overtime' From Belgium with Booklove

PRAISE FOR SARAH SULTOON

WINNER of the Crime Fiction Lover Best Debut Award
LONGLISTED for the CWA John Creasey (New Blood) Dagger

'You won't read another book like this in 2022! Raw, authentic, powerful ... you won't see the end coming!' E C Scullion

'As searingly an authentic thriller as you are likely to read ... Passionate, disturbing storytelling at its best' James Brabazon

'Brilliantly conveys both the exhilaration and the unspeakable horror of life on the international news frontline' Jo Turner

'Authentic, provocative and terrifyingly relevant. It will stay with you' Will Carver

'Sensitive handling, tight plotting and authentic storytelling make for a compelling read' Adam Hamdy

'A taut and thought-provoking book that's all the more unnerving for how much it echoes the headlines in real life' *CultureFly*

'A powerful, compelling read that doesn't shy away from some upsetting truths' Fanny Blake

'Tautly written and compelling, not afraid to shine a spotlight on the darker forces at work in society' Rupert Wallis

'A gripping, dark thriller' Geoff Hill, ITV

'A stunning debut ... a powerhouse writer' Jo Spain

'So authentic and exhilarating ... breathtaking pace and relentless ingenuity' Nick Paton Walsh, CNN

'My heart was racing ... fiction to thrill even the most hard-core adrenaline junkies' Diana Magnay, Sky News

DIRT

ABOUT THE AUTHOR

Sarah Sultoon is a journalist and writer, whose work as an international news executive at CNN has taken her all over the world, from the seats of power in both Westminster and Washington to the frontlines of Iraq and Afghanistan. She has extensive experience in conflict zones, winning three Peabody awards for her work on the war in Syria, an Emmy for her contribution to the coverage of Europe's migrant crisis in 2015, and a number of Royal Television Society gongs. As passionate about fiction as nonfiction, she completed a Masters of Studies in Creative Writing at the University of Cambridge, adding to an undergraduate language degree in French and Spanish, and Masters of Philosophy in History, Film and Television. When not reading or writing she can usually be found somewhere outside, either running, swimming or throwing a ball for her three children and dog while she imagines what might happen if...

Her debut thriller, *The Source*, was a Capital Crime Book Club pick, won the Crime Fiction Lover Best Debut Award, was nominated for the CWA's New Blood Dagger, was a number one bestseller on Kindle and is currently in production with Lime Pictures. It was followed by the critically acclaimed *The Shot*. Follow Sarah on Twitter @SultoonSarah.

Also by Sarah Sultoon and available from Orenda Books
The Source
The Shot

DIRT

Sarah Sultoon

**ORENDA
BOOKS**

Orenda Books
16 Carson Road
West Dulwich
London SE21 8HU
www.orendabooks.co.uk

First published in the United Kingdom by Orenda Books, 2023

A catalogue record for this book is available from the British Library.

ISBN 978-1-914585-46-3
eISBN 978-1-914585-47-0

Typeset in Garamond by typesetter.org.uk

Printed and bound by CPI Group (UK) Ltd, Croydon CR0 4YY

For sales and distribution, please contact info@orendabooks.co.uk

For Jonny, Samantha, Max and Clara

And Michelle, Joseph and Lola

Prologue

The chickens were used to pecking. Especially in chicken house number one. It was the most overcrowded of all the warehouses, deliberately constructed on the fringe of the kibbutz to keep the worst of the smell at bay. But wasn't that of the *refet*, the cowshed, stationed a little further up the hill, arguably far worse when the wind blew in a certain direction?

It was a topic of constant debate around the communal tables in the kibbutz dining room. You were either inherently in favour of chicken or beef. And most people's choice had nothing to do with the smell.

The truth of it was that most small farming communities really needed to concentrate on doing one thing well. Put all their eggs in one basket, if you'll pardon the pun. But the kibbutz is a subsistence farm. A communal enterprise – appealing to both the heads and hearts of its members. So it needs to be all things to all people to ensure it survives. At least, it needs to appear that way.

Those chickens in house number one had to work for their feed. There was always plenty of it, spread low amid the sawdust, away from the pens at the back where they would settle to lay their eggs. But house number one was overcrowded for a reason – the highest ceiling meant the best aerial playground, the loftiest beams on which to roost. Essential for birds that can't fly very far. It didn't matter that it was noisiest – especially with missiles flying overhead from the Lebanese border a few hundred yards away. It didn't matter that it was the dirtiest, covered in the inevitable layers of grime that accompany too many animals in too small of a space.

House number one had the most real estate. As with all animals, it was about ownership. The fight just made the territory in question seem like a more valuable prize.

And so the chickens gravitated to it, skittering across the gravel courtyard between the overflow houses two and three, to lay claim to a little patch of melee. These were the chickens that got fatter faster, laid the most eggs, and met their end in the kitchen first.

Then in flocked the next round of chickens. So much for territorial supremacy.

Even for chickens as practised as these, today there was a feast of irregular proportions. The body steamed gently in the heat as the birds pecked their way around it, the fetid smell of chicken feed mingling with the sulphurous whiff of smashed eggs. The pecking became indecorous as the hardest-working chicken, a champion amongst fowl, found an eyeball. Then another. The used condom, an equally irregular delicacy dropped amongst the sawdust, swiftly filleted and discarded.

Still the chickens pecked, pecked and pecked themselves sick.

By the time the body was found, it was unrecognisable, but there was no mistaking who it was.

And the chickens, they knew what it had been hiding, but had so effectively disposed of the evidence, almost no one would ever understand.

Chapter One
Wednesday, 17 April, 1996

Just before dawn

Lola shades her eyes, chasing any shadows further down the path. The sun is just beginning its aggressive climb over the hills to the east, shooting watercolours through the sky above the sea behind her. The Mediterranean is all flirtatious languor, despite the tensions a few degrees further north, where Israel's border with Lebanon slopes abruptly beyond the kibbutz's perimeter fence.

To the uneducated eye, it might seem as if the territory changes hands just past those sharp spikes of razor wire. As if it really is as simple as tracing out a line in the sand. When Lola first arrived, those metal loops and curls seemed to gleam far too malevolently. All the guard posts, all the hardware, it all felt too conspicuous and overblown. Wasn't the kibbutz just a communal farm? A much-revered socialist idyll that didn't exist anywhere else in the world? Why was there a fortified perimeter around the fields themselves, encircling nothing but bananas and avocadoes? A watchtower at the heavy steel entrance gates that only opened and closed for known faces or designated visitors? To say nothing of the steep hill of no-man's land beyond the fence, before the red and white stripes of the Lebanese flag replaced the Israeli Star of David, often hard to pick out against the similar blue of the sky?

Now that buffer zone doesn't feel nearly wide enough for the current tensions. In the six months since Lola arrived, there have been seismic changes to the political landscape. She remembers the moment round one of their campfires back in November when everyone else on the kibbutz started screaming. The news that the Israeli prime minister himself had been shot dead by an extremist from his own side reverberated not just around the country but around the world. When suicide bombings returned to the streets of Tel Aviv in the spring, it turned out a kibbutznik's cousin had been one of those killed. And now missiles have been flying into Israel from over the border in Southern Lebanon for more than a week.

Lola knows when this particular round started, but still can't pinpoint exactly why. There was an explanation – some allegedly accidental deaths on one side necessitated a response from the other. And so the tit-for-tat began. But up here, on her hallowed spot on the clifftop, she is so close to the border it feels impossible that life on the other side can be so opposed. That the simple matter of traversing a hillside can mean the difference between one way or another. Up here, with industrial-scale farming machinery positioned at every turn, the personalised trauma kits they carry at all times just seem like common sense, and not armour in case of attack.

And so it follows that daily life continues on the kibbutz, albeit punctuated by the regular rush to take cover in a bomb shelter. As the kibbutz isn't just a communal farm. It's a collective way of life. A successfully functioning community can't just stop operations at will. The stakes are that high.

Lola sticks out her chin, as if to prove it to herself too. For the story of the land slowly undulating its way east, all the way to the high plains of the Golan and beyond into Syria, can't fail to be forever part of her story now, even if it isn't her true ancestral home. But still the white and blue of the Star of David fluttering in the distance remain ephemeral against the dawn light.

The dog noses at her calves, sniffing every available inch of bare skin. Lola reaches down to give her rough head a little pat before hurrying down the path to work.

They call them volunteers, her and others like her, come to live and work in these small farming communities for varying amounts of time while they figure out what they want to do with the rest of their lives. They call themselves that too, even though it doesn't always reflect why they're really there. Some believe in the project, some don't, but none of it matters so long as they commit to the land where they live. Lola isn't Jewish, but Sam most definitely is. And Sam's been her best friend forever, through the dog days of puberty all the way to being a legal adult, now allegedly free to do whatever she pleases, so long as it does nothing other than demonstrate her unswerving commitment to the State of Israel.

Of course Lola was going to follow Sam out here, see if she could find a way to belong too. What else would she do? Her mother is completely obsessed with her half-sister, Holly. The only person in her family who ever seems to notice her is Richard. And no, she's not going to call him Dad, even though her own disappeared when she was a baby. The truth is that Sam's the only person Lola's ever felt like she belongs with. Sometimes best friends are more than family. There's a reason they are also known as soul mates. They're partners. Especially when your real family is so toxic.

It turns out the kibbutz is a project with international appeal, to Jews and non-Jews alike. The rest of the volunteers come from all over the world and aren't Jewish either. Dave arrived from deepest, darkest America, carrying two identical sets of clothes and a suitcase filled with books. Tom brought his surfboard all the way from Australia, only for it to become a sofa, propped up by the tree stumps next to their fire pit. And then there's Andre and Johan. Joined at the hip, even if one is twice the height of the other. Their shared past in South Africa still isn't clear to everyone, but that doesn't matter either. Volunteering on a kibbutz is instant membership to a club where the only entry requirement is being in a certain place at a certain time. There's a level of enigma that no one wants to acknowledge, as to do so would be to ask the unsayable, even the unthinkable. When all you need to do to belong is work, no one wants to give honest answers to questions about where they've really come from. Much less what they're really looking for.

No wonder it's so appealing. Even with missiles flying overhead. There's an air of invincibility that comes with being part of a community so entrenched. When you want to belong to something, there's no better way to do so than picking a side.

In exchange for room and board, the volunteers rise with the sun to tend the banana fields, to cultivate the greenhouses, to harvest the orchards – alongside those who choose this as their way of life forever. There's indoor work too: washing and folding a community's worth of laundry, preparing and cooking the three meals a day that are all eaten together in the shared dining room. It's a window on a particular kind of utopia – can life truly be as simple as communal subsistence farming? As straightforward as a group commitment to the same piece of land, knowing that everyone in the circle has the same rights and rewards, even if they carry out different jobs? The months roll blissfully by while they are convinced that it is – until it's not.

This is the only part of the thought Lola ignores as she hurries into the heart of the kibbutz. A volunteer who is late, who isn't totally committed, has a marked card. Hardly a worthy volunteer. The dog trots a few paces ahead as if to remind her.

'Hey, Lola. Wait up!'

She slows, catching her brow before it furrows. Tom is jogging over to meet her from one of the low-rise housing blocks that line the path.

'Catching another sunrise, huh?'

She pulls off her bandana to fluff her hair at him. 'You know me. I'm a sucker for the sunrise. From up on the clifftop too. It's different every day.'

'Even with gunpowder in the air, huh?' Biba shies away as Tom reaches down to pet her.

'Come on.' Lola starts to walk again. 'We're going to be late.'

'Like that's ever bothered you before.'

She shoves him. 'Listen, I'm never deliberately late.'

'Right. I tell you what, if we were in Australia—'

'I'd always be late?' Lola parrots the end of his sentence. She's heard this story a thousand times before. They'd all be convinced Tom was here on behalf of the Australian tourist board if it was feasible the Australians needed any more help getting people to visit. But no – Australians all seemed to be looking for a more tactile horizon. Something more tangible than their infinite red centre. Little wonder, Lola supposes, as otherwise they might have to confront the fact that much of their vast land, their so-called *terra nullius*, was anything but uninhabited when the British arrived to claim it for themselves. She starts to jog past the familiar outlines of the kibbutz kitchens and dining room.

'Too right,' says Tom. 'There ain't no sunrise like an Aussie sunrise—'

'And it doesn't smell of chicken shit either.'

'Exactly.' Tom smiles. 'Hey, check you out. You've been listening after all. And there I was thinking I didn't have any effect on you.'

Lola shoves him again. A small sigh escapes as she notes Biba disappearing in the opposite direction. 'We can watch the sunset together later, if you want?'

Tom's smile widens. 'Like you've got anywhere better to be, huh.'

They pause in the courtyard, where the float trucks are idling, waiting for the last stragglers before heading to the banana fields and orchards further inland. Tom always seems to have a way of finding Lola, even though he works in the greenhouse, set back from the courtyard in the opposite direction. Behind him, she can see that Andre and Johan are already heading inside.

'Don't work too hard, OK?' She re-ties her bandana. 'I'll see you at breakfast.'

His grin fades at the shouts from the group beckoning to Lola from the far float. She squeezes his arm before jogging away. She doesn't need to turn to know he's watching her take Fouad's hand as he hauls her up on board.

*

Sunscreen is passed around as the float rattles past the orchards. The cherry pickers loom high and frozen between the fruit trees, marked out like hunched skeletons in the dawn light.

'You miss a little,' Fouad says, improbably blue eyes glass clear and twinkling in his dark face. 'Right here.' He points to his own nose. 'You want to peel it like a banana?'

Lola stripes herself with a zinc stick, tucking a strand of fair hair behind her ear. She's the only volunteer who works in the banana fields. In fact she's basically the only kibbutznik. Moti, who is in charge of the bananas, runs command and control from the dining room rather than do any of the actual manual labour. Apparently he did plenty, once upon a time. Apparently he cultivated these fields from the ground up, when he was part of the group that founded the kibbutz itself many years ago. Now most of his team is made up of Druze Arabs who all come to work on the kibbutz from their village a few miles away. The wage is good – better, they say, than some jobs in the big cities across the north.

The volunteers can see this anomaly. Not everyone who works this land like it's their own can also live on it. You don't have to be Jewish to volunteer. But if you are Bedouin or Druze, or any of the other religions that account for the Arab citizens of Israel, it seems like you just get to live to work. Fouad may be an Israeli national, but he's still an outsider in this particular community.

Lola knew about the friction between Israelis and Palestinians before she arrived. And she thought she understood the wider tensions with the Arab world in general – the only tranquil border Israel seems to have is with the sea. But Lola hadn't grasped this particular nuance at all. She finds it even harder to understand now she's living amongst it – up here in the north, there seem to be as many Arab villages as there are *kibbutzim*. To Lola, the warring sides seem more similar than different. To Lola, all this particular nuance does is prove it.

'Better,' Fouad says, reaching for the tube of zinc to mark his own face, bright stripe flashing neon against the brown skin. 'See? Even I must do this.'

She smiles as the others laugh, cocking her head in expectation of another morning ritual. Fouad can tell the time to the nearest minute just by mapping the sun's position in the sky on to the ground. It feels impossible, but he always gets it right. Of course it could be an elaborate feint, put on for her benefit – is one of the others signalling to him from behind her back? Lola finds that explanation as appealing as the trick itself.

'What time is it?'

'It is...' He squints past the corrugated tin roof of the float at the shimmering sky. 'Nine, no ... ten minutes after five.'

A whoop goes up from the rest of the team as he beams at her.

'You make us late again, Miss Lola.'

'Only by a minute,' she says, frowning down at her watch. By her count it's by at least four. Even when her watch is fast she seems to lose track of the time. And she can ill afford to keep being late, much less make others late too. 'What are we doing today? We'll easily make that time up.'

'Petrol,' he replies, wrinkling his nose as the float turns down the track into the field itself.

She groans, already tasting the acrid smell. 'Isn't it too soon for petrol? It's only April.'

Fouad waves a weathered hand at the thick rows of banana trees, overgrown as jungle canopy. 'Already the trees are too big. They need more space to make flowers...'

He pauses to answer another question in rapid-fire Arabic. Lola's mind fills with the purple pendulum flowers that have to form for the bananas to develop higher up the stem. These are plants only worth the fruit they produce. There are no fringe benefits in the banana fields.

'You must count carefully, Miss Lola. We kill only one tree in five.'

Issam, Fouad's deputy, jumps from the float with an armful of petrol guns, beckoning with his head that they all follow. He directs her down the nearest line of trees, planted with rigorous precision but now as unwieldy and aggressive as bindweed. Strapping a full plastic tank of petrol on to her back, Lola runs the hose arm with the gun on the end over her shoulder, feeling suddenly queasy. She must inject the chosen trees right at the base to kill them. Once they are withered, there will be more back-breaking work taking their corpses out.

She doesn't know which is worse. The slow, sweaty administration of poison into healthy, thriving plants, or the bone-crunching excavation of their roots.

Lola turns back to the float for a hopeful moment, the steel of the injection gun already burning in her hand. Sometimes they are allowed to pair up, each walking the length of their allotted row on the inside lane so they can chat. Sometimes they can idle, massaging sore shoulders, giggling as they shake out cramping hands.

A shiver goes through her as she thinks it. It feels as forbidden as it is.

But the trees have closed ranks. Everyone has already disappeared.

Chapter Two
Wednesday, 17 April, 1996

8:30 a.m.

'Nothing else for you today, Smurfette? Not even a soda?'

Jonny Murphy forces a smile as he hands George a fistful of shekels in exchange for his breakfast kebab. The menu postered on the wall next to the sizzling meat rotating on its spit screams of eighties Hollywood rather than a Jerusalem street-food stand. Knickerbocker glories for dessert. Hotcakes with butter and maple syrup. Even a banana split. Why would anyone choose pudding after eating an entire Jerusalem-mix kebab? It's like expecting to have room for a whole packet of digestive biscuits after a full English.

'You know no one in America actually watches *The Smurfs* at all? It's that bad. Even English kids are starting to give it up.'

Jonny can't stop his eyes rolling when he answers. George calls him Smurfette whenever he wears his red cap. Doesn't matter that it is now bleached a mucky shade of brown. It was box-fresh red when Jonny arrived in Jerusalem last summer. And that seems to be all George can remember. Never mind that Jonny was able to reply to him in perfect Hebrew. The fact is, almost everyone in Israel speaks Jonny's language as well as their own, even if it's with the caveat that they've all learned it from naff cartoons. The American influence is that pervasive.

Jonny eyes the menu again, its laminate coating shining with grease. Maybe that's also why George thinks advertising hotcakes with maple syrup after a large kebab seems like a good idea.

'Does that mean you don't want your extra English onions?'

Jonny peers over the counter into the steaming paper bag waiting in George's weathered hand, eyeing the metal containers of chopped-up vegetables and other traditional Middle Eastern condiments in the tray below. He can't see any crispy onions, either on his kebab or on the drip tray below the spit itself. He's sure he's the only customer around here who eats them. Let alone being the only customer around here who eats shawarma for breakfast.

Jonny likes to think he's as native as they come. He has an Israeli mother. He speaks fluent Hebrew. He's entitled to Israeli citizenship by birth, even though he was mainly raised in the UK. Not to mention the fact his father was apparently so Irish that his blood may as well have run green. But the truth is that no Israeli starts the day with a kebab. Much less covers the whole thing in onion scraps. It's only strong Arabic coffee and an even stronger cigarette. The truth is that Jonny is trying just a little bit too hard.

'Short-changing me *and* calling me Smurfette—'

'Just the extra-hot chillies for you, then?'

Both men snort as Jonny reaches over for his kebab, dropping a couple of crumpled bank notes on the countertop.

'You'll be back for lunch?' George fingers the money briefly before dropping it into the till.

'If you're lucky.' Jonny dips his head into the heady aroma wafting from his overflowing paper bag. The slightly burned smell of spiced yoghurt on chicken just the right side of charred. No street corner in this part of Jerusalem's Old City would smell right without it. He is pleasantly surprised to find a stray dog salivating at his feet rather than the usual cluster of skeletal cats. You deserve an extra piece just for that, Jonny thinks, nudging a couple of juicy morsels over the lip of the bag and on to the ground. Round here, the price of survival is that high.

'You'll be the lucky one. I'll change the sauce just for you.'

Jonny straightens up as George clangs the till shut.

'Not on my account, buddy. Two shawarmas a day is my limit. I have to draw the line somewhere.'

'OK, Smurfette.' George grins. 'Dinner it is. I'll make some more onions, too.'

Jonny hides his grimace in his kebab rather than say anything else, touching a finger to his visor by way of goodbye. *Smurfette*. It's enough to make him tuck the long strands of fair hair plastered down his neck back under his cap with his free hand.

Jonny would get himself a new cap if he wasn't so superstitious. But this one has been just too lucky. He's been wearing it since he arrived, even showing up for his first day on the job with it already jammed on to his head. Israel is a country where everyone's head is covered most of the time – the Jewish *kipah*, the Palestinian *keffiyeh*, and of course, the military-issue hard hat. So what else could a journalist wear other than a completely neutral cap? Especially a cub reporter like Jonny. One who can't afford to put a foot wrong.

Jonny pulls down the frayed visor as if to prove it to himself. For this cap has successfully helped hide every emotion that has threatened to cross his face in the line of duty. The shock and disbelief when the Israeli prime minister was assassinated by one of his own people. The horror and pain of last month's terrorist attack in the heart of Tel Aviv. The alarm at the rapid escalation of the Israeli military's bombing campaign in southern Lebanon since it was announced last week. They are calling it the Grapes of Wrath. Except every single rocket Lebanon's Hezbollah militia launches into northern Israel seems to elicit an aerial bombardment in response far bigger than just a bunch of fucking grapes.

Jonny yanks at the visor as his own opinions threaten to take hold, reminds himself to remain objective. The journalist's sacred oath. And Jonny's had to apply it to plenty of painful personal discoveries he's made over the last year. He pulls his cap down even lower, tries to block them out, but just succeeds in showering more of his kebab on to the ground. This time it's the army of stray cats that take the undeserved spoils. By the time he pushes open the swing door to his office just outside the Old City walls, it's more than his breakfast that's left a bad taste in his mouth.

The thrum of activity hits Jonny as soon as he walks into the newsroom, crumpling his paper bag into the nearest bin. The Jerusalem offices of the *International Tribune* newspaper are always busy. The creation of the State of Israel in 1948 was an international matter to start with, and it seems like almost everyone still has a political stake in the place. The *Trib* set up shop shortly afterwards and has since established itself as the region's definitive global voice – at least that's what its masthead would have its readership believe. Jonny snorts softly as he takes in the black letterhead plastered in huge letters above the door. For a profession that lives and dies on objectivity, news journalism's opinion of itself is about as subjective as it comes.

He pauses, taking in the shiny black lettering as if he's seeing it for the first time all over again. For someone so young and inexperienced, Jonny was lucky to get his foot in this particular door – but isn't good journalism always a matter of both luck and judgement? He's a smart kid, entitled to both British and Israeli citizenship, with associated connections to boot. He speaks fluent Hebrew, a smattering of Arabic, and is brimming with questions about the place, desperate to deepen his own understanding of the complexity of his roots. Journalism is a profession built on getting the right people to answer the right questions. Someone like Jonny is surely the most natural choice that any news editor in this city could make. Activity in this particular newsroom went nuclear when former Prime Minister Yitzhak Rabin was killed late last year. Since the Israelis launched Operation Grapes of Wrath ... well, let's just say Jonny has had an equally intense baptism of fire. And all it has done is made him hungry for more.

Dropping into his chair, Jonny shifts his gaze to the map of Israel and surrounds that he has pinned on the low wall separating his work station from his editor's. The so-called Green Line, picked out in dots around the perimeter of the West Bank. *Disputed Territory*, he reads from the map's key in the bottom corner. He wishes for at least the eightieth time he had brought a few more maps with him from home in London, even though he hardly needs to remind himself that the various factions here would have labelled them with a range of different names. His eyes wander the patchwork of villages and towns, listed in both Hebrew and Arabic. Jonny could lose himself for hours in this map – from the north's ancient city of Nazareth, where the angel Gabriel apparently told Mary she was going to bear a child, past Jerusalem to the historic town of Bethlehem, where the child himself was born. Once upon a time, the three wise men apparently hiked directly between the two. Not on this map, with all these dots in the way.

Hunching forward, Jonny traces out the solid black line separating northern Israel from Lebanon with a finger. It's been two weeks since the Israelis began their aerial bombardment, and still the rockets are flying. Israeli firepower dwarfs that of the Hezbollah, yet the missiles continue regardless. This particular paper, with its right-leaning international executive management in America, isn't going to spend any time thinking about why. So neither is he. Which is a shame, since he spends most of his time wondering about the nuances of exactly that.

Jonny clasps his hands together, folds them into a toy gun. This conflict is so loaded with different perspectives, applying weapons to it feels impossibly crude. *Bang bang you're dead*. Like it's as simple as a game.

'Shawarma for breakfast again, huh.' His editor stands up suddenly from behind the low wall.

Jonny jumps, forgetting to apologise for daydreaming in his haste to check his T-shirt for scraps – let alone reply in anything other than English. Since he arrived in Jerusalem, he always prefers to speak Hebrew if he can. But Allen's English is almost better than his. The *Trib* is international as its masthead. 'How did you know?'

'You stink.' Allen wafts a hand in the air with a smile.

'I do not,' Jonny mumbles, reaching for the half-full bottle of water still open on his desk. He doesn't stop to consider whether it's actually his.

'And that's mine,' Allen replies, just as Jonny takes a full gulp. 'But don't worry. Looks like you need it a lot more than me.'

'Sorry.' Jonny winces as he swallows. The water is warm. The bad taste is still lingering. 'Thanks, I mean. And sorry. I should have checked.'

But Allen is already concentrating on something else.

'We need to update all the data. The statistics on the rocket attacks. Who, what, when and where, etc.'

Jonny leans forward, flicks on his computer. 'I can do that—'

'No, you can't,' Allen interrupts. 'That's the problem.'

'What do you mean?' Jonny frowns. He knows most of it is hidden under his hat.

'There have been no civilian deaths as a result of the rocket attacks into Israel. Plenty of damage and injuries, but no one has been killed. While on the Lebanese side of the border...'

'Ah.' Jonny sees it now. 'So won't the statistics just make that clear?'

'No.' Allen's eyes bore into his. 'Because that might read like we are making an altogether different point.'

Jonny considers this. The rocket attacks are a problem. Just because they haven't killed anyone in Israel yet, doesn't mean that they won't. To say nothing of the damage and injuries already caused to communities across the north, its many Arab villages included. Israel says its subsequent air raids and shelling are necessary to stop the rockets for good. But at the expense of the dozens of lives they have already claimed in southern Lebanon...? To say nothing of the displacement of thousands of civilians.

'Well,' he begins, 'isn't that point equally valid?'

Allen snorts. 'Of course it is. What do you take me for? That's exactly it. It's more than equally valid. It's a story we should be telling. It's the kind of story that should define the *Trib*. This particular escalation in the conflict is objectively one-sided. We can't tell that story in a table of statistics. We need a balanced investigation, with voices from both sides.'

'Can I at least have a go?' The question is out before Jonny can stop it.

'Ha!' Allen snorts. 'I should have known those would be the first words out of your mouth.'

'Please.' Jonny tries not to sound like he's begging. But the truth is, that's exactly what he's doing. He longs not just to explain the conflict but to truly inhabit its complexities. In many ways, he's living proof of it – raised in the UK rather than Israel after his mother was disowned by the rest of her family for having the nerve to fall in love with – worse, *reproduce* with – a Catholic.

Marrying out, she had once explained, with a pained expression on her face – it looked to Jonny as if the words themselves tasted as bitter as they sounded. Apparently one of the many legacies of the six million Jews murdered by the Nazis during the Holocaust was the urgent need to rebuild the Jewish population as substantively as possible – a load of big numbers and words that Jonny didn't understand at the time and has never been able to reflect on properly since, due to the equal extremities of behaviour his father was said to have displayed on their arrival back in the UK. Not that Jonny has ever had a chance to ask him about that. There's still so much Jonny doesn't know about his past. The need to fill in the gaps, to try to understand, is all-consuming.

'Don't be ridiculous.' Allen sounds anything but conciliatory. 'I can't just commission an investigation into the ethics of this particular military operation when I've just been instructed from on high to update the statistics. Much less commission it from a cub reporter. What are you, nineteen? Spare me.'

Jonny pulls at his cap as if it can hide the blush creeping up his neck.

'Actually I'm nearly twenty-one,' he replies, immediately wishing he hadn't. It just draws attention to the fact that if his Israeli passport had actually translated to residency too, he'd still be deep in the mandatory army conscription that awaits all Israeli teenagers when they come of age. The place may be the most militarised nation on earth relative to its size, but it's in large part made up of kids holding guns.

'Sorry, anyway,' he adds hurriedly. 'Is there anything else I can do?'

'You can make the calls and update the statistics!' Allen roars at him, before stalking away towards the graphics desk.

But Jonny is smiling as he reaches for the telephone on his desk.

For he knows exactly who he is going to call. He hardly needs the excuse of another rocket attack. And when Allen finds out about this particular connection, the conversation is going to get a whole lot more interesting.

Chapter Three
Wednesday

8:30 a.m.

Lola wipes banana sap onto her shorts as she climbs down from the float. Almost every item of clothing she brought with her to the kibbutz is indelibly stained by now. But those stains are a badge of honour. This community is only as strong as its connection to the land. Its outsiders need to work doubly hard to prove their worth. Lola's messy clothes are in her favour.

She rolls her head on her neck, already stiff from lugging her petrol tank around the banana fields for the past two hours. The queasiness hits again with another waft from the jerry cans and guns stacked in the middle of the corrugated floor. They're back on the kibbutz and supposed to fuel up with a hearty breakfast. But food is the last thing on her mind.

'Aren't you coming too?' She eyes Fouad and Issam, still lounging on the benches to the float's either side.

Fouad wags a finger at her. 'Not today. After breakfast, you will see why.'

He slaps a playful hand on his thigh, grinning across at Issam.

Lola stalls. Everyone is invited into the kibbutz's communal dining room during the working day. That's the whole point of the place. All meals are eaten together – breakfast, lunch and dinner. It's one aspect of communal life that takes no getting used to. When is eating alone any fun, much less cooking for one? And on a kibbutz, there are precious few cooking facilities anywhere outside of the main, industrially equipped kitchens. There's always more food than you can shake a stick at in the dining room. It's the one location that just screams 'welcome'.

'You're not hungry?'

'Of course,' Fouad cackles, rubbing his stomach. 'But for something else. You will see.'

Issam jumps down from the float with a wink, removing his petrol-stained T-shirt to safely spark up the cigarette dangling from his lips. The flash of his washboard abs sends Lola hurrying away, trying not to look.

She knows all the Arab Israeli workers are welcome during the working day too – she's eaten breakfast and lunch with them countless times. Except she can't shake the feeling that they don't always feel that way.

Tom calls out to her as she pushes open the dining room's heavy swing doors. He's already pitched up at their usual table underneath the nearest windows, larking about with Andre and Johan. Those three all work in the greenhouse together – endlessly planting, weeding, sorting and picking. Managing tray upon tray of identical-looking seedlings, the only things flourishing under the sweltering heat of the glass.

The rest of the kibbutzniks tend to sit away from the volunteers. Lola can already see Oren, the manager of the greenhouses, glowering at the boys from his seat a few tables away. Tom and Andre are cackling wildly at something, hands waving in circles over their heads. But Oren doesn't have much of a sense of humour when it comes to his greenhouses. He's a founder member of the kibbutz too. And it's his greenhouses that produce the hundreds and thousands of olives that the kibbutz profits from all over the world. Come to think of it, the only joke Lola has ever heard Oren laugh at is the one about the place being built on olives, not milk or honey. And it's not even funny.

Nodding back at Tom, Lola grabs herself a plate from the stack next to the battalion of dishes set up side by side in the centre of the room. Industrial-sized trays steaming with heaps of boiled eggs. Vat after vat of fresh chopped salad – a neat dice of tomatoes, cucumbers and peppers, sprinkled with curls of parsley. Large tubs of harissa, both the fiery, red kind and the mellower coriander-green. Bowls of soft cheese and yoghurt. Loaves of sliced bread. Piles of avocadoes. Pyramids of squashy green pomelos.

But Lola's stomach flips again. The giant kibbutz dining room suddenly feels like a shop window. Its bounty may be on full display, but the reality inside is never quite the same.

She makes herself grab an egg and a couple of pieces of plain, sliced bread.

'That's hardly going to get you through till lunchtime,' Tom fusses, making a face as she sits down. 'Christ, babe. What the hell have you been doing all morning?'

'Sorry.' Lola pulls at her vest. 'It's petrol. I know it stinks. We have to inject some of the plants to make sure they actually die. There's way too many of them already.'

Andre snorts from across the table, fork clattering. 'Right. It's that easy, hey.'

'Not really.' Lola starts to peel her egg. 'How's the greenhouse?'

'Rancid,' Andre continues. 'Hot as balls already. You think you smell bad. Try getting up close and personal with this lot. With a hangover too.' He jerks his fork at Johan and Tom.

'Has Sam eaten yet?' She twists round, searching the open entrance to the kitchens at the front of the room. Sam is the only volunteer who works there. At first, Lola wished they had been placed together. But the relentless cooking and cleaning of the kitchens would be far too claustrophobic for Lola, even with Sam by her side. Lola has spent most of her life waiting on other people. Conforming to their expectations, if only in the hope that they might change. Out in the open air, deep in the banana fields, she feels freer than she ever has before.

Johan shakes his head. 'She's still boiling eggs. Like there aren't already enough on the table. And Farid isn't even here yet to crack the bloody whip.'

A shiver runs down Lola's spine at the mention of Farid's name. The survival of this particular kibbutz is founded on three industries: Moti runs the bananas. Oren is master of the olives. And Farid is in charge of the chicken houses.

But unlike the other two men, Farid isn't a founder member of the kibbutz. He's a Druze Arab, the only outsider in charge of a division.

When Lola has asked about it before, Tom has always pointed out that chickens are the subsistence part of this particular farm. They pretty much look after themselves. Which even came first, the chicken or the egg? he laughs. Ha-ha, very funny. The fact is it's only the bananas and olives that actually turn a profit.

But Lola knows Tom is just being petty – for reasons she'd prefer not to think about too long. He seems to get jealous of every male Lola interacts with other than him. The fact is that chickens produce both meat and eggs, help fertilise the soil too. Lola has already pointed out this is a saving – profit by a different name. To Lola, that just means the chickens are worth far more than crops that are only good for one thing. And Farid manages most of it alone.

Another anomaly it seems only she can see. In a community where everyone and everything is supposed to sit on the same plane, these hierarchies hide in plain sight.

'He's not here yet?' she asks lightly, as if she hasn't already given the dining room the once-over. 'Weird. It must be busy—'

Tom cuts her off with a snort. 'Busy with birds, hey.'

Andre and Johan roar with laughter. Lola tries not to blush, starts to make herself a sandwich, wrapping the bread in between two paper napkins.

'Babe. Are you alright?' Tom's fork stills on the way to his mouth.

'Fine, fine.' She tries to brush it off. 'The petrol has just been making me feel sick all morning. I know I'll need to eat something later though.'

She shoves the sandwich into her pocket, pushing her chair away from the table. In the same moment she realises Dave hasn't arrived in the dining room yet either. He works in the cowshed, further up the hill from the chicken houses. All the animal warehouses are deliberately built as far away from the heart of the kibbutz as possible. Their float must just be late picking them up. But she can't wait any longer. She knows she has to get back to work.

'Have fun,' she says, walking away before Tom can say anything else.

*

Fouad and Issam laugh and joke in Arabic as they head back out to the banana fields. Lola smiles even though she doesn't understand a word, painting more zinc on to her face. Another four hours of back-breaking petrol injections are ahead, but Lola doesn't mind. Out here, deep in the banana fields, all she really needs to understand are the plants.

She feels disoriented barely two steps back into her lane. The trees loom tall on her either side, their thick canopy overhead acting like a greenhouse, already heavy with heat. More banana sap, cloying and sticky, stains her fingers as she hunches at the base of the next condemned tree, driving in her gun to deliver her poison injection. The stench rises almost immediately. She thinks about how nothing grows properly without its own space.

A sudden crackle of leaves snaps her back to the present as Fouad emerges from the adjacent lane with a bunch of dwarf bananas in his outstretched hand.

'Bapples,' he says, beaming at her frown. 'See? Half banana, half apple. Today, *this* is our breakfast.'

Lola reaches out for the fruit, turning it over and over in her fingers. A banana so small and fat it could be an apple in a different light?

'Try it, *yalla*.' Fouad takes it back to peel for her. 'We make as an experiment...'

'But how?' Lola wonders.

'Mix the apple plant with the banana. Why not?' Fouad munches on her fruit, shaking the rest of the bunch at her to snap off another. '*Alhamdullilah*. Delicious!'

Lola feels herself blushing as Fouad fixes her with those eyes, jewel-bright in his dark face.

'Eat, *habibti*, come on. Do you like it?'

She reaches over, plucking and peeling quickly. The banana – or apple – tastes powdery and sharp on her tongue.

'Very clever,' Lola replies, swallowing. She can't bring herself to say delicious. There's none of the sweetness of a banana, much less the juice of an apple. But the fact he's brought them for her makes them easier to stomach.

Fouad continues through another mouthful. 'We are trying out different things to show Moti. These plants, they are smaller, they make flowers even in winter. And they make fruit no one has ever seen before. Think how much he can make from that.' He cackles to himself.

'Does he know yet?' Lola makes herself swallow down another bite.

Fouad wags a finger at her. 'Only when they are perfect, when we know he can sell them. Otherwise he will just be cross, say we are wasting his time.'

Lola folds the banana skin between her fingers, picturing Moti's inevitable fury. If it isn't his idea, it doesn't fly until he has made it his own. What if it turned out Fouad and Issam were better at turning a profit than Moti himself? That could never be allowed to happen. In a community as tight as this, its commanders can't afford to be seen as anything other than in complete control.

'I'm sure he won't,' she says lamely.

Fouad's snort turns into a smile. 'You are too nice, Miss Lola. You think the best of everyone.'

Her blush fades cold as he cocks his head, searching the glare of the sky, raising a hand to silence her before she can ask him why.

And then she hears it.

A low, unmistakable whistling, keening through the sky with the thrum of a distant jet engine. Lola throws herself face down, instantly terrified – doubly so because of the slosh of petrol against her back. Is she expected to take cover while she is literally covered in ignition fuel? Now comes the dull thud, reverberating somewhere further inland – south, right on the coast, maybe?

Cries dart back and forth overhead in Arabic, but Fouad has disappeared by the time she's raised her head. She shouts weakly after him, soil gritty in her mouth. He's going to leave her alone, when that can only have been another Katyusha rocket? Another whistle now, lower. She's sure she can feel the ground vibrate as the missile swoops and lands, closer this time, the very air around her curiously distended by its thud.

The mantra she's heard around the dining room every mealtime for the last two weeks clatters round in Lola's mind. We are too close to the border itself to be hit, the kibbutzniks insist, laughing and pointing at the short, steep hill separating Israel from Lebanon. These rockets, they are the crudest of crude weapons. They can't be programmed to clear the hill and then land immediately on the other side. What else do you expect from an enemy so weak?

Even when one of these crudest of crude weapons did manage to breach the perimeter, the kibbutzniks were defiant, insisting on escaping the air-raid shelters for hasty smokes on its breezeblock roof. Lola quivers as the mournful wail of the air-raid siren rents the air, suddenly longing to be huddled with the other volunteers in their thin sleeping bags on the concrete floor, as they were just a few short nights ago.

They said it could never happen until it did. And now they couldn't be more exposed, all alone in the fields in the open air, explosive charge still crackling all around them.

Relief floods over her with the buzz of a radio. Fouad's face appears between the plants in the adjacent lane.

'Come, Miss Lola,' he urges her with an outstretched arm. 'We go back, now. Come on. Stay on the ground.'

'I don't understand,' she murmurs, shivering involuntarily as a large, cool hand closes around hers. 'There's no bomb shelter this far out in the fields, is there?'

'We have to go back to the kibbutz,' he repeats, tugging her towards him. 'It is an order.'

He folds his body around her as a third whistle tears overhead, tangling with the rise and fall of the siren. She tenses for the thud, Fouad's heart banging against her cheek.

'We can't move,' she mumbles into his vest. 'If we can't get to a shelter then—'

'We must,' he growls, letting go of her hand to wrap his other arm around her. 'That is the order.'

This time the whistle is so low Lola can almost feel its trajectory, the hairs on her arms standing up to meet it. She is mashed so tight against his chest she can barely breathe.

'It will be OK,' Fouad whispers into her hair. 'I promise you, Miss Lola. A short drive, then we will go underground. We are safe to move now.'

'You don't know that,' she whimpers, picturing the discarded petrol tanks strewn all around them, turning the already parched banana fields to tinder.

'*Yalla,* of course I do. Four rockets is four too many. You know what will happen next. The Israelis are already in the air. Move like this, look.' Fouad rolls on to his stomach, waiting for her to follow suit, a shot of panic dimming his electric-blue eyes. 'Please, Miss Lola. I must take you back. You don't understand.'

'But I do,' she says, the prickle of adrenaline pushing her to freeze rather than fly. 'I know we should stay still until the siren stops. We should shelter in place if we can't get underground. That's what Moti said—'

She cries out as his hand grabs roughly underneath her armpit. 'I must take you back. Please, Miss Lola. I must do this.'

'Were we hit? Is that why?'

Fouad drops her as if she's suddenly radioactive. Another hierarchy hiding in plain sight. Out here, 'we' doesn't apply to everyone.

'It is the order,' he repeats after a moment. 'We are all in danger if you don't follow it. You know this too. So come on.'

Lola shrinks into the ground. Only when his hand hooks under her armpit again does she propel herself forward. She feels Fouad deflate beside her.

'*Yalla,* just a little more,' he says as they haul themselves away. The siren screams overhead, mercifully uninterrupted. 'You can do it, Miss Lola. We will all be OK if you do.'

Chapter Four
Wednesday

11:00 a.m.

Jonny's hand stills on the receiver as the newsroom suddenly explodes with activity. Everyone else's phones are ringing off the hook. The bank of televisions mounted on the wall overhead all flash up the same sickening image, increasingly familiar – a plume of acrid smoke rising from deep inside a heavily populated residential area.

Jonny has to take a minute to make sense of the Hebrew letters bannered across the bottom of each screen, but Allen is already shouting their meaning out, back at their workstation in a flash, a phone pressed to each ear.

There's been another rocket attack in the north.

Jonny hunches forward again, stares at his map as he listens to Allen. One missile has apparently destroyed a house on the outskirts of the port of Akko. Beautiful, ancient Akko ... that's pretty far down the coast for a rocket launched from southern Lebanon, he thinks, straining to pick out details in the rapid-fire Hebrew ricocheting all around him.

Three injured, mercifully no dead. And all Arab Israelis too ... not the look the Hezbollah will have been going for.

He stands up, tries to get Allen's attention, but the conversation is still moving too fast. The *Trib*'s reporting team are already on their way to the scene, heading straight from their base in the northern city of Haifa. What on earth were they still doing at their hotel? Having a leisurely breakfast? Smoking their way through an entire shisha pipe? They aren't up in Haifa for the view!

Now Allen starts deploying a volley of swearwords. Enough with the excuses now, come on. Don't we have anyone who can get there any faster? Is the whole team planning to walk? It does not take that long to get from Haifa to Akko!

'Jonny.' He jumps, Allen switching back to English to instruct him too from over the wall. 'Where are we on the statistics? We need this latest attack included for the next edition. Annotated map, attack radius, total number of injuries, you know the drill.'

He snaps into action, flipping open his notebook, calculating as he scribbles. These latest injuries are to Arab Israelis. Jonny knows more partisan newsrooms might already be arguing over whether they should be included in the overall toll. The decade that started with the peace treaties is rapidly spinning out of control. These latest attacks are pushing even the simplest of calculations to the brink. But Arab Israelis hold full citizenship and serve in the Israel Defence Forces. There is no question in Jonny's mind. And he knows there is no question in Allen's either. Still his pencil pauses as he considers this. Just the fact that it has started to become a question at all is a terrifying indication of what might lie ahead.

Jonny only realises he has slipped into reverie when he registers the shrill ring of a phone is actually coming from the one on his desk. He swaps pencil for receiver, hand stilling on the black plastic when he sees the incoming number and realises who is returning his call. His heart, having stood still at the sight of those treasured few digits, resumes operations with a thump. He only needs to listen rather than talk for two minutes before replacing the handset with a soft click, brow furrowing at both the map in his eyeline, and the unexpected new nugget of information slowly turning over inside his head.

'What the hell are you waiting for?' Allen's face reappears above the wall between them. 'It's a simple fix. You should have it done already. I've got a list as long as my arm of other data that needs updating.'

'Sorry,' he mumbles, making a show of flipping open his notebook again, rooting around for another pencil. This is usually when he reminds himself Allen isn't deliberately being rude, it's just that Hebrew doesn't translate well into English. Both the grammar and vocabulary are sparse. There's no room for standard politesse.

'What's up with you?' Allen leans over the divider to peer at him. This is also usually the time Jonny starts to beg and plead to leave the office in Jerusalem, to go and actually cover the latest developments on the ground, instead of just processing other people's information.

'It's just—'

'Don't start.'

'It's not what you think.'

'Whatever it is can wait until you're done with your day job.'

She silences him with one of her famous glares, reserved for everyone that assumes she is a man before they actually lay eyes on her.

'Allen...'

Her frown softens as he switches to Hebrew.

'I just got a tip. Can we...' Jonny trails off deliberately, jerking his head in the direction of the water machine in the far corner of the room.

She scowls at him before stalking away, not even checking he's on her tail. Only when they reach the back wall does she slow and allow him to fall in step beside her.

'Make it quick, come on.' She folds her arms across her chest.

'I just got a call from someone in the north,' Jonny replies, switching back to English. He wants this next part of the conversation to be as private as possible. 'There's ... Well, a body has been found, up near the border.'

Allen pulls up short before the water machine, turning to face him.

'A body? What do you mean? A casualty?'

'Sort of, yes—'

'Where? We have the official numbers on the rocket attacks already—'

'It's got nothing to do with that.'

Allen searches his face for a moment before replying. Jonny takes the respite to further consider how much to tell her. Allen may never know the name of this particular source, but she sure as hell knows their value. She just doesn't know exactly how much it is worth yet.

'So who is it, then? What is it to do with? And why would the *International Tribune* care about it, in the middle of an Israeli military operation in Lebanon?'

Allen elongates every word of the paper's title to make her point. This better not be an eighty-year-old dead of a heart attack in an armchair, is what she really means.

'It's just ... Look, Allen, a body has been found on a kibbutz right on the border – Beit Liora, you know the one. The location couldn't be any more relevant. And it's an Arab Israeli who works there. Young, shouldn't just drop dead—'

Allen cuts him off with a burst of laughter as she starts to walk again.

'I know it sounds crazy—'

'No, what it sounds like is a waste of my time.' She pulls a disposable cup from the column strapped to the side of the giant plastic water container. 'I prefer your usual speech. You know, the one where you claim to be starved of oxygen because of all the time you spend sitting in here doing your actual job.'

'It just doesn't smell right to me. Rockets flying over the border, and an Arab citizen turns up dead on a kibbutz that may as well be part of the line itself?'

'Put like that it doesn't smell right to me either.' Allen pauses for a sip of water before continuing. 'But if you think you can go chasing up there while we're still crushing these so-called Grapes of Wrath then—'

'It could so easily be connected, though, don't you see?'

'That's a whole lot of conclusions you're jumping to.' She fixes him with that glare again. 'What aren't you telling me?'

'That's all I have, honestly.' Jonny reaches for a cup for something to do with his hands, rolling the plastic rim between his fingers. He dare not meet her eye. There is so much he's not telling Allen that his tongue suddenly feels thick in his mouth. But this particular source is worth so much more to him than just furthering his career.

'Well, if that's it, this is five minutes of my life I'll never get back.'

Jonny feels her eyes burning into the top of his dipped cap.

'Come on, *Yonatan*.' She switches to Hebrew. 'You think I'm going to push you out of the door on a wing and a prayer? When do I ever do that? When does anyone ever do that, here? Especially if it means I'll have to account for another sorry ass in the line of fire.'

'Like we're not all in the line of fire just by being here.'

Jonny knows he's floored her for a moment with that. There's no need for him to be any more specific. They all know how many people were killed by a suicide bomber in Tel Aviv just last month. On the eve of a major Jewish holiday, outside one of the most popular shopping malls in the country. They wrote the obituaries, they detailed every last horrific injury. They invaded the privacy of those shattered families for colour that would sell the paper. Jonny has to swallow down rising acid before he can continue.

'Just let me go and meet my source in person. I've got somewhere to stay up there, so it won't eat into your budget. Twenty-four hours, tops. I promise. Sniff around, come back.'

Allen snorts. 'If you're bunking in with a source, you need to be doubly sure you're not being played. This is the source you've alluded to before, correct?'

'I know other people up there too.'

'Who? You know the drill, Jonny. I just need the general direction. I'm not looking for names – well, not yet, anyway.'

'Doesn't everyone know someone who knows someone else in this country?' He holds her gaze with that, just for a second. 'They're all related in the end, aren't they?'

'Amen,' Allen replies after a moment. 'Fine. You can have your twenty-four hours, but only on account of the journey. Unless you've grown wings since the last time I looked? Then I expect to see you back here, post-shawarma as usual, doing your actual job.'

He smiles at her, even as she turns her back on him to walk away, his eyes finding a patch of sky through the window opposite, a glare of the sun so bright it is almost blinding.

Chapter Five
Wednesday

Fouad hunches over Lola, holding her down on the truck's grimy floor. The air is as thick with tension as it is with intensifying heat, the siren painfully amplified in the confined space between their bodies. There's a pool of blood coming from somewhere – some*one*, Lola realises. It must be – she can sense it growing and thickening against her cheek. The float lurches as it starts, jolts of pain scudding through her hip bones as they judder against the corrugated floor.

A sudden burst of static spurts from a radio. Lola can only identify a couple of words, and none help her understand. What possible order could override shelter in place? Who is injured? Is that why they are moving? Won't this tin can of a float tear them all to pieces if another rocket lands anywhere close? Every time Lola thinks she understands the rules of engagement around here, they seem to change. But only the metal below her cheek hears her protest, Fouad shouting over the rattle of the engine.

'We go all the way back. We must. That is the order. Stay down, Miss Lola...'

There's iron on her tongue as the truck speeds up along the tarmac of the kibbutz driveway, and suddenly the hand jamming her hard against the floor is hauling her upward, bundling her off the truck and straight into the dark, open mouth of the concrete bunker at the centre of the courtyard's turning circle.

Lola feels herself moving like a rag doll. Only when she

stumbles on the steep stairs is she able to collect herself, bracing a shaking hand against the stone wall, growing colder with every inch it slopes deeper underground.

Fouad charges past as the steps level off into the dank enclosure, hands whirling in the alien-yellow light flickering overhead. Issam limps awkwardly behind, blood trailing from his boot. Lola cries out, the hand reflexively flying to her mouth coming away stained with the blood left on her face. Is she injured too? Is anyone else? She tries to catch them up, but Tom's blocking her path in an instant, cupping her cheek with a sweaty hand.

'Shit, Lola, are you OK? What happened? Thank God you made it.' He sighs, wrapping her into a hug. 'Man alive, I was so worried.'

Lola squirms, but Tom's grip is too tight. She peers over his shoulder. Fouad and Issam have already been swallowed up into the crowd gathered on the far side. Another round of static clamours off the breezeblock walls. She wipes the remains of the blood on her face on to his T-shirt.

'We just cut and ran straight from the greenhouse,' Tom continues. 'The lot of us. Soon as we heard the whistle—'

'Where did they land? Do you know? Fouad said we had to come all the way back, I think Issam is injured.'

Tom is shocked into letting her go. 'Who? Really?'

'Can't you see there's more blood on the floor than on my face?' Lola can glimpse enough now to see that Issam is being taken care of, sitting on a plinth cut into the opposite wall. She searches the rest of the crowd, hoping to find Sam, knowing that she won't. The kitchens are almost a bunker of their own, with their vast subterranean larders. Simultaneously she realises Dave is missing too.

Tom lets out a low whistle. 'So a rocket landed in the banana fields? Holy shit. That is closer than ever before.'

'I didn't think any had.' Lola relives the thud, still fresh in her bones, twisting round to see if she's missed Dave in a dull corner. 'They felt quite far away, to be honest. Issam must have fallen while running away, or something.'

Lola pauses as Fouad re-emerges from the crowd, shouldering past clusters of people to march back up the stairs without even giving her so much as a backward glance.

'Those fellas.' Tom jumps in. 'You can lead a horse to water, and there'll always be a donkey that doesn't drink. Wait – Lola? What the hell are you doing?'

It's only with Tom's shout that Lola realises she is following Fouad out of the air-raid shelter and back into the courtyard. She can't help herself. This latest salvo isn't making any sense at all.

It hits her with the sun warming her face. The siren is no longer wailing, air curiously suspended and still.

Lola turns on a compass. What has she missed? The pockmarked hillside hulks intractably at her back, shadow lengthening over the kibbutz buildings at its foot. To the east, the orchards quiver, lush and expectant. Her beloved banana plants are creaking in the wind on the exposed southern slopes towards the sea. And Fouad is rapidly disappearing down the path, back into the kibbutz in the direction of its western clifftop edge.

Lola cocks her head, sure she can make out the distant wail of a hound. So order has been restored? Except it hasn't…

'Come back inside.' Moti's deep voice echoes in the weighty silence of the completely deserted courtyard, still as a painting. 'Now, Lola, come on.'

She turns to find his heavily bearded face emerging from the dark of the stairwell. 'We must all stay underground, you know this.'

Lola grinds her feet into the gravel. How come Fouad can just walk out but no one else can? Especially now the siren is off? She didn't complain while he held her down, did she? And if it's still too dangerous to be out in the open air, then why isn't anyone worried about him?

Moti rolls his eyes as if she's asked all her questions out loud. 'He can break all the rules he wants.' He takes a heavy step towards her, reaching out a meaty hand. 'But you know the difference. You must come back downstairs.'

The hand stiffens at the end of his arm; it's as if Moti is daring her not to take it. Suddenly Lola finds she has to clamp her mouth shut. Surely she has the right to ask, just as surely as anyone else who lives to work here? But she already knows the answers won't be what she wants to hear.

Moti's expression softens slightly. He suddenly looks to Lola like some subverted version of Santa Claus. 'You do not need to worry about the rockets. They land far, far away from here, like we tell all you volunteers. The Hezbollah cannot hit the kibbutz unless they run down the hill themselves. But you must come back downstairs. Stay out here and all that happens is you will burn.' His hand waves at the sun overhead, as if that in itself should make sense of everything he's saying.

But Lola falls in line. By now, she knows she has no other choice unless she wants to leave.

At the bottom of the stairs, Moti practically hands her over to Tom, who is standing as close as he can get without breaking any rules by actually taking a step up. She smarts as he grabs her.

'I can stand up by myself, you know.'

'For yourself, you mean.' Tom's arms fall away; he looks as if Lola has slapped him in the face. 'What the hell do you think you are playing at? Trying to get us all sacked?'

A wave of misgiving breaks over her. She brushes herself down rather than meet his eye, takes in the stains on her clothes all over again. Lola may as well have *loyalty* tattooed down her arm. But Tom isn't so lucky. The only physical evidence he displays is the fact he's still here.

'Well, they've turned the siren off. It's already over, I saw it for myself.'

'Like hell it is. We can't go back out there. Not at least until I'm damn sure we won't get blown to bits by some lunatics trying to make a point. We're not here to be collateral damage.'

Lola folds her arms, but can't look up. 'And since when is anyone just here to be collateral damage?'

Tom chastens her. 'Look, we get to live here by just showing up, I get that. Half of the labourers here don't, even though they speak the same languages, have identical claims on the place. I get that too—'

A snort escapes her before she can stop it. And now it's only jealousy flaring in Tom's voice.

'Is this about him? It is, isn't it?'

Lola's long-rehearsed reply is almost off the tip of her tongue, but she is mercifully silenced by a loud clap ringing around the room. It's Oren who steps out of the gaggle in the centre, speaking in Hebrew first, then in his perfect, American-accented English.

'We need to stay down here for a while longer, folks. Just until we've combed through the outer perimeter—'

'Were we hit?' Tom interrupts almost immediately, panic still trembling in his voice. 'Where? Is everyone OK?'

'Everyone is fine.' Oren holds up his hands, looking around the room. 'As far as the rocket attacks are concerned, anyway. No one needs to worry that they'll be sleeping in here tonight. We just need to make sure of a few other things before we can go back to work.'

But Tom is still belligerent. 'How can you folks ever be sure it's safe? Out in the far orchards, or the banana fields, for starters?'

'We'll only go back outside when we're sure you're as safe as can be, Tom. But we all have to get back to work. We cannot allow ourselves to be paralysed at will.'

Oren's deliberate use of language is not lost on Lola. Still, all that ripples through the rest of the group is a murmur of assent. Moti even steps out to stand shoulder to shoulder with Oren.

Heads swivel in her direction as Lola clears her throat, takes a deep breath before she asks, 'But Moti, shouldn't someone at least go out and look for Fouad? If you're still not sure it's safe to be out in the open air?'

'He'll be just fine,' Oren replies instead. 'The rockets aren't a threat now.'

'Mate, come on.' Now it's Tom stepping forward. But his support just makes Lola shift from foot to foot. 'What the hell is going on? We're either all inside or we're out. Which is it?'

Oren laces his arms behind his back, shoulders bulging. 'Well, Tom, you yourself can be either. You're a volunteer. You're the one choosing to live here, in the middle of a major military operation. You can leave before your time is up, should you so wish, no question. You're under no obligation to stay here if you don't feel it is safe to do so.'

'Oren, mate...' Tom holds up his hands. 'That's not what I meant at all.'

The most curious expression crosses Oren's face before it closes over. Lola only realises she's been holding her breath when it all comes out in one go.

'I understand,' Oren finally replies, tight-lipped. 'It's a lot to take in. We realise that. And we welcome your work as much as you welcome our way of life. I'm afraid it just comes with a certain degree of risk attached to it.'

'I get it, mate, I do. I just—'

'We are simply resolving an incident on the other side of the kibbutz, before we go back to work. That is why we are here. Not because we are afraid of paper aeroplanes flying over the hill.'

'So we *were* hit? Where? What happened?'

But Oren ignores Tom in favour of the radio squawking at his belt. And the moment he pauses, the hubbub around them restarts immediately.

'Can you believe that guy?' Tom grumbles. 'He's like that in the greenhouse all the time. One minute he's your best mate and the next – bam. Closes over like a steel trap. All because you've dropped an olive in the wrong place or something.'

'And what does he mean by "incident", hey?' Lola bristles as Andre and Johan pile in. She's still straining to hear any words she understands.

'Who the hell knows,' Tom replies. 'I thought there was only one reason we'd ever hear an air-raid siren, especially now. And I sure as hell thought I knew the only reason we'd ever be told not to go back to work.'

A sudden commotion breaks out at the mouth of the stairwell behind them. Lola's heart flutters staccato as she turns to find Fouad marching back inside. But he walks straight past her towards the back wall, Issam tottering upright immediately at the sight of him.

'Well, would you look at that,' Tom mutters as Fouad rounds on Moti and Oren, hands whirling above his head.

'What are they saying?' Lola leans closer as she listens intently. The words she understands never seem to be the ones she needs.

'Chickens, I think...'

'Tom!' Lola's frustration finally boils over. 'How many times do you have to—?'

'No, babe.' He wraps a warm hand around her elbow, catching her arm before it whirls in fury over her head. 'It's the chicken house. I think that's what they're saying. Something's gone down in the chicken house.'

Chapter Six
Wednesday

11:45 a.m.

Jonny hurries out of the office, ducking to avoid George lolling on his shawarma stand countertop as he cuts the corner of the Old City. George is always full of questions. Useful, as Jonny only answers them by asking more uncomfortable ones, but he can't afford to get into that now. He simultaneously congratulates himself for having a shawarma for breakfast, since now he won't have time for lunch. Turns out marinating himself in the culture has practical advantages.

Rather than grabbing a change of clothes from his nearby apartment Jonny heads straight to his usual taxi rank, hoping to find Amer. As much as he has to think about, it's still a four-hour-plus drive to the northern border. Not only can Amer can be relied upon to provide steady conversation when needed, he has a strong enough stomach to head north right after a rocket attack.

A stream of horns blares as he crosses the road, even as he chooses a perfectly legal spot to do it. Any car staying in its lane in Jerusalem is a car with something to hide.

The butterflies that always tremble in Jonny's stomach at the sniff of a story give way to relief that Amer is on the stand, eyes lighting up immediately at the prospect of a mega-round trip, a bonanza fare. It's one reason Amer will let his minivan idle, hoping for *Trib* employees chasing a tip. No one other than journalists is catching taxis to the far north right now.

Jonny keeps it light, colloquial Hebrew mixed with even more colloquial Arabic. You are on rocket watch, *habibi*? Yep, *Insha'Allah* the injuries aren't too bad. No photographer this time? Nah, I'm meeting everyone up there, they just needed another body.

Even the van has to negotiate its way through Jerusalem's gnarled streets to head west on the cross-country highway. The map Jonny spends hours gazing at flashes back into his mind. There's no direct route to the north. That dotted line means they have to head to the coast and then turn right. A steady stream of curses drifts through the open window as Amer changes lanes without looking, speeding past knots of traffic as the outer reaches of the city fall away behind them.

'You know it is going to get worse before it gets better, *habibi*.'

Amer's deep voice echoes around the van as he closes the window with a thump. The motorway lengthens around them, cutting a path through the hills to Tel Aviv.

'How do you mean?' Jonny knows, but asks anyway. Perspective is everything, especially in this country.

'They are so angry, *ma'sha'Allah*.' Amer bangs a hand on the steering wheel, accelerating. 'The Hezbollah and the IDF. There will be some big bonanza bang in the south of Lebanon before this is over. Something so bad it means both sides have to stop. Already it is getting worse with every rocket.'

'I guess it is, hey—'

'Of course it is!' Now it's the horn rather than the wheel that takes the bulk of Amer's frustration. 'The Israelis multiply the shells by ten, then twenty, then thirty. For every rocket that lands in a field. And none of it makes an equal sum.'

'Mmmmm.' Jonny keeps his eyes on the hills in the distance, already parched rather than green, even this early in April.

'They have been waiting for this. Those crazies in the government. This is how they make their point. *Ma'sha'Allah*, if Rabin was still here—'

'Do you really think that would have made a difference?' Jonny interrupts. 'With rockets actually destroying homes across the north?'

This is a question he asks whenever he can. Yitzhak Rabin's assassination is still so fresh. The Israeli prime minister himself, shot in the back by one of his own people at a peace rally only six months earlier. His assailant was a Jewish extremist determined to stop the most advanced peace talks between Israelis and Palestinians since the creation of Israel itself. And the answers swing from one end of the spectrum to the other and more often than not, in surprisingly opposite directions. Another one of the place's irresistible paradoxes.

'Rabin was a man of peace. And in the end it was his own crazies that got him.'

'Do you think that means his response would be more proportional? I mean, Rabin was still a politician, whether he was one of peace, or not. Like you say, it was one of his own that killed him.'

Amer straightens his arms on the steering wheel as he leans back into his seat. Jonny reminds himself for at least the eightieth time of how Amer is a Palestinian living in Jerusalem. Which entitles him to far more freedom of movement than those living in the West Bank, behind the dotted line. Those living in the Palestinian Territories – or Occupied Territories, as they'd be first to point out – were far more restricted by checkpoints and the like than those living in Jerusalem, whose residential papers afforded them more privileges. Which is one reason why Amer may feel … Jonny catches himself before he makes the assumption. To assume anything out here is not just dangerous, it is often inflammatory. He can't be that person. He isn't that person.

'Of course there would be a military response,' Amer concedes, with a shake of his head. 'Yes. Of course there would. We are not fools. The Hezbollah cannot keep firing over the border and expect nothing to happen. But he would do more talking first.'

'And where would that get him?'

'To the same place, in the end. Yes.' His leather seat wheezes as Amer pushes himself further back into it. 'But we are going to get there faster and harder without Rabin in charge. Remember, the Americans hold half the cards, and they trusted him the most. Now he is gone, everything has to start again, and the Israeli side just stepped a lot further away from the middle. You will see.'

The car swerves as Amer turns to look at him with a grin. Jonny grits his teeth to smile back, tyres squealing around them. He's been meaning to look at the stats for ages. He's sure more people die in a week on Israeli roads than have ever died in rocket attacks.

'Does ... does everyone feel like you? Where you live, I mean?'

Jonny tries to keep the wince out of his voice as cars speed to their either side. Both Israelis and Palestinians claim Jerusalem as their capital. The Old City itself actually has four quarters – Jewish, Muslim, Christian and Armenian. Just walking from one quarter to the next covers thousands and thousands of years of ancient history. Even calling it the cradle of civilisation itself doesn't feel expansive enough. The place's opinions are kaleidoscopic and vary with the same colourful, and often sharp, regularity.

'*Lah*, of course not.' Amer slams the horn again. 'Like your people. No one can agree on anything other than the fact we cannot be expected to live under occupation forever. How do we fix things? If we fight, no one wins. If we don't, nothing changes. Even our leaders cannot say one way or the other. But *Amer* knows...' He taps his nose with a finger before continuing. 'Your uncle Amer, he knows that talking is always better than no talking, even if you don't like who you are talking to.'

'Amen,' Jonny mumbles, rubbing an eye as his mind digs out a grainy photo of his father posing in front of the Irish flag. There's a conflict apparently as factional than this one. Every day another political acronym seems to enter into the talks with the British.

The digital clock blinks on the dashboard. He's got at least another three hours in the van before he can really get started.

'Close your eyes, *habibi*,' Amer winks at him through the rear-view mirror. 'There will be a lot more traffic before I get us anywhere close to Akko.'

Jonny lets his head loll as he nods back, gazing again at the hills in the distance. Plenty of time to tell Amer where they are really going. His eyelids flutter closed, heavy with the weight of expectation.

Chapter Seven
Wednesday

10:30 a.m.

The shouting gets louder, a mixture of Hebrew and Arabic, echoing off the breezeblock walls. Lola eyes the reinforced ceiling, so implacable and low, it's as if it is pressing down on to her head. She only realises she's started for the stairs again when Tom pulls her back.

'You heard the man,' he says, frowning, grip tightening on her arm. 'It's a risk—'

'Of what?' Lola smarts, trying to shrug him off. 'Oren said it himself. The rockets aren't a threat now.'

'Babe, come on.' She tries not to stiffen as Tom wraps his other arm around her shoulders. 'No way am I letting you walk out of here while we don't know what's going on. We should have been questioning the risks long before this. It's been, what, nearly two weeks? And we've been sitting ducks in the fields, under glass, you name it. We have rights. We should have—'

'What could we have done?' Lola shifts on the spot. Beyond, she can see Oren's face colour as he squares up to Fouad, tensing militarily opposite the taller man. 'We don't have any right to stay. A few days refusing to show up and we'd have been fired—'

'Never.' Tom's squeeze tightens. 'Look at Doron. That kid can't hold down a job for longer than a month. Where hasn't he worked? They lost fridges' worth of food when he was in the kitchen. He ate more avocadoes than he ever picked. He even got fired from the dishwasher and they found him something else.'

'Doron isn't a volunteer though. The rules are completely different for kibbutz families.' Lola tenses, the shouting reaching fever pitch. She thinks about how rules always change based on who you are, not what you're doing.

'I think someone's had an accident in the chicken house,' Johan mutters to Andre next to them. 'Isn't that what they're saying?'

Lola tries to untangle herself as the greenhouse boys gab back and forth, but Tom's still holding her fast.

'Babe, please. I'm just worried about you, that's all. I'm worried about all of us. Can you blame me? There are actual missiles flying over our heads, for fuck's sake. None of us have family out here except each other.'

'I just don't want to be stuck down here for any longer than we have to be, that's all.' Lola scuffs at the concrete floor. 'It gives me the willies.'

'You think I don't know that?' Tom's smile turns her stomach afresh. 'It was my sleeping bag next to yours that night, remember?'

Lola shivers reflexively. Those pitch-dark, cold and uncomfortable nights under concrete. Made only fractionally warmer by Tom's body pressed up against hers. Trapped together in that dark, airless room, with the threat of missiles flying overhead, her own defences were at their lowest ebb. Tom has spent the best part of six months trying and failing to disguise how he feels about her. She was scared, and he was there. And the thing about a community as tight as this one is that everything seems like a new and potentially exciting idea after a while. Even ones that have never felt advisable before.

'Look, babe.' He looks furtively over his shoulder before continuing. 'I know we haven't exactly discussed what's going on between us, but I think you know – damn, you should by now – how much I care about you. We've been doing this for months – working here, I mean. Living here. Together. With the other volunteers. Not, you know...'

Heat rises up Lola's neck like an allergic rash. She suddenly longs for Andre and Johan to interrupt again, but they are still intent on talking to each other. Tom continues unbowed.

'I'm not trying to corner you. Really, I'm not. We're all figuring ourselves out, huh? That's one thing we've all got in common. We've come here to be part of something without having to fully commit other than to earn our keep. And isn't that what's so beautiful about it? About this whole concept? The idea that we can all become family by just being here together, by just working on the place itself?'

And now he's smiling, as if the bright, white teeth and artfully surf-bleached hair are the answer to the question themselves. It could be so simple – why can't Lola feel lucky that someone like him wants to hold someone like her? While they all shoot the breeze on the clifftop, watching the sun melting into the sea with icy cans of Goldstar in their palms? Or while they're trapped, underground and under fire? But in that moment all Lola sees is oppression, the muscular shadow falling over her rippling with possessive intent. Tom hasn't come here to find himself. He's come here to find someone else.

Lola is always wondering if that's what she wants. If that's all she needs to feel settled and content. But somehow, whenever she has someone, it never works out quite the way she thinks it will.

'Steady on.' Tom's smile finally dips with her pause. 'You know I don't mean anything serious. Between you and me, I mean. I just—'

A sudden clamour at the back mercifully cuts him off. Tom's grip slackens as Oren shoulders past, the rest of the shelter on his tail. And now Lola doesn't have to make any excuses for following, because that's just what they do here, they all follow because it's a communal enterprise, all their tasks focused on one goal, the same goal, the one they all share ... Tom lifts and drops his hands in despair, but of course he's following along too, Andre and Johan by his side. There's no pause for thought or wonder, even as the familiar path into the kibbutz takes on an otherworldly shimmer, its usual rhythms replaced with the eerie hum of worry.

By the time the crowd reaches Lola's hallowed spot on the clifftop, the dog's howl is so loud it could take on the siren itself. Biba bolts for her immediately, barking like a popgun. Panic kicks at Lola's chest – not here, not now, not in front of all these people. Most kibbutzniks usually expect any dog to be dispatched with a well-aimed kick, and Lola could never do that, not to Biba, not to any animal. Pulling out of the throng, she tries to draw the dog away, heading for the wire fence separating the warehouses from the perimeter road. It's all the encouragement Biba needs, racing ahead only to skid to a halt directly opposite chicken house number one, where she starts howling again. Beyond, Lola can see Fouad tangling with Moti and Oren in front of some yellow-and-black-striped hazard tape, stuck feebly across the warehouse's open entrance. The panic rises as Lola jogs back to where Tom is standing, clustered with the others behind the open gate into the driveway.

'There must have been an accident of some kind,' Tom is saying.

'In a chicken house?' Andre snorts. Johan immediately puts himself between them, holding up his hands, gaze flicking nervously back and forth.

'It must be something to do with Farid. He's in charge of the chickens, hey? Something must have happened to him. No one else would be up at the warehouses that they would bother stopping the whole kibbutz for.'

The rest of the crowd suddenly surges forward. Lola spots Fouad disappearing inside the warehouse in a feeble flutter of hazard tape. She only realises they have all started to follow when a sharp, high-pitched wail brings her up short, stumbling as a cascade of chickens come flapping and squawking towards her. The discord is suddenly deafening, ringing around the courtyard and echoing off the clifftop like a repeating chorus, drowning out all thought and reason.

'This is bad,' Tom mumbles from somewhere behind her, the others grunting assent. 'We shouldn't be here, guys, come on. Whatever's happened, it doesn't feel right.'

Lola shrugs him off, unable to tear her eyes away from the mouth of the warehouse and the hunched figure shuffling back out, only to fall to his knees amongst the birds.

'Fouad!' she shouts, even as heads swivel round to question her. What does she think she is doing? How dare she, a volunteer girl, make a spectacle of herself at a time like this? What questions could she possibly have that merit asking, especially now? She wipes sweat from her eyes, wondering if it really is Oren who is dropping to his knees too, swiping away chickens to loop a bulky arm over Fouad's shoulders as they heave with sobs. Moti too, out of nowhere, appears at his other side. Biba claws at the fence as she howls.

'Let me go.' Lola stops Tom before he can restrain her, panic trembling in her voice. 'I just want to find out what's going on.'

'It's obvious, isn't it?' Tom lifts his hands in surrender. 'Something's happened to Farid. Why else would the other guy be so upset? And his stupid mongrel may as well be weeping actual tears.'

'What the fuck are you talking about?' Now it's Andre in her way, Johan arriving on cue to back him up. Where's Sam when she needs her? Lola knows she is gasping, but can't seem to regulate her breathing.

'They're brothers, man,' Johan explains just a little too eagerly. 'Fouad and Farid. I was talking to Oren about it a while back. It's how we run farmhands in South Africa too. All the Arab workers on the kibbutz come from the same family. And it cuts both ways, hey – gives the outsiders almost as much of a stake in the place as if they lived here themselves. It also encourages trust – same family, same motives.'

'Motives?' Lola stammers, gulping. 'What do you mean?'

'You didn't know they were all related?' Tom can't disguise his irritation. 'What, you spend all that time together and he's never mentioned it?'

Lola's hand flies to her mouth. She sways into Tom's arms as he steps towards her.

'Babe, steady on. Are you OK? Help me with her, would you? What is it, Lola? Is it the heat?'

She nods weakly as the boys guide her over to the wire fence, so grateful to be given the obvious excuse that she thinks she might pass out for real, crouching down to rest on her heels. Biba wails in the background, suddenly the loneliest sound Lola has ever heard.

'Is she alright?' Moti's deep voice interrupts from nowhere.

'She's fine, mate, fine,' Tom fusses.

Lola shivers as Moti's bulky shadow falls over her.

'I just felt a bit faint, that's all,' she murmurs, trying and failing to sit up straight. 'A lot ... a lot's happened this morning.'

'Yes.' Moti silences them all. 'Yes, it has.'

Time slows for a moment as Lola stares – at Fouad still hunched on his knees between Issam and Oren, at little Biba's head thrown back as she howls. Even from a distance Lola can tell how desperate the dog is to bolt inside, fur rippling with the strain. A single tear escapes as she thinks about how enough love and encouragement can train even stray animals to do almost anything. To Lola, it suddenly feels like these past dreamy, rainbow-hued months have instantly condensed into a single bubble about to pop.

She swipes the tear away with an angry hand, feels her mother's unseeing eyes on her even from hundreds of miles away. To Lola, it really shouldn't have come as a surprise.

Moti lets out a long, deep sigh. 'You must leave now, all of you. Go on, go back to your rooms. Wash up, drink some water, there will be some food out for everyone in the dining room. We will find you when it is time to go back to work.'

'Mate.' Tom's voice is heavy with dread. 'What's happened? Has there been an accident?'

Moti takes a moment to look up at the sky, over his shoulder at the hill rising behind them, then back out to sea, before he can continue.

'It is Farid. Farid is dead. And it is not—' He stops short, has to take a few breaths before he can say anything more, belly wobbling with effort below his red vest.

'It is not what we thought. It is not what we thought, at all. His brother is sure that somebody killed him.'

Chapter Eight
Wednesday

3:45 p.m.

Jonny wakes with a start, into the deafening blare of a horn, mouth dried sour by the van's air conditioning. He swallows a few times, circling his head on his neck as he focuses out of the window, Amer screaming abuse at the car cutting him up in front. There's the sea to the west. He squints into the lowering sun – great, they can't be far out now. Still, they are quite high above the shoreline. He twists round to see the cluster of buildings that make up the centre of Haifa, the biggest city in Israel's north, receding in the distance behind them.

'Not far now,' Amer mumbles to himself, before Jonny catches his eye in the rear-view mirror. 'Welcome back, my friend. I drive so fast we will have time for a shisha.'

'Where are we?' Jonny swallows again as the words stick in his throat.

'Very close, very close.'

'To Akko, right?'

Amer doesn't answer, just swears as he leans on his horn.

'This is the real problem around here, Jonny. This! Not a single person who lives in the north knows how to drive properly. They have no experience of a real city...' Amer lets his hand gestures do the rest.

Jonny snorts as he rubs his neck, collecting his thoughts. Sleep came easily, which is good. He's obviously been a journalist – no, a reporter – for long enough now that his body has caught up to the fact you sleep whenever the opportunity arises. Just close your eyes and go under. Because when you hit the ground, you better be running. Adrenaline tingles up Jonny's spine at the thought.

'I know a better shisha on the other side of Akko,' he says, rooting around in his backpack for a bottle of water. Amer lets out a roar of laughter.

'How long have you been here now, *habibi*? Six months, a year – and you think you know a shisha better than your uncle Amer? Tell me, what is the difference between a shisha and a nargile? Is it the pipe or the tobacco? Who do you think invented hummus? *Y'ani*, it was not the Israelis!'

'So who was it, then?' Jonny enjoys this explanation. It could apply to the entire region. But it's only the outsiders who ever seem to see it that way. Simultaneously, he finds himself wondering whether there really is a difference between a shisha and a nargile or whether Amer is just winding him up – again. Aren't they both just elaborate smoking hookah pipes filled with equally elaborate and over-scented tobacco? He pictures their ornate bulges and curves, often clad in silver, even gold, wonders if there is yet another historical argument of immense territorial significance hiding in their different chambers.

'Let us see now.' Amer taps his nose again. 'How long have we had this ... this State of Israel?'

Jonny plays along. 'Since 1948. Nearly fifty years—'

'*Khalas!*' Amer interrupts. 'Enough. It is bad enough I have to explain this to you in Hebrew.'

Jonny laughs back. He could tell Amer to carry on in Arabic, Jonny knows the explanation well enough not to give away how much he still doesn't understand. Hearing it in a variety of languages makes the story even more appropriate. But Amer is already continuing.

'Hummus, my friend, is one of the oldest foods in the world.

Older than Israel will ever be. So how can the Israelis have invented it?'

Jonny clears his throat; he's still having trouble swallowing. 'Wasn't it actually the Greeks?'

A lorry-load of Arabic clatters around the van. Jonny holds up his hands in mock surrender.

'Let me tell you once again, *habibi*. The Lebanese, they say it is theirs. The Egyptians, they say they make the oldest recipe of them all. We find it in the Qur'an, also too in the Bible. The Greeks – did they find chickpeas growing under the Acropolis? The Parthenon? *Lah*, they did not. And that is the point, of course. Hummus, it belongs in the Middle East. Like we all do. That is the thing your people must remember.'

'My people?'

'Journalists, you know.' Amer waves a dismissive hand, but Jonny's heart just swells in his chest at the thought. Nothing – well, other than incompetence – can take away his membership of this particular tribe. And Jonny has proved he's most definitely competent for going on a year now.

'Your people come here to tell our stories, like it is just about who did what, when and how. *Lah!* No.' Amer bangs a hand on the horn, even though there are no cars on the road in front of them. 'We all belong here. All of us. No matter who did what and when. It is like the hummus, you see. We are all more the same than we are different.'

'Amen.' Jonny claps a hand against the back of Amer's leather seat, noting again how the older man wheezes through his chuckles. Who, what, when and how. Amer is only missing the why. There Jonny allows himself a small smile. That's what makes Jonny the journalist and Amer the cab driver. But the smile fades almost immediately as he remembers that the stories don't always turn out to be quite what he's looking for.

'Turn right here, would you?'

Amer frowns through the rear-view mirror, rooting a hand into his shirt pocket for a cigarette.

'I actually need to go up to Nahariyya first,' Jonny explains, passing over his own packet. 'Sorry, I should have said. It's getting too late for me to get anything done in Akko now, and the others are already there.'

'Nahariyya?' Amer asks through his teeth as he lights up, tucking the rest of Jonny's cigarettes into his pocket for good measure. 'There is nothing in Nahariyya. Nothing but old people and bad shops. There is not even history.'

'You just have to drop me off there, don't worry.' Jonny hopes the gift of cigarettes will help with his reassurance. Nahariyya barely merits its label of tiny, sleepy Israeli retirement village. Not exactly a hostile town. But this far north, barely ten kilometres from the far more hostile border with Lebanon, the communities stay separate. They keep themselves to themselves. There may only be a few miles between one village and the next, but residents only mix if they have to. They bump along next to each other, not together.

'And there is no shisha in Nahariyya,' Amer grumbles, cracking open a window as the patchwork of exquisite buildings that make up the ancient city of Akko start to flash past, the late afternoon call to prayer to its Muslim residents lilting on the breeze.

'I'll make it up to you when I'm done, *habibi*, I promise. You'll have to let me direct you, though. I can't read or write in this language, not a scrap.'

Amer howls, the idea he'll have to be directed worse than the lack of fragrant tobacco. But Jonny meets a pair of smiling eyes in the mirror.

Almost there, he thinks. And he's ready to start running.

His stomach suddenly twists. It's all that talk of hummus, Jonny remarks to himself. He's just hungry. It's nothing else. Nothing else at all.

One hour later

The smell is always what Jonny remembers. The curiously salty hit of jasmine mixed with sea spray, hanging heavy in the air whether the wind is up or not, so heady he can somehow conjure it from deep within the choking fumes of Jerusalem traffic – any traffic, frankly – if he chooses to. It's a memory so potent he knows it must have been laid down in early childhood, during those sepia-tinted flashes of being a baby in the Israeli sand, before he was upped and moved to the UK. Much like the language his brain must have learned first, still so agile amid the English that has long dominated and taken up permanent residence in his brain since.

What did he do with his days here? Where did he spend his time? What of those years spent as a baby, then a toddler, before the memories started to stick? Years that are near-invisible, except for the senses, which never forget.

The apartment block itself is a couple of rows back from the edge of the beach – right by the school he would have gone to before his mother decided that moving closer to his father's family might fix the obviously unfixable problems in their short marriage. For a low block it still feels as if it is looming tall in front of him as it did when he was a child, running in and out of the entryway with a bucket and spade, perhaps? Or an ice-cream? He reflexively brushes non-existent sand from his hair as he eyes the black squares of windows punched into the white concrete façade.

Was one of them his bedroom? Or was it where he would sit for dinner, gawping at the sky turning crazy colours as the sun set? He will find a way to ask. There must be a way of phrasing the question that will give up some useful detail, even if it's just about the architecture.

Jonny sways ever so slightly as he considers this, gulping another draft of salty, perfumed air. It will be far easier to ask the questions if he sees them as a simple test of his professional ability, a simple test of the job that means everything to him. He's a journalist. Better, he's a reporter. It's his job to ask questions. It's his job to keep asking them, even when they get harder.

He gives the windows one last look before heading back down to the beach itself, walking the fifteen or so minutes along the front to find the apartment that he was never allowed to go to, the apartment that is precisely nowhere in any sepia-tinted snatches of memory that he searches. Jonny tries to regard the housing block itself as dispassionately as it regards him, exactly the same shape, size and design as every other purpose-built housing unit in Nahariyya, including the one he's just come from. Yet out pop the goosepimples, pricking his arms the second he steps into the concrete entryway to ring the bell.

It's just the shade, he tells himself, buzz of the opening door suddenly keening in his ears. Concrete does that. Especially in April. It's still not as hot as it's going to get up here in summer.

Jonny tries to make his feet catch up with his heartbeat as he climbs the leaden steps to the first floor.

Chapter Nine
Wednesday

11:15 a.m.

Moti has shuffled off. The siren has been long silenced, but Fouad's cries have the same effect, heavy in both weight and sound, reverberating between the slatted walls of the three chicken houses arranged in their horseshoe up on the clifftop. Lola blinks furiously – hoping it's sweat, knowing it's tears – tracing out their shape with her gaze, remembering how exacting the description was when it was first explained to her. Why hadn't she pointed out then that horseshoes are only lucky when they face a particular way? Held upright and full or upside down and empty? Is that why she suddenly feels like she is dissolving from the inside out? A few seconds ago the technicolour beauty of the landscape still seemed so enhanced Lola felt like she could literally touch it. Now all she sees is a watercolour washing away, the promise of its vivid colours slipping through her fingers, as fragile and ephemeral as she should have known they always were. Up until she got here, the entire fabric of her life has felt the same.

'This is fucking terrible,' Tom murmurs beside her, dipping his cap reflexively.

Lola struggles to contain herself. The last few months of happy memories are already a blurry stain.

'Up here of all places.' Andre sweeps a hand towards the sea, glinting aggressively under the merciless sun. 'Although I suppose we're not exactly in a benign location, hey.'

'But ... murder?' Johan adds. It's as if one can't speak without the other, clipped South African accents identical. 'How can they possibly be sure it was deliberate? Why would anyone want to kill Farid? You find me a friendlier guy that shovels chickenshit for a living—'

'How would you know? You've never so much as set foot in the chicken house, have you?' Tom interrupts.

'Ya, I have, just for a week before I was sent down to the glasshouse. And no, I wasn't fired, they asked me to move over, something about crops and seasons, I don't know, hey. They even made a gag about too many cooks in the hen house—' Johan breaks off to wince as Andre hoots with laughter. 'Sorry.'

'Mate, don't apologise to me,' Tom mutters, dipping his cap further in Fouad's direction, still bent and wailing on his knees. 'Good thing he didn't hear you, though—'

'Tom?' Lola finally interrupts, faintly. 'Tom, I think...'

And with that the rest of her sentence evaporates into an uncontrollable retch.

Lola's mind empties of everything other than bringing her roiling stomach under control. Wiping her eyes, she spots Oren approaching, immediately allows herself to be manhandled upright. Her only goal: to get herself away from the crowd.

'I'm so sorry,' she whispers, resting against Tom. 'I must be dehydrated. It was already so hot in the banana fields.'

'Babe, don't worry, don't worry at all, I've got you, OK?'

Tom shouts over his shoulder to Andre and Johan as they stagger away.

Questions are scudding through Lola's mind in a nauseating whirl, answers hovering just beyond her reach. Oren has mercifully fallen back.

'I'm OK, I'm OK,' she mutters before he can ask, continuing their stumble down the path to the volunteers' accommodation block. Relief floods through her when she realises the rest of the rooms are still empty.

'Let's get you some water.' Tom bustles into her shared bedroom, motions towards her cot, its patterned sheet still crisp and tucked in tight. Lola pulls out an edge, tries to rumple it, before settling for just collapsing on top. Surely he won't notice it hasn't been slept in? Panic overrides the nausea in her chest. The cot on the opposite wall is demonstrably unmade, Sam's belongings strewn all over the place.

'Aha!' Tom peers around the doorframe separating the sleeping area from the small hall and bathroom, brandishing a bag of sliced bread and a jar of Nutella. 'Guess these are the benefits of sharing with someone who works in the kitchen. What else has young Samantha got stashed in here? Shall I do you some toast?'

Lola gathers the sheet beneath her as she pulls herself to sitting, the bed instantly unmade and messy. 'Not sure I can keep it down,' she croaks out shakily. 'Sam won't mind if you help yourself though. You're doing her a favour. She ... she can't stay off that stuff.' The nausea rises again at her attempts at a joke, however feeble.

Tom just nods as he flicks on the bar heater fixed to the wall above the door. 'Funny, isn't it?' He holds a piece of bread against the heater's grill with a fork. 'These things are basically useless. Have you ever known them to make the room even a centigrade warmer? But leave your bread on them a second too long and – bam.'

He makes a sizzling sound through his teeth, pulling his face and body into an approximation of being electrified. But all Lola can do is stare. Her face feels rubbery and slack yet she can't fix it into an expression of anything other than shock.

'Are you sure I can't make you some? Be good for you to eat something.'

'Could I...' Lola has to stop to clear her throat. 'Actually, Tom, could I have that drink?'

This time the expression on his face is genuine as he realises he's forgotten her water.

'Be right with you, babe, sorry.'

He puts the toast on her bed and heads to the bathroom. Finally Lola's head drops, all her breath streaming out in one go. Gathering a clump of cotton into her fist as if it will steady her, she squeezes it tight, plays a series of images through her mind:

She'd met Farid in the usual place, at the usual time. Even now a shiver of anticipation runs through her just thinking of it – the most delicious secret she's ever kept. Lola did everything right, followed every instruction – and now he's dead? Her shiver dead-ends into the reek of bile.

She swallows, rewinds, starts again. Half past midnight in the far corner of the furthest orchard, almost completely hidden by avocado trees. That's the blind spot. The only place where Farid can climb into the kibbutz unseen, and only if someone else is providing the rope ladder, slinging it silently over the high wire fence. Lola pictures herself throwing it over in exactly the way he showed her. Were they seen – or heard – regardless? She reflexively looks over each shoulder only to find tattered wallpaper rather than moonlit shrubs.

Now for the separate routes they always take up to the chicken houses, just in case they're caught. A hand flutters to her cheek – yes, this is how he cups her face first, as fleetingly and gently as the silky night air, before disappearing in the opposite direction. They skirt the outer edge of the kibbutz like sprites, mirroring each other's movements, until their paths cross again at the very top of the cliff. The only sounds ... Lola's brow furrows. She has to think hard about this, as she's usually too consumed with nervous excitement to hear anything other than what she's intent on hearing. There's the swish of the sea. The creak of the breeze through the banana fields. The occasional appreciative whine from Biba when she catches Farid's scent afresh. That is, until the scrape of the loose panel that lets them into the cottonseed warehouse, the world's largest mattress. There, Farid finally takes her hand, leading her higher and higher through the fluffy bales until the only things that can see them are the soft husks themselves. He caresses her just as gently, like her whole body is made from clouds.

Lola shivers again, lingering on the sensations of every detail, a hand drifting under her vest to find the stray seed-heads that always seem to stick there afterwards as if they will prove to her Farid isn't dead after all. Her fingers search every crease until she gasps, a punch to her chest, as she realises there are none left. Not a single one.

'Are you alright? Lola?'

She only realises she has screwed her eyes shut when she opens them to find Tom standing at the foot of the cot with a glass of water.

'Thanks', she mumbles, reaching out. 'I just...' She tips her head back, the need to finish her sentence disappearing as she glugs down the lot.

'More?'

Lola shakes her head, handing the glass back. Tom smiles, then presses the play button on the tape deck. Familiar guitar chords flood the room: Oasis, the definitive soundtrack to their last few months, a kaleidoscope of memories attached to every song.

Lola's fingers suddenly twitch with the impulse to turn it off. Every lyric suddenly seems to mean something far darker, far more complicated.

'Man alive. That poor guy. Of all places to cark it. Done over in the middle of a hen house, chickenshit everywhere.' The bread sizzles as Tom toasts another slice on the bars of the heater.

'I wonder why they think it was deliberate,' he continues. 'They must have found the guy in a right state – Jeez. And no doubt we'll all have to account for ourselves now. It's not like random folks can just drive in and out of here.'

Now it's the geography of the kibbutz that's flashing through

Lola's mind. The border, the clifftop, the heavy iron gates that clank closed at the end of the main driveway every night.

The tangles of razor wire edging almost every fence.

The armed guards.

The hidden cameras.

She sees the realisation in Tom's eyes the moment he turns away from the heater.

It hits Lola in the same moment with a dazzling, painful clarity. Every single other person on the kibbutz will have realised the same thing.

'Hang about. What was that guy doing here in the middle of the night anyway? He doesn't live here, does he? So he must have been here well before sun-up. Which means someone must have let him in. Unless—'

Tom suddenly curses, the aggressive bar heater making short work of his flimsy slice of bread. An acrid waft of smoke drifts through the air.

Lola rubs at her temple, has to clear her throat again. 'Could I ... could I have some more water? Do you mind? I just ... Sorry, I still feel a bit woozy.'

Tom's irritation melts away as he reaches for her empty cup. Lola flops back down on to her cot the moment he's disappeared, twisting and pulling at the allergy bracelet on her wrist. And now all she can think about is how Farid used to tangle with it too, but only to circle the tip of his finger over her pulse with such exquisite gentleness it would have the opposite effect on her heart rate.

Lola has to yank her hand away, claw at her bedsheets instead. Is the first person to see her so clearly really gone? Farid used to gaze at her like he'd found a soul she didn't even know she had herself – and now she's somehow got to pretend none of it ever happened? That she never even cared? Lola's breath starts to come in little gasps, the concept too huge to fathom. Except it isn't, because she's connected to it, she must be. He wouldn't have been here at all if it wasn't for her.

A cold sweat prickles down Lola's back. Somewhere in the background, Oasis is singing about cannonballs, landslides and supernovas.

'What an unholy mess.' Tom rounds the doorframe again, water sloshing over the brim of the cup in his hand. 'As if an actual war wasn't already enough to deal with. Now people have obviously been coming in and out after hours. So much for a ring of steel – what a crock of shit. Who are they? And what have they been doing? Everyone will want to know, not just us. And there's no way of hiding it, not with a body on the ground.'

Lola reaches for the water before any more of it spills, dipping her head to hide the tears leaking from her eyes. All the nights she's spent fending off Tom's advances, a few beers in, campfire burning down to fireflies. What about the few nights she's given in? Handsome, hearty Tom, who just wants to love and protect her. She wasn't leading him on. She was giving herself a chance.

Or is it just the fact she seems to do things for people after a while, especially if they ask her in the right way. Lola swallows down the water in sudden, angry gulps.

'Better?' Tom's gaze meets hers, wide blue eyes brimming with hope and opportunity.

'I think so, yeah. Thank you.' She reaches a shaky hand out to the larger one resting on the mattress beside her.

'What is it, babe?'

She lets her head drop into the other hand reaching out to cup her face. Tom's own edges closer, breath tickling her chin.

'The thing is ... Tom?'

He silences her with a soft kiss, a brush of lips against hers. She pauses for moment before pulling away, squeezing his hand down into the mattress.

'It's just ... I need to tell you something.'

Chapter Ten
Wednesday

5:30 p.m.

The unmistakable funk of stale, sour air hits Jonny even though the heavy door is barely open a crack, his whispered greeting lost in the creak of the hinge as he pushes it wide. Immediately he has to flap a hand around to try and move clouds of cigarette smoke through the air, hanging in the room like a fire blanket, blotting every other atom out.

'Safta – what happened?'

A coughing fit stills Jonny on the threshold before he can continue, marvelling in equal measure at the quantity of smoke in the tiny apartment, and how natural the Hebrew word for grandma already feels for a woman he had no memory of ever meeting a year ago.

'What do you mean?' a voice answers him from somewhere by the windows, closed fast against both the glare of the setting sun and any hint of a sea breeze.

Jonny squints into the fug. There's an outline of a small, bird-like figure perched improbably upright in the faded patchwork armchair under the sill.

'Why—' But Jonny's question dies off into another splutter. He crosses the few steps through the room to the wall of windows, scrabbling at one of the catches.

'Leave it. I don't like the noise.'

'Noise is going to be the least of your problems if you don't let me open it.'

There's an almost physical quality to the rush of salty, fragrant air pouring into the room as Jonny wrenches the sash free. But his grandmother just scoffs.

'See? What did I tell you.'

The chatter and bustle of the crowds drifting from the beach below mingle with a wave of curses from the figure sharpening in the armchair.

'Now they will light a fire. Then they will get out the guitar. Ach, it will go on all night.'

'Better than suffocating to death.'

Jonny hangs his head out of the window for another gulp of air. Clusters of young people laugh and joke while they kick at the sand below, string vests hanging off their shoulders, six-packs of cans stacked in columns around them. The tableau finds him almost immediately, as it always seems to, anywhere in Israel – a strikingly beautiful girl, dark curls rippling down her back, artfully frayed denim skirt riding high around her hips. Opposite her, a similarly-aged man, bright singlet top, surf-hobo tan, bare brown feet. Too rangy and relaxed, with hair far too long to have been through the army, he tosses his head and laughs as the banter flows. No one seems to care they are well in range of any incoming rockets from southern Lebanon.

Jonny pushes the window wider as he wonders, was this how they met? His father, brimming with exotic-stranger confidence, keenly aware of his appeal as someone who hadn't been through the three years of conscription that await all Israeli teenagers as they come of age? Someone with the promise of distant shores, alternative horizons, the same dreams, just shaded in a different colour. From a literal far-flung island nation – the emerald isle, a jewel-coloured one at that. Patrick Murphy, he may as well have had a shamrock tattooed on his forehead. Maybe he did...

And there would have been his mother, fresh out of the air force, hungry for new thrills and experiences. The reason so many

Israelis found themselves tripping their lights out on Thai beaches straight out of the army. Find any place, do anything that would transport them somewhere else, blot out institutional memories as fulsomely as possible.

Jonny tunes out more grumbling as another male approaches – no mistaking this one with his square shoulders, army-straight back, buzz-cut dark hair. The girl turns her whole body towards him, face bright with white teeth. Not the scenario he'd imagined, then.

He returns to the smoke of his grandmother's apartment, berating himself. Jonny's parents met when his father volunteered on the very kibbutz Jonny would be visiting tomorrow morning, while his mother was still living there with her parents. That much he already knew. His mother and her family were apparently kibbutz originals. The lot of them only left the place and decamped to this faceless town once the disgrace of his mother's affair got too much, merely to fracture even further into their single component parts.

Marrying out, Jonny muses, for at least the thousandth time. What a hideous, warped term for simply falling in love. Did any member of his so-called extended family ever appreciate quite how far its consequences would extend? Jonny is still miles away from putting together what happened to them all next.

'You were fast,' the old lady observes, her frown sharpening with her wrinkles as the clouds of smoke start to clear.

'There wasn't...' Jonny pauses for another cough. 'There wasn't as much traffic as usual. Can I leave at least one of these open?'

'Only if you get me another cigarette.' She fixes him with her dark eyes rather than smile. Jonny chances a grin anyway, tapping his empty shirt pocket.

'I'm all out, sorry.'

But his grandmother just inclines her head in the direction of the white kitchen cabinets lining the opposite wall.

'In the middle.'

'Sorry?'

'The middle one.'

Jonny raises his eyebrows, glancing at the cabinets then back again.

'You keep your own stash right here?'

She doesn't answer, frowning out of the window in distaste instead. Jonny sighs before clumping the few steps over to the cupboard. They still hardly know each other, he reasons, brow furrowing as he removes a carton of two hundred cigarettes from the stack inside. So how can he expect to understand why she chain smokes her way through the strongest cigarettes on the market? Or get away with judging her for it? At least if he complies he can get away with asking her a few more questions. There's still so much he doesn't know about why she wasn't part of his life until he managed to find her himself.

Jonny unwraps the box, cellophane crackling through his fingers. *Noblesse*, he reads on the lurid green cover. The French would read it one way, the English the same. He's not sure they'd agree with how the Israelis have appropriated it. Nobility doesn't necessarily equal strength in this part of the world.

'Here you go.' Jonny is all falsetto brightness, walking back across the room with the packet in his outstretched hand. He leans on the windowsill, out into the open air, watching her lighter flare.

'So, how are you? I hope the rocket attacks haven't disturbed you too much? Where are the bomb shelters in this apartment block, anyway?'

Jonny asks even though it feels pointless. He's come up here on a summons. Which is a development in and of itself, but still. He's had to instigate most of the previous visits. He's still basically a stranger in all but name to this woman. The same as he'll be to the rest of his family, if he ever finds any of them too.

His grandmother answers with a funnel of smoke. Jonny tries to continue without breathing.

'Thanks for asking me up. There's a lot of ground to cover between us, after all this time—'

'*Lo*.' No. The Hebrew word seems so much more emphatic than the English as she silences him. 'Not for this.'

Jonny nods, trying not to let his head droop too much. Order isn't restored. The past has happened. This still isn't a joyous reunion. He still hasn't got any more information, of either the personal or professional kind.

A small smile plays around his grandmother's wizened mouth as she surveys him. Below the open window, a burst of noise spurts in from the boardwalk.

'You are a good boy,' she answers eventually. 'She was like that too, once.'

'Mum, you mean?'

His grandmother turns away, blows smoke at the sea. She won't say her name, Jonny knows that. For at least the thousandth time, he wonders whether she really hasn't said it since his mother had the temerity to fall in love with the wrong person. There are a thousand things that should matter more to his grandparents than the fact his father wasn't Jewish. But to some people it seems that it matters more than anything else, more than being a good person, a present father, a non-violent, nay, loving husband – to name the usual, normal fundamentals.

Jonny smarts. After all this time, it still doesn't make any better sense. He has to swallow down the acid of betrayal before he can try again.

'Why did you call me up here, Safta?'

'Your Hebrew is perfect.' She nods as she inhales again. 'You learned it in school, over there?'

'No. She taught me.' Jonny doesn't use his mother's name either, doesn't trust himself with it. 'We spoke it at home, together. It was just me and her, so it made sense. She actually refused to speak English to me even when I was tired and couldn't find the right words in Hebrew. Stayed quiet until I found another way to say what I meant. I think she knew it would die in me if she didn't, and she was right. There wasn't anyone else who spoke Hebrew where we lived—'

'Of course there wasn't!' Jonny jumps as his grandmother interrupts, tiny body suddenly filling the frame of the armchair in fury. 'She did not belong there. With him.'

Jonny doesn't dare answer. He's come here enough times now to understand the rhythm of these visits. Once the door is open, all he can expect to do is stand in the frame. Once he is over the threshold, it's about sitting and listening, rather than answering. Only when Jonny has demonstrated he understands enough is he going to be able to ask questions of his own. And there are still so many. Sometimes it feels like the questions are the things choking him, not her ever-present clouds of cigarette smoke.

'And of course, now you are here,' his grandmother adds. 'You have come back. Because you belonged here all along. That is why.'

'Mmmmm?' Jonny nods, eyeing her cigarette. Suddenly sharing a smoke feels like the logical next step, even though the room is still coated in her last packet.

'You can have one if you want, of course.'

He leans to pick the packet off the windowsill next to her. Chatter and laughter laps through the air as he waits for her next move, considering his own.

'So there has been a business. At the kibbutz.'

'That's the only reason you called?'

'You are a journalist, yes?'

Jonny exhales through his nod.

His grandmother's dark eyes gleam through the haze. 'It is a good job,' she says, examining the cigarette in her bony fingers.

'I think so,' he replies softly, peering back out of the window. The girl and her buzz-cut companion are long gone, singlet-man smiling at someone else. Jonny finds himself marvelling for at least the eightieth time at the transcendental glimmer of the sea in the background. This sea does not look like the type to churn you up and spit you back out again if you so much as dip a toe into its waters.

'Yes, yes. You want to find out the truth, even when no one wants to tell you.'

'By business, do you mean what's happened at Beit Liora?'

Another name that might set him back with her, but Jonny says it anyway. Much like his mother's, his grandmother may have excised its name from her memory too, but there's one certainty in Jonny's life out here, and that's the job he's got to do. And Allen set the clock, after all. He can practically hear it ticking as the minutes grind by.

'Yes.' Those dark eyes find him again, like lasers. 'And it is not what you think.'

'I don't think anything.'

'Yes, you do. I tell you a body has been found, an Arab worker, in a kibbutz on the border. You must think something...'

'Well, I think it sounds suspicious.'

'That is because it is.'

'And are you going to tell me why?'

A firecracker pops below the open window into a volley of laughter.

'Only if you do not ask how I know.'

'Well, I can figure that part out myself,' Jonny replies lightly. 'You've lived your whole life either there, or close by, in a country where practically everyone knows everyone else. It stands to reason why stuff might reach you.'

Years seem to flash by in the nanosecond their eyes meet through the haze. Jonny's mother was never supposed to find out the secrets of what both her parents did for the Israel Defence Forces, and continued to do long after their conscription ended. Much less tell anyone else what she knew. But secrets and lies are things that even the youngest children can understand. Especially when dressing them up as military intelligence makes them sound like an exciting game.

A small smile turns the corners of Jonny's mouth. Thanks to his mother, here he is, more than a decade later, understanding the value of information that comes from certain sources without having to be told why. It's also thanks to her that he's found a job that feels a bit like a family too. He continues, emboldened.

'This body. Was it a revenge killing because of the rocket attacks?'

Nettled as his grandmother's scoff turns into a coughing fit, Jonny silently justifies the question to himself instead of her. Residents along the border have been terrorised the most by these recent attacks, he reasons, picturing the mad dashes into air-raid shelters, the echoes of World War Two in every siren, the sleepless nights on concrete. You don't have to look hard to find Israelis that see their minority Arab citizens as inferior, even though they hold the same citizenship. Jonny can see it happening, sure he can. A death in retribution. Especially in light of how the Israeli prime minister was assassinated himself. An old grudge boiling over into a crime of passion, maybe. Making the point in another way. Why not?

Jonny tries again. 'OK, but was it deliberate? This guy was killed? He didn't just die?'

'He did not.' Another cough. 'On this, you are right. There has been a murder.'

'And why would I care about it? Or more importantly, why would the *Trib*?'

Another firecracker bangs, further in the distance this time. Below the window, someone begins to strum a thin tune on a guitar.

'Because this man...' his grandmother says, stretching out an arm to point her lit cigarette directly at Jonny. 'This man was using our tunnel.'

Jonny stares at the ember glowing at his chest like the centre of a target. And all of a sudden he realises that she isn't directing it at him at all.

She is pointing north, up the coast beyond the border.

But now all that comes out is a whispered 'no'. Lola forces herself to remember that fighting back doesn't always make it stop. Sometimes it just makes things a hundred times worse. Go limp, her body tells her. Escape more punishment. Submit.

'Then what is it?' Tom hesitates.

Lola clinks mugs, presses buttons, puts on a show. She knows Tom's ego will stop him being any more direct unless she's explicit. She waits another beat, curiously revolted by her own behaviour as she is relieved her plan is going to work.

'It's about Farid.'

'What about him?'

Tom stares, questions written all over his frown. And they're not unreasonable: why would they need to discuss Farid any further beyond what's just happened? Neither of them work in the chicken houses. None of the volunteers do. On the face of it, all any of them know about Farid is his hard-earned reputation: the only Arab Israeli in charge of an entire kibbutz division; his legendary commitment to his chickens. And just like that, Lola is picturing Farid all over again – his tawny frame, his improbably bottle-green eyes, his broad smile twinkling around the communal dining room, the puppy in the room trying to root out and convert the last humans still indifferent to him. In the flash of a blink he is replaced with Tom, his blush cooling unevenly into blotches.

Tears prick her eyes as she sighs, has to pause and look away.

'Aw babe, come on, it's OK.' Tom's across the room in less than a second, arms tight around her. 'It's a shock. A big one. But you don't need to worry. These guys, the Israelis, they don't mess around. They'll find out who did this in a nanosecond. Hell, they probably already know. They'll question everyone just for appearances.' He lets out a dry laugh. 'We'll all have to go over what we were doing last night, at least, for sure. Everyone will have to account for their movements. Hell, I'd love to be in the room when they get to Andre. Maybe he'll finally 'fess up to making googly eyes at Sam all night, huh. At least Jo can fall back on spewing his guts up – literally. Bits of his dinner are probably still around the fire pit if they poke around enough.'

Lola stiffens against him. Suddenly she sees their hallowed stone circle high on the clifftop for what it really is – broken deck chairs half buried into the ground, cracked and overflowing ashtrays, all strewn with crumpled beer cans. 'Looks like we had a good night,' the volunteers always joke as they pitch up again. But what it actually looks like is a snapshot of disrespect and denial. And the volunteers are the ones still welcome here.

Lola opens and closes the kettle, staring into its empty recesses as if it will somehow fill itself. 'So what'll you say? When they question you, I mean? Do you think they'll start immediately?'

'Who the hell knows.' Tom cosies himself up behind her. She tells herself it's just his trauma kit that she can feel bulging against her lower back. 'They only just found the guy. There's probably all sorts to do with the body first. And the place still has to function – no doubt we'll all end up back at work in short order. Can't have the avocadoes rotting in the trees.'

A little whine escapes before she can stop it, the image of overripe fruit turning putrid alongside a decomposing corpse almost too much to bear. But all Tom hears is encouragement, pulling her even closer.

She snaps the kettle lid closed, gulping a deep breath into the clunk. 'It's just ... The thing is, I ended up going for a walk last night. I felt so sick after Jo got the rocket fuel out...'

Tom snorts, breath hot on her neck. 'Hah. I forgot about that.'

'I just ... I had to walk it off before I could lie down. You know how I get. I would just spew if I tried to sleep after that much vodka. So I walked around and around the kibbutz until I sobered up enough to nap before work.'

'Did you stay up all night?' His hand snakes back under Lola's vest. 'My little anarchist.'

'No, I...'

'So when I saw you this morning on the clifftop, had you even been to bed?'

'I did pass out eventually, just for a bit. But I must have been wandering around for hours. I don't remember much apart from it being around 3:00 a.m. when I got in.'

Tom spins her round into his chest, massaging her back.

'No one will give a stuff about that, babe. Like you're ever on time anyway, huh? So you went for a little moonlight walk. Round the houses, till your head stopped spinning. Kicked a few of the strays into touch to boot. No big deal.'

No big deal? Finally Lola buries her face in his chest if only to let the tears flow. Resting on top of hers, Tom's head feels heavy as a helmet.

'We don't even know why they think it was deliberate,' he continues. 'It could just be the other guy overreacting, you know, his brother...'

A mouthful of sweaty cotton muffles her attempts to say Fouad's name.

'That guy, yeah. We actually don't know a thing until the cops get here. Or whoever they call this far into the bush. Might even be the military.'

Lola is shocked into pulling away. 'The military? Are you serious?'

Tom's expression creases with surprise. 'Why not? Is there even a difference around here? What's the point of cops if half the people around you are in the army anyway? Are those guys marching around up the hill border police or soldiers? It's all the same, isn't it? Whoever shows up here will have questions, sure, but I doubt they'll care about our pissed-up campfire beyond the fact we were having one, together, before we all went to bed.'

Lola squirms under his stare, gazing past him at the photos stuck all over Sam's side of the room, happy families in technicolour. Not for the first time she finds herself wishing for Sam's simple fix – behaving exactly as an observant Jewish girl is expected to. Lola was just lucky that Sam fought to bring her along while she was doing it. Sam didn't have to.

Tom cocks his head. 'Is there something else you're trying to tell me, babe?'

'No!' It comes out a little louder than Lola planned and Tom's surprise furrows to something more pronounced. 'Not unless you want to count the hours I lost rambling around the perimeter in circles.'

'We were all as wasted as each other,' he mumbles, finally looking away.

'It's not a good look, is it?' Lola takes her chance, cradling his hand in hers. 'I guess none of us could categorically say we remember for sure who went one way and who went the other.'

Tom pauses, twining his other hand into her hair, tracing stray strands away from her forehead. Lola holds her breath. Has understanding passed between them, or is there more left to say? The hand on her forehead moves to cup her face, tipping her chin towards his just a little too deliberately.

'Let's just see what happens, shall we?'

Lola closes her eyes as Tom's lips brush hers, goosepimples springing out of her bare arms.

Chapter Twelve
Wednesday

6:00 p.m.

'What do you mean, a tunnel? Like, underground?'

Jonny is so floored he can't even curse himself for asking such an infantile question. He gazes out of the window, lets the setting sun blind him for a minute. A tunnel? From inside the kibbutz? Why? And where to? His grandmother suddenly laughs, sharp and brittle.

'A tunnel,' he repeats, more to himself than to her. 'Starting inside Beit Liora?'

Another laugh, more of a wry snort this time.

'Wait a second.' Jonny pulls himself straight, not having realised the extent to which he was leaning against the windowsill. Chatter rises from the beach, grating against the thoughts jangling inside his head.

'You're telling me that under one of the most fortified borders in the world – controlled by a literal army, no less – there's an open tunnel connecting one side with the other? So in theory a load of Hezbollah militia commandoes could run through it at any moment and shoot the place up in seconds if they wanted to?'

Smoke wreathes between them as Jonny peers at the figure in the armchair, still such a stranger to him and yet so significant a new presence in his life he is suddenly furious that he can't see her properly, can't read her expressions, can't try to recognise shades of his mother, better still, himself. How dare his grandmother call him up here just to land him with this information? He wrestles a little though – because he can see it both ways. As a journalist covering the current tensions between Israel and Lebanon, his grandmother is handing him dynamite. But is that what he really wanted from her?

She nods. 'Yes. And the Israelis should have destroyed it years ago. It would all be buried inside the mountain, if I had my way. All the secrets. Gone.'

'What way? W-what do you mean?' Jonny can't stop himself stuttering. He peers into the smoke, out of the window at the horizon, then back again.

'The minute we found it, we should have destroyed it. It was too big a risk. Compromising the border? Leaving a pathway wide open to a hostile army? Forget it.'

The embers fly as she waves her cigarette, sparks of light dancing in Jonny's eyes.

'But, instead, all those idiots saw was opportunity. A way to spy on the enemy. A giant strategic advantage, they said. Never mind that it was far more likely to be a giant strategic mistake.'

Jonny rubs his eyes, trying to put the pieces together. 'So you're saying the dead guy had found it?'

'Yes. Worse, he was using it. Communicating with the other side. That is why he is dead. Which is also why we now have an even more giant problem. For who knows what he gave away? And to who? Right as we're fighting again.'

The sharp edge of the windowsill jabs Jonny in the stomach as he has to turn away for another gulp of air. This information feels so explosive it can't possibly be true. He leans out of the window again, peering up the coast, at the land sloping sharply up to the border, picked out by the sky itself.

'That's ridiculous,' he murmurs to himself before ducking back into the room. 'How can there possibly be a tunnel under that mountain? You'd need heavy machinery to dig anything resembling one, for starters. And there's no way to do it unnoticed, no way at all.'

'You are not listening. It was already there. We don't know how old it is, but that doesn't matter. The Israelis are the ones who found it.'

'Since when?' Jonny runs a sticky hand through his hair. 'It's just so hard to believe.'

He starts as the figure moves from sitting to standing to leaning next to him in almost one, fluid movement. Two tiny, worn hands tug at Jonny's arm.

'What is unbelievable is the fact we didn't destroy it immediately. It has been sitting there open for years. How stupid can you get? Why do you think I left the service? I could not stand by and watch after that. Finding a back door unlocked and open to one of the most hostile nations on earth? Deciding not to close it so we can run a secret intelligence operation instead? Spy from two feet away? Never mind the fact it could be used to transport guns, bombs and murderers? And it's me who had to leave the military in disgrace!'

'Because you refused to follow orders?'

Rather than answer Jonny immediately she puffs on her cigarette as if it's providing oxygen, blowing the smoke out through her teeth.

'That's what they'll tell you. I'm some madwoman, on the edge of treason. But only I know the truth. Not that there's anyone left that will listen to me. And now we have those idiots up there, in that, in that ... place.'

'Beit Liora?' Jonny prompts her without thinking, shrivelling in on himself as her coal-black stare inflames with rage.

'Yes,' she practically spits at him. 'Those idiots who think all that matters is their way of life together. Even after all this time, you think I don't know what they are really like? What they really care most about? These are people who will sacrifice anything and everything just to live on those stupid farms, rotting their brains away with their fruit and vegetables. Someone there thinks they have killed a traitor, as if that will be enough, as if that will end this whole thing. As if it is impossible the tunnel could still be a risk. Never mind that the entire kibbutz has spent the last two weeks in and out of air-raid shelters dodging rocket fire.'

She spits for real this time, a bullet out of the open window.

'And do you know what is even more stupid? Those kibbutzniks don't want anyone to find out, because then the IDF will come in and raze their farm. It was only built there in the first place to secure the access on our side. No, they prefer to leave us vulnerable just so they can keep growing their stupid olives.'

'So you're saying there are other people on the kibbutz that know about it too? I don't understand.'

'That is your job – to try and understand. And then to tell everyone. Imagine if the rest of this country finds out that their beloved military knew of this weakness all along? Imagine if they find out *after* a load of crazies have used it to slip into Israel undetected and shoot up everyone and everything they can see?'

'I ... I know, Safta, but—'

'You dare to come here, after all these years – you dare come to find me, my long-lost grandson – just to laugh in my face? To tell me I know nothing about my own country? About our enemies, and how to defeat them? About just how far they will go to take this land for themselves? Ach, I should not be surprised you are as stupid as her!'

Vertigo suddenly seizes Jonny's legs, instantly quivering with the impulse to pitch his body out into the open air, away from this woman, away from all that she is suggesting. He has always reasoned that seeking his mother's family out was a necessary evil. He would never be able to reconcile himself with living here unless he searched for them at some point. It would always be lurking in the back of his mind if he didn't do it, waiting to ambush him in his dreams.

And Jonny hasn't even told her that his mother is dead yet.

This is the thought that propels him back into the room, plants his feet more firmly into the floor, only for his grandmother to start pushing at him, tiny fists like birdshot.

'Stupid, stupid, stupid—'

Jonny holds his hands up, as if it will make her stop.

'Please don't say that about her. You hardly knew her, in the end.'

'She was my daughter! Until she betrayed our country with that man. And now here you are, reminding me of everything she could have been.'

'Do you mean that?'

Jonny's heartbeat quickens, if only for a second. But all his grandmother's fists do is fall, tiny arms suddenly limp by her sides. He holds his breath, till she turns away, sits back down into her chair. Resumes her position. Lights herself another cigarette. Blows smoke towards his face.

'Go up there. See for yourself. If you do your job properly, you will tell everyone. You will have to. But do it fast. There are already too many bodies. We could have buried it all inside the mountain if those fools had listened to me.'

Jonny turns back to the window, gazing down at the cluster of people below, singing along with the splash of waves on to the shore behind them. He hardly needs any encouragement to go up to Beit Liora. But he doesn't feel ready for what he might find. Not one little bit. Time slows as he considers his choices, as if he even has any at all.

'Do you mind if I use your phone?'

His grandmother tosses her head in the direction of the unit on the kitchen counter.

'Of course. You will eat first, yes?'

He blinks at her through the smoke, no need for an answer to propel her to her feet.

'Sit down, sit down. You are hungry.'

A statement, not a question. It's only then that Jonny registers the still-steaming bags of fresh pitta bread and tubs of chopped salad on the counter that she must have readied for his arrival.

The smoke clears as she totters past him, waving a hand in the air.

Chapter Thirteen
Wednesday

12:45 p.m.

'Hah! What did I tell you?'

Lola pulls away from Tom as the door flies open. Andre walks in carrying a large bowl of hard-boiled eggs, Johan following with a plastic-wrapped loaf of sliced bread.

'Here...' Andre holds out the bowl with a triumphant gleam in his eyes. 'We brought you lovebirds some food. I bet Jo that you'd be at it, hey. Feeling better?'

Lola takes the eggs with a small nod. Tom's hand rests on her back, heavy and warm. She doesn't always tell the truth. Sometimes she leaves things out. Sometimes important things. That's all this is. Everyone tells the stories they want to tell. Not necessarily the ones they should. Still she feels suddenly cold as Tom removes his hand to wave at Andre.

'How's the mood in the dining room?'

'Terrible. Man, the place is groaning with food and people are too scared to touch it.'

Andre flips the tape in the deck as he sits down on Sam's unmade bed – Pulp, the one about common people. For a moment Lola wonders if there'll ever be a time in her life when songs don't seem to be telling her something. This access-all-areas aspect of their shared accommodation block used to feel like a cocoon. The lack of privacy made her feel safe – secure, even. This was no place for secrets. There was nowhere to hide. But her axis has shifted now. Suddenly Lola could not feel more exposed.

'So everyone's out of the bomb shelters?' she asks.

'Just about, hey. All of them had shown up by the time we left. The greenhouse, the orchards. Even the laundry dudes.'

Andre reaches out for an egg to peel, dropping shell on to the floor. 'No need for that look. She won't mind, and I know you don't.'

'Sam is tidier than you think,' Lola mumbles, frowning at the underwear poking between the clothes all over the floor. 'She's just not very good at keeping on top of it.'

Jo snorts from the doorway, holding a piece of bread against the heater, face falling almost immediately that Andre's eyes narrow at him.

Lola gazes between them. Andre and Johan's emotional balance is the complete opposite of their physical one. Johan dwarfs Andre but hangs on his every word. It's like he can stand taller when they are together, hunching and shrinking whenever Andre leaves the room. Are she and Sam the same and she's just never noticed? What if their friendship is just as far out of balance? Lola's stomach clenches all over again as she considers all the places Sam's true loyalties lie. She lets Tom take her hand, follows him over to her cot, where they both sit down.

'Made any progress on that front yet, mate?' Tom laughs.

'Wouldn't you like to know, hey,' Andre crams a whole egg into his mouth. Jo passes Tom a piece of toast without another word.

'Thanks, bru. She's a hard nut to crack, young Samantha.'

'Shut up,' Andre mumbles through a mouthful of egg.

'Sorry.' The toast crunches as Tom takes a bite, continues talking while chewing. 'I know you'll front up when you're good and ready. You've been trying it on for long enough. She's still in the kitchen, I take it?'

Jo nods. 'We talked for a sec on the way back. She was still boiling eggs when she found out. Makes you wonder whether we should be eating them today.'

'Don't be so soft, man.' Andre leans over for another egg. 'Like this has got anything to do with chickens or eggs.'

'Too right,' Tom adds, swallowing. 'Have the cops or anyone official-looking shown up yet?'

Lola tenses but Andre shakes his head. 'Sooner or later, hey.'

'We'll all be grilled, too,' Tom continues. 'We've just been talking about it—'

Andre cuts him off with a snort, nodding at Jo. 'Man, I told you the rocket fuel was a mistake. On a weeknight too. And don't pretend you can remember anything.'

Jo drops the bread from the heater, pretending he's burned his fingers. Relief suddenly cascades through Lola with an intensity that's almost painful. *No one can remember anything*.

'You weren't exactly compos mentis either, mate,' Tom snorts back. 'I seem to remember you throwing vodka shots over your shoulder rather than into your gob.'

'That's an Aussie trick, *mate*.'

But Andre's smile doesn't reach his eyes. Lola tenses further. Still, Tom doesn't rise to it, just peels the egg white away from its yolk. 'Whatever. We were all wasted. It's the same old story. Fire pit, sunset, bad tunes, too much of the strong stuff. It won't sound particularly interesting even if they hear it six different ways.'

'You think?' Jo wonders, folding a slice of bread in half. 'I don't know. They might be a bit more forensic if it stops all the late-night singing.'

'You'll have to admit to hurling up your guts then!' Andre hoots from the other side of the room. 'I think you even put the fire out in the second wave.'

Jo grimaces. Lola watches him try not to tear the bread between his fingers with a growing sense of dread.

'You're right though, bru.' Andre tosses his head towards them. 'It's what we do every night. It would be weirder if we pretended we'd done something different. But I suppose Dave will have to think about how to explain going to bed early with nothing but a book again, hey.'

'Tom can account for that, though.' Jo jumps in a little too eagerly. 'He was probably still up reading when you rolled in.'

Lola finds herself squeezing her plastic bowl so hard in anticipation of Tom's response that the eggshells at its edge start to crack. Now Tom can reasonably get away with saying he'd spent the night outside with her, just to get some time alone.

But all Tom does is hedge. 'Mate, the problem is Dave's book is the *Satanic Verses* at the moment. What if he has to prove what he's reading? That thing is banned in a bunch of places. We're damned if we do and damned if we don't, huh? He smuggles it over in his smalls, pulls a sock over it and everything, only to wave the fucking thing around whenever he can't be arsed with your banter.'

And with that Tom stuffs the yolk into his mouth to a resounding roar of laughter.

The thick white curls of discarded egg white glint nauseatingly under the strip light as Lola realises Dave will know immediately if Tom is lying. There is no way he can give her an alibi. And Tom knows that too. He might sound like he's joking around but he's actually just reminding her that he can't.

Andre smirks knowingly at them both. 'You two kill me, hey.'

Lola tries to roll her eyes, but knows she just looks suspicious. But don't they all, she wonders? Unanswered questions suddenly start popping in her mind, bursting out one after the other like they've been trapped for months. What is the real story behind Dave's obsessive reading? Why are Johan and Andre quite so obsessively dependent on each other? What must have happened to Tom in the past that has made him so intent on making her commit to him? She realises living and working together as closely as they have has only given them the illusion that they know each other inside out. When in fact, it's just been small talk, surface stuff, covering up any cracks or inconsistencies with commitment to whatever menial task is actually at hand.

'Whatever you reckon,' Tom answers for them both. 'We'll be fine if we look after each other. We're not the problem out here. No one gives a stuff about us beyond whether we're doing our jobs properly or not. We just need to keep our heads down and stick together, just in case. We could still end up in the bunkers tonight, which now I think of it, wouldn't necessarily be a bad thing.'

'I forgot about that.' Jo rummages in the bag for another slice of bread. 'Sam said the same. They were all talking about it in the kitchen. Plenty of rockets went over too this morning, landed just outside Akko apparently.'

'Young Samantha sure is talented, isn't she?' Tom winks at Andre. 'Shame she isn't around to translate for all of us when we need her.'

'Ja, her Hebrew is better than you think,' Andre adds. 'She just pretends not to understand when she wants more information than she's got...'

'Don't we all.'

'Right.' Andre's gaze shifts to Lola, eyes suddenly hard as flint. She looks at the floor. 'And it all comes out in the wash in the end, hey?'

He tangles a shoe into the clothes between them again, deliberately ferreting out the underwear to nudge in her direction.

Lola shrinks into the curve of Tom's arm, clinging to the bowl in her lap. None of the different stories or explanations clanging around in her head matter anymore.

Andre knows she wasn't in her bed last night.

Because he was in here with Sam.

So he'll also know if one of them is lying.

Chapter Fourteen
Wednesday

7:30 p.m.

'Well? What have you got?' Allen barks down the phone.

Jonny notes a small smile escaping from his reflection in Safta's shiny laminate counter top. He could put it down to another translation quirk, English slimming right down as it changes to Hebrew. But he knows it's not. This is just Allen. The sister he's never had.

'How did you know it was me?' His eyebrows raise at himself. Safta must wipe the place down every day. Once a soldier, always a soldier, disgraced or not. His smile fades.

'I didn't. I've got the same question for anyone calling this number from a northern area code. And now I know it's you, it better be good.'

Jonny nods to his grandmother shuffling past, back to her armchair by the window. He waits for her to sit down before continuing.

'I'm not on top of the whole story yet, but—'

'Why the hell not?'

'I wanted to talk things over with you first—'

'So talk.'

'I need more time.' Jonny shoots a sidelong glance at his grandmother, still impassive in her chair. 'I need to get inside the kibbutz, and there's no way I'll be allowed in if I pitch up in the dark.'

'Do I need to remind you what we're up against back here? I

don't have time for you to take some extended beach holiday, Jonny. You either figure it all out tonight or you're back at your desk as usual tomorrow, and I don't care if you have to drive through the night.'

Jonny squints at the back of his grandmother's head. Has it moved so she can hear him better? He takes a deep breath.

'Look, Allen, I know this is going to sound crazy but—'

'Spit it out, will you? You are the least important number from a northern area code to call me in the last ten minutes, and I've already been on the phone to you longer than the others.'

'There's an allegation that the dead guy had found a tunnel.'

Safta's head jerks a little, he's sure of it. Jonny presses the plastic receiver against his ear, listens to the background noise of the newsroom lapping in and out before continuing.

'I wouldn't usually pass on something like this before checking it out more than I've been able to so far but—'

'Hang on.' Allen switches to English as she cuts him off. Jonny's heart gives his chest a thump. It's all he needs to hear. Everyone in the newsroom has some English to work with, but only a few are close to being properly fluent. This small switch is enough to signal Allen is taking him seriously. A beat passes between them, newsroom bustle fading out into the distant slam of a door.

'Start again,' she snaps. 'What do you mean, the dead guy had found a tunnel? Where? From one end of the kibbutz to the other?'

Jonny hesitates. 'No, under the border.'

'With what? There's nothing else up there—'

'The border, Allen. The border between Israel and Lebanon.'

Silence. Jonny pictures Allen's eyebrows peaking under her glossy black fringe, mind whipping through a thousand possibilities.

'What on earth are you talking about, Jonny?'

He replies just a little too quickly. 'It sounds insane, I know. But that's the allegation. Obviously I have to get inside the kibbutz and check it out—'

A sudden burst of newsroom noise cuts him off. Allen lets out a sharp volley of Hebrew before she replies.

'Who the hell else knows about this?'

'I don't know yet. My source only knows about the tunnel itself. And that the dead guy was using it.'

'Using it? What do you mean?'

'I'm not sure exactly. Betraying its location for a start, I guess.'

Allen swears as she sighs, a low thrum through the receiver. 'Presumably your source has come by this information in a manner that isn't hearsay?'

A pause, loaded with subconscious understanding, hangs in the air. Allen knows the value of Jonny's source too. Which is also why she knows he can never openly discuss it. Even in newsrooms, classified sources are just that. Classified.

'And presumably you don't need me to school you on how to handle a tip like that.'

Jonny nods as if Allen can see him. 'Of course not. I'm going to use the rocket attacks as cover. I've been given the name of someone to ask for at the gate and everything. There's no way I'll be allowed in if I say I'm there about the murder.'

'You're telling me you want to head up there first thing? On your own?'

'Yep. It's a kibbutz. The place starts at dawn.'

Allen sighs again, handset growling. 'I'm not sure about this, Jonny. Not at all.'

Jonny's hand tenses on the receiver. 'It'll be OK. It's just a kibbutz. How wrong can it go? Especially if I just pitch up on my own with a feature in mind.'

'That's what you're going to say?'

'Yes.' Jonny opens and closes the door to the cabinet above his head. 'I'm just scoping out a feature piece on the consequences of living under fire. Where better to do it than the farm that sits on the border? The gate will swing right open—'

'Not if your source is anywhere near correct, it won't.'

Jonny slams the cabinet door closed. His heart goes from nought to sixty in a nanosecond. There are a million reasons why he cannot let this opportunity slip through his fingers – both professional and personal. Jonny's never been inside Beit Liora. When he actually considers the facts of how his parents met, he has nothing but a blank inside his head. He braces himself against the cupboard door.

'I can handle it, Allen. How can we not at least try to check it out? I just need to give the slightest of hints that I suspect something is up and they'll have to give me something to send me on my way.'

'Kibbutz folk are more than just curious, Jonny. They want to have their cake and eat it. Why else would you set up home so close to the enemy? They'll be running cable-car rides to the top of the cliff just so they can gawp across the other side next. If there is honestly a suggestion this allegation is in any way correct then they will want the threat fully neutralised without even a seedling being disturbed.'

Jonny moves his sweaty hand to his head, whipping off his cap to wave around. 'So I'm your best shot, then, aren't I? A completely non-threatening junior reporter with nothing but a pencil behind his ear. You can't send in the cavalry—'

'Have you forgotten who you are talking to, Jonny? I damn well can, and make no mistake, I will do a whole lot more than that if there is even the slightest evidence of—'

'But it's my source.' He throws his cap on to the floor, immediately grateful that Allen can't see him behaving like a petulant child. He kicks at it, wishing he could see her face at the same time as thanking the stars she can't see his. A beat passes between them, a phone ringing off the hook somewhere in the background. When Jonny finally looks up, his grandmother is still sitting implacably still.

'That's true,' Allen replies at last. 'But what's also true is I've got a fair few of my own, and don't forget the little bit I've just figured out about yours too. There's an agenda there, that's for sure. Spilling to a junior reporter at the *Trib* instead of the cavalry, for starters? Seriously? I need to make some calls. At least establish if this is within the realm of possibility—'

'Calls to who? What if—?'

'What? Are you worried the IDF will charge straight up there and close the place down before you've thumbed a ride? Please. I have some experience of handling sensitive information. And you seem to be forgetting the most important thing...'

'I know,' Jonny mumbles into the phone, but Allen continues as if all he's done is sigh.

'...That if even part of this is true, we're in more danger than we've ever been out here. We all are. But the people living on the kibbutz itself – shit, let me think for a minute, would you?'

Jonny holds his breath, hunching over the receiver, resting his bare forehead on the shiny cabinet door. The setting sun is piercing through the windows so hard it suddenly feels possible it might set fire to his T-shirt even though it is plastered to his back with sweat.

Finally Allen continues. 'Right. What number can I reach you on? I'll call if I have anything you need to pay attention to before dawn. But you can proceed in the meantime. Don't even think about heading up there before sunrise – once it gets dark you'll just get the gate slammed in your face.'

'Can't I just call you again before I leave?' Jonny curses the wheedle in his voice, but isn't ready to give away Safta's number. He's fought so hard to get it in the first place. And now it's a huge professional advantage as much as it is personal treasure. To Jonny, the prospect of cementing his position, even hoisting himself up a level in a job he values above all else, is worth as much as anything he learns in the process. But Allen isn't letting it drop.

'No you fucking can't, Jonny. Well, you can, if you have anything else to tell me, but my point is, give me the damn number. Do I have to spell out how dangerous this could be? I need to be able to contact you. I don't need to know whose number it actually is. And take down this number too, would you? This is the direct line into our workspace in Haifa.'

Jonny whips the notepad and pencil from his pocket, scribbling at the same time as gabbling digits back down the phone, hunching lower like it might muffle them.

'Right.' Finally Allen sounds satisfied. 'Leave me to it, now, OK? I'll call you with any updates. For now, your plan is sound. Stick to the script. See where it takes you. I've got your back. And you can call me anytime, I do mean that. Just make sure you don't wake me up for no reason. Get some sleep if you can.'

The peaks and troughs of the newsroom punctuate the final beat passing between them.

'And Jonny?'

He nods to himself, all the sweat he's left on the cupboard door changing his reflection to nothing more than a messy smudge.

'Be careful. I expect to hear from you by noon.'

'You will,' he replies, but she's already hung up.

Jonny replaces the handset with a soft click. Turning to the window, he sees his grandmother's head relax on her neck.

Chapter Fifteen
Wednesday

1:30 p.m.

Lola keeps her head down as she hurries, stumbling on uneven patches of gravel. Spurts of Hebrew dart around her from the others on the same path to the communal dining room. She doesn't need to understand them to know exactly what they mean. *Did you hear about Farid? Do you know what happened?* The more strident spurts will be the ones asking what he was doing on the kibbutz overnight. She needs to get to Sam before anyone else does. There's a strange tension in the breeze, tangling strands of hair loose from her ponytail, as if the siren has left a charge of its own.

Farid was devoted to his chickens, to all animals for that matter. He'd even chosen to train – no, to *love* – a stray dog, rather than deliver the sharp kicks anyone else around here would use to send her flying. Just the thought of Biba sends tears springing back into Lola's burning eyes. She swipes them away, as if she can physically elbow self-preservation to the forefront of her mind.

If it comes to it, couldn't she say that Farid had told her he wanted to check on his chickens after hours? Is that an idea that might excuse her behaviour? If a man with a reputation like Farid's was the one asking, especially if he was asking a volunteer? What rights do any of them have when it comes to their jobs? The outsiders have all got that in common.

There Lola has to stop, a sharp pain coursing through her ankle as a stone catches her sandals out. Nothing could be more ridiculous. In the unforgiving light of a Mediterranean spring day, it couldn't be more obvious: if Farid had wanted to check on his chickens at night, there were plenty of kibbutzniks that would have agreed to it.

That's the kind of reputation Farid had.

But is it the kind of reputation she's got?

And there the pain bites further into Lola's ankle.

For the fact is that on this particular night, it was Lola who let him in, and did it secretly to boot. It was Lola that helped Farid break every decree in the kibbutz rule book. It's been Lola that's helped him do it countless times, without asking why he couldn't just come through the main gate. Without asking why he needed to keep doing it in secret. Without wondering why the whole thing had to be such a secret at all.

The fact is, Lola just didn't want to know the answer.

The fact is, it was all just too exciting not to do it.

Half-formed arguments and justifications begin to whirl through Lola's mind – all dead-ending into the same inescapable conclusion.

That at best, a volunteer girl – a non-Jewish one, by the way – has been regularly compromising the security of the kibbutz, at a time when security could hardly be more important. And at worst, she must have had something to do with a murder.

With that, Lola feels her breath start to come in raggedy gasps.

For the coldest, hardest fact of them all is that on a kibbutz, nothing is done alone.

Everything is shared.

Everything is communal.

And the person who killed Farid must be living amongst them.

Lola lets the sun into her eyes for a minute, willing that dark spots block everything else out. But the questions flickering inescapably at the edges of her mind just start to warp and flare in the shadows.

Why would anyone want to kill Farid, let alone anyone on the kibbutz? And why would it happen where and when it did – if it had nothing to do with her? The idea that this beloved spot of hers is truly, universally communal ... Lola knows the concept is as inconsistent as the geography itself, doesn't she? Lola's the one who works with an entire team that doesn't even live within the perimeter fence. The fact that her so-called love affair with Farid cannot have been at all incidental is suddenly staring her in the face, even as she conjures the only image she never wants to forget – an impossibly handsome man, in the prime of his life, gazing at her as if she's all he ever wants to look at. He can't have been playing Lola for a fool. He just can't have been. Except the doubt persists, now growing as it morphs and shifts, little sparks of light popping and dancing in the dark no matter how hard Lola stares into the sun.

'Waiting for me, hey?'

Instantly Lola knows it is Andre who has caught up with her first, even though she can't see him properly.

'Hey yourself,' she mumbles, rubbing her eyes, scattering little crescents across her vision.

'Wait – are you crying?'

'Of course not.' Lola starts to walk again, just concentrates on moving one foot, then the other. 'What are you doing here, anyway? And without Jo, too – wow, what's the occasion?'

'Same as you.' Andre falls in step beside her, gravel crunching beneath their feet.

'Really. And what am I doing?' She hears herself parroting back at him, wonders if she even knows herself.

'Hey, you told us you were going to find out whether it was time to go back out to the banana fields. Except here you are walking to the dining room instead of the courtyard. And I have a sneaky suspicion that where you are actually going is to the kitchen.'

'That's where you're going, is it?'

'Ja, I promised Sam I'd come back as soon as I'd delivered your eggs. What's your excuse?'

Lola feels the anger rising again. How dare Andre, one half of a pair, practically a clone, feel like he can ask her a question like that? All the nights they've joked that the boys can finish each other's sentences flash past in a blink. Both Andre and Johan know what the other one is going to say before he's even said it. And it's only ever been funny, rather than creepy. Even though neither of them will ever be drawn on exactly why they are quite so close, why they each seem quite so dependent on the other. Much less what brought them so far away from home in South Africa. This is the thought that helps Lola to round on him.

'Why would I need an excuse to chat with Sam? Do you need an excuse for sharing every single little detail about your life with Jo?'

'Well, that depends, hey.'

The sunspots dwindle as Lola blinks. He's the same height as her, so they are eyeball to eyeball, until Andre drops her gaze in favour of fiddling with his fingers. A whisper of tension starts to leave Lola's chest before she remembers she's the one who actually blinked first.

'See, I promised Sam that we'd keep it a secret. She made me swear not to tell anyone.'

Lola opens her mouth to try and deflect again, but all that comes out is a juddering sigh. She can't pretend she doesn't know exactly why Sam would want – no, need – this particular secret of hers to be as safe as possible. Because there's a reason Lola and Sam are as close as Andre and Johan. There's a reason they are as dependent on each other too. And unlike the reasons that bind the two South Africans together, Lola knows this one as well as she knows her own heartbeat, thumping ever more painfully inside her chest at the prospect of Lola manipulating it to her own end.

'Look, Lola.' Andre finally glances up. 'I know you weren't in your room last night.'

She lets out a little laugh, but it just sounds brittle and forced. 'Ah, and here I was thinking you wanted to keep your little thing with Sam a secret.'

'Come on, man. You don't think it's worth getting our stories straight?'

'For who? For you two? Or for me?'

'You don't want Sam to find out either, hey. You know better than anyone how she's going to feel about it. Do you really need me to spell it out? Or is the pile of spew by the chicken house enough of a clue?'

Lola stares past Andre into the sun again, a beat passing between them. She can't help but remember how her body has betrayed her before, even when her mind has insisted on the exact opposite. It shouldn't be called muscle memory, she thinks bitterly. It's not memory. It's reflex. It's just an unconscious, repetitive pattern. For if it were memory, nothing would ever happen in the same way again.

'Listen to me, Lola. It's not about me and Sam. Or about you and Tom.'

'That's none of your business either, so—'

'You weren't with him, so don't pretend you were. Unless you want us to go and find Dave, and ask him together? Ja, let's go and see what he has to say.'

'What is your problem, Andre?' Lola asks even though she already knows.

When Andre speaks next, there is nothing left that can disguise the threat in his voice.

'I saw you, Lola. I mean, I've seen you. I've seen you and Farid together, acting out your little love story. I know exactly what you two have been doing – all of your dirty little secrets. And if I have, then I guarantee it won't just have been me. So we need to start talking, and fast. Because it won't take much for someone to slip up and then...'

He fades as she breaks into a run, clouds of dust kicking around her heels on the track down to the kitchen.

Chapter Sixteen
Thursday, 18 April, 1996

2:00 a.m.

Jonny stares hard into the dark until the shapes start to pop. If he can just hold off blinking for another few seconds ... there. He screws his eyes tight shut, revelling in the explosions of dots, the phosphorescent shadows morphing and changing inside his eyelids before the blackness descends again, briefly smiling to himself in the dark.

The tricks that children learn to pass a sleepless night. He's going to need all the tricks he can remember since the single bed in his grandmother's second bedroom doesn't have a mattress.

Wriggling uncomfortably on his back, Jonny laces his fingers together across the sheet draped over his chest to consider the events of the last few hours. He can practically hear Allen's clock ticking with the night rolling by, only drowned out by the air conditioner above the door randomly jolting in and out of gear even though the window is open. The sheet pools on the floor as he gets up to turn it off, choosing to lean against the windowsill rather than lie back down on what is effectively a plinth made of stone rather than anything resembling an actual bed.

All this fidgeting is going to get Jonny nowhere. The truth is he was always going to have to overnight somewhere, and he wanted it to be here, concrete slab or not. He has nothing to gain by pretending to himself that isn't part of the reason he's come.

Jonny explores this thought as gingerly as he moves, allowing it into the forefront of his mind instead of fighting to keep it to one side. The minute his grandmother called they both knew he would jump. She, for reasons he hasn't yet been able to unearth, and she, perhaps, doesn't even realise herself. And Jonny doesn't need to remind himself why he needs no encouragement.

In terms of developing any semblance of a relationship, there are still miles to go for both of them. But even the tiniest of nuggets of new information about his mother sustain him through night after night of wondering.

Does their re-acquaintance enthuse his grandmother even half as much as it does him? Does she see that meeting her grandson after all this time, her only daughter's only child, no less, affords her the chance to make peace with her past choices? Only if she regrets them, Jonny thinks. But what about giving her the opportunity to see how it could have been different? Giving her the chance to pick up somewhere further down the line?

He picks at a fingernail, wondering for at least the thousandth time how it came to pass that his mother's parents disowned her simply for falling in love with the wrong person. How could anything be so terrible that a parent would pretend their own child was dead? And they didn't even know how wrong that wrong person really was. Those terrible days after his mother died, Jonny had to go into care. His father had been gone that long there was no hope of finding out where he actually was. Much less whether he would take in a child he hardly knew. There were no cousins. And of course there were no grandparents.

With a foster family, the social workers had explained when he'd asked where he would live – as if that made any better sense. Didn't these people already have their own kids? What would they want with another one when their family was already complete? Was he expected to just slide into place and start calling someone else's mum his own? Jonny didn't think he could bear it. So the social workers just sat him down with a McDonald's and told him all over again. To this day all Jonny can really remember about that time was that his mother died and he ate a McDonald's. He's avoided even looking at those so-called golden arches since.

Jonny was lucky, his social worker explained in a later visit, that he was placed so quickly with a couple open to long-term care. A different social worker, obviously. They were never the same. Only the buff file on the desk between them seemed to be constant, even if it was a kind of instantly forgettable beige, surely the opposite colour of anything referring to care? Shouldn't it have been a warm pink, or a dusky violet? And it was there in black and white, on the pages poking out of the top, that Jonny would read off words like 'contented', 'happy' and 'settled' – and find himself wondering if they were really true. It was only when he heard stories of other children in similar situations to his that he became determined to make his story end differently.

A curious heaviness settles in Jonny's chest as he thinks about the Hammersons – their kindly hands, their warm and crinkly eyes, their strange conviction that a higher power guided their every benevolent move. The Hammersons weren't Jewish either. But they had a God. They lived by a similar moral code. In the end, isn't that all that matters? Jonny was loved. First by his mother, then by a set of perfect strangers. Who cares what any of them believed in other than that?

Jonny pulls at the skin on his thumb, knowing how to draw blood even in the dark. He suddenly feels treacherous by simply being in Israel – worse, being in the company of this gnarly old woman who chose not to love at all. There is so much still to tell her, or decide whether to tell her. The brutal truth of it is that this gnarly old woman's disgraced daughter is, in actual fact, as dead as she has long pretended she is.

And there the thought sits, suddenly easier to deal with as an uncomfortable fact rather than as an unproductive distraction, hovering at the edge of his consciousness every time he tries to think about something else. Satisfied with this at least, Jonny turns into the open air.

The moon is so high and bright in the sky that the beach is lit silver, stretching deserted the length of the coast before the land starts to slope up towards the border. Jonny peers out of the window, looking in both directions, noting the emptiness either side of the small town of Nahariyya, itself barely a patchwork grid of streets and low apartment blocks. He lingers to the north, picking out the curve of coast dipping inland then out again as the land starts to rise into cliffs, sharp and sheer against the gentle swell of the Mediterranean. He muses briefly on the majesty of a calm sea by night, as serene as it is sinister, able to turn with the tide, to swell with the storm. What secrets are those waters hiding? What have those waves seen, if only to wash the evidence away?

A tunnel. Jonny is instantly picturing all kinds: does his grandmother mean a burrow, the size of a rabbit? Suddenly his brain is full of cartoon bunnies, cotton-ball tails bounding as they gambol in green fields under a countryside-spring sky. Not a rabbit hole then ... a fox, perhaps? A hardscrabble hole at first, rough and ready, lengthening into something of a tube? Now all he can see are badgers, for some reason, glossy black-and-white bodies undulating as they dig and disappear into the ground.

A tunnel, Jonny, not a fucking fox-hole. For humans. That's what she means. He considers the hulking shadows of the cliffs, bulky and immovable against the fluid lines of the waves. Any viable tunnel would have to be reinforced, and properly – steel beams, no doubt, and maybe even wired with electricity, for power and for lights. A matching surge goes through Jonny as he considers the implications of this. Why would there need to be power and lights? For what? Heavy weaponry? To recharge and reload? In which case are there shelter points in this tunnel too? Little nooks and crannies carved off the main drag? Is it possible this is some wholly subterranean command-and-control centre? An underground complex fit for an army? Jonny shakes his head, trying to rein in his galloping imagination. He can't help feeling like the moon is laughing at him too, twinkling in the velvet sky.

Staring instead into the gloom of the small room, Jonny rolls out his shoulders, arching his sore back. If only he had been able to get himself into Beit Liora before nightfall. But a small, close-knit farming community butted up against a hostile border? The fact that he thinks he can even show up at all is laughable. These are families that live and die by their land. Trust is cultivated in their soil, year upon year. It isn't just afforded to any smiley face that shows up with an open mind.

Anyone who doesn't live and work there is at best, an outsider.

At worst … a trespasser doesn't even cover it.

And now Jonny has a live grenade's worth of information in his possession, far more explosive than anything he could have imagined.

Jonny digs knuckles into his eyes, phosphorescence popping all over again as he goes over it one more time. The cover of recent rocket attacks is obvious – living under the constant threat of incoming fire is exactly what these communities expect journalists to show up and ask about, isn't it? He can hear the interviews already: we have to work, if our crops die, then we don't eat. We're sleeping in air raid shelters. Gosh, aren't they uncomfortable? Jonny feels his own back twinge at the thought … Yes, but better to be safe. We will not be terrorised. These are our homes, this is our livelihood. We will not let them be taken from us.

There Allen's voice mercifully chimes in Jonny's mind.

If what his grandmother says is true then the whole charade provides the perfect cover for anyone trying to bury what's really happened in the last twenty-four hours.

Give the earnest journalist equally earnest chapter and verse.

Show him the terror, the damage, the sadness, the pain.

Give him as much florid detail as possible.

Send him on his way with enough to write a double-page spread, with photographs that will sell magazines. He'll leave faster than he arrived.

Smiling, Jonny gives Allen a little mental nod. Eyelids finally heavy, he lies back down on his stone slab, sleep descending as wholly and fully as ocean fog.

Chapter Seventeen
Wednesday

1:45 p.m.

Andre is still on her tail as Lola reaches the back door of the kitchens. Ducking inside the doorway, she turns immediately into the dishwasher plant room just in time to register Andre clattering off in the opposite direction. Clouds of steam hide her as Lola skirts around the industrial-sized steel tunnel, following its scorching metal casing from back to front where she can loop out through the dining room and back into the kitchen. Wiping the moisture from her eyes, she heads straight into the first open fridge – a room all of its own, stacked floor to ceiling with perishables. Only as its heavy door slams shut does it occur to Lola how long she'll have to hide in the freezing cold if her gamble hasn't paid off. The goosepimples are already spread across her arms like Braille when Sam whips round in surprise from the stack of crates in the far corner.

'Hey,' Lola says, breathing hard and hugging herself, cold immediately starting to bite. 'Sorry, I know these don't open from the inside, but I had to talk to you and figured you'd be putting lunch away. And I know you'll be missed, so we won't be in here for long.'

Sam lets the top of the crate she was lifting drop back into place with a sigh. Lola winces as a couple of plump tomatoes pop underneath, their seeds leaking through the holes in the side.

'You'd better hope you're right.' Rummaging behind the stack of crates, Sam retrieves a tarpaulin, shaking the folds of material out of their messy heap. 'Here – wrap up, quickly, come on. Everyone's still slumped all over the dining room. I was only in here putting away the stuff we'd got out for lunch as there's still so much breakfast left over. We're just going to leave it out. I don't think anything formal is going to happen for the rest of the day.'

Lola wraps the rough cotton around herself while Sam does the same, rolling themselves inward until their bodies are pressed together.

'What would you have done if I wasn't in here?' Sam grumbles, breath hot on Lola's neck. 'They don't just routinely open and close these massive fridges, you know. Let's hear it then. Although I know what you are going to say.'

Lola dips her head. She can't bring herself to meet Sam's gaze, risk souring something so comforting and familiar. The packed shelves surrounding them suddenly feel like they're bearing down. Enough fruit, vegetables and meat to feed an army. There must be a million cows behind all this milk, cheese and yoghurt. Can a place with so much plenty ever really feel hardship? Lola feels all her breath leave her in another one of her stupid, shaky sighs. She wishes she didn't already know emotional hardship is a very different beast. It doesn't care much for bounty.

'You're too soft for your own good, you know,' Sam answers for her, their telepathy bringing Lola none of its usual joy. 'Farid will have been up to something dodgy, that's for sure. People don't just die without a reason up here. And it was always going to be a risk putting someone like that in charge of anything.'

'You hardly knew him.' Lola can't help herself, even as the cold seeps into her bones.

'Well, I didn't have to!' Sam exclaims, squirming inside the tarp. 'I know his sort. Everyone up here should feel exactly the same about people like that. How can any Arab ever be a true Israeli? There's still too many people around here that believe in the wrong dream.'

Lola struggles to contain herself, suddenly nauseated by the earthy smell of vegetables. If she had a family as devoted as Sam's, wouldn't she agree with whatever they said too? Wouldn't Lola accept their prejudices as her own? She pictures Sam's parents perched expectantly on their flowery sofa at home, as in love with their spiritual community as they are with their so-called only daughter, who is just as well versed in covering up any behaviour that might be seen as transgressive – especially after what happened to the sister: the unmentionable one, the one cut out of all the technicolour photographs plastered over their bedroom wall. 'Samantha,' Sam's dad would say, 'when you walk into a room those people are lucky to have you there.' Sam would tell Lola she was lucky not to have to deal with expectations like that. Lola never felt lucky. Just invisible.

'And besides,' Sam continues, huffing. 'We still need to find out what happened. All the boys said was they were sure he was killed deliberately but no one knew why.'

'Not yet.' The thought of Andre helps Lola pull herself together, meet that familiar gaze head on. 'That's why I needed to talk to you.'

Sam stiffens, arms pinned to her sides inside the tarp. 'Me? Why?'

'Were you with Andre last night?' An altogether less comforting spark flares in Sam's eyes, but Lola forces her own to stay focused.

'You know I could never be with someone like him—'

'And you know the fact he isn't Jewish couldn't bother me less? Since I'm not either, and I love you more than anything in the world?'

A flood of anguish dampens the spark as Sam stares back. But still, Lola holds fast. A beat passes between them before the tarp loosens with Sam's sigh.

'So you *were* with him?'

Sam turns away, nods almost imperceptibly towards the closed door.

'And you know they'll never find out unless you tell them?'

Still Sam doesn't say anything, just keeps looking at the frozen door. Lola waits, flinching with cold, knowing the pain of the memories running through Sam's mind as if they were her own:

The catatonia of Sam's parents' grief and shame after the truth came out about where their elder daughter had gone, and who with. The heat of the bonfire where all evidence of her very existence was burned to ash – the tiny bonnet she'd worn as a new-born, all her beloved soft toys, her treasured first finger paintings – vapourised, along with her birth certificates. The acrid smell of fresh paint on the walls of her old bedroom. The holes in all the photo frames. The destruction of every family snapshot. The wall of silence. Finally Sam mumbles, resting her forehead on Lola's shoulder.

'It's like they know already. I can literally hear their screams, all of them, the whole extended family. Tell your kids something enough times and the guilt ends up tattooed on their faces. They'll spot it the second I walk through the door.'

'Which isn't for months, so...'

Sam sighs again. 'Well, wait till they get hold of this. Sleeping in bomb shelters for two weeks, and now a murder? Don't pretend you don't know my parents better than your own. They're only tolerating the fact you're here too because it's spreading the gospel, apparently. The more *gentiles* we can bring to experience the struggle, the better – so long as I don't marry one.' She leans on the word *gentiles* to soften it, as usual, but Lola doesn't care. Using that word is the least of what Sam's parents have done in the past. And all in the name of honour.

'So you were with him? Last night?'

Sam squirms inside the tarp.

'Did he stay with you till the morning? Or was it just for a bit after the campfire?'

'He stayed,' Sam finally whispers. 'I told him you must have already slipped out when we woke up.'

'What else did you tell him?'

Both their bodies are rigid now, stiff with all the secrets and lies.

'What do you mean?'

'Just ... Did you tell him I was with Tom?'

Sam flinches – or is it Lola herself? It's so cold now she can't be sure of anything. Even the fact Sam has been the best friend she's ever had feels suddenly out of reach, beyond her increasingly numb fingertips. She takes a deep breath, forcing down every last bite of the ice down her throat, into her stomach.

'You know when you told me I had to stop ruining it for myself? That sabotaging things every time they start to work out, just because I'm too scared of what'll happen if they stop, is only ever going to end in tears?'

'Did I say that? We were pretty drunk.'

'You also said you were sick of picking up the pieces. And that at some point everyone would be if I wasn't careful.'

'Like I said, we were pretty drunk.' Sam twists round, eyeing the implacably closed steel doors. 'We say all sorts of things when we're pretty drunk. Not that it matters, since we're going to freeze to death.'

Lola grinds her teeth to stop them chattering, inhales another gust of frozen air instead.

'I didn't go with Tom last night. I haven't been with him for ages now...'

Sam's head snaps back on her neck. 'Ummmm, have you forgotten about our little mini-break under concrete last week? We may have been blind enough in the pitch-dark but did you think we were all deaf?'

'Nothing happened,' Lola says reflexively, as if denying it will make any difference to what happened next. 'We were just holding each other.'

'Like we're just holding each other now?'

That familiar, comforting gaze dissolves to shock as Lola starts to cry. She can't help herself, hot tears running tracks through the frost that feels like it's forming on her face.

'Oh, hon, I was kidding. You know that, right? I love you even when you lie to my face.'

'One day you won't,' Lola chokes out between icy sobs. 'One day you'll give up.'

'Shut up, would you? I would never do that. Ever.'

Lola feels Sam's hands twitch in their bindings, tells herself she'd hold hers if she could.

'It's just … I was with Farid last night, Sam. I was with him, up by the chicken houses. He's just been so kind, been so lovely to me that I—'

The rest of her sentence catches as Sam yanks herself as far away as the tarp will allow, expression frozen into a rictus of horror.

'You were with him? What do you mean, you were *with* him?'

Lola has to pant into her collarbone before she can continue, a toxic cocktail of panic and the beginnings of hypothermia. What little breath she has left leaves her chest.

'He said we could hang out together if I let him in at night. That it was the only way we could ever be alone. That he could hardly bring a kibbutz girl, even if she was English, into his village at night. And that he wanted to get to know me better.'

'Lola, are you fucking kidding me?'

Sam's conker-brown eyes blaze improbably hard at her.

'You … and Farid? Together? Here, on the kibbutz, at night?? Do you even know what you've done?'

Lola's teeth clatter together.

'How did you even do it? He leaves after work every day, doesn't he? Or at least, after dinner … Oh, my God.' Sam's gasp comes out in a visible puff. 'You were letting in him? You were actually meeting an Arab in the middle of the night to let him back in after hours? Just so you could be together? Somewhere deep inside that twisted brain of yours, it was all just too exciting not to do it?'

'I know ... I know I screwed up. You don't have to say it—'

'Don't I? Because the only thing I know for sure right now is you have zero – no, less than zero – comprehension of how bad this is.'

'Well it doesn't get any worse than being dead.'

Sam laughs, high and mad, even as Lola starts to cry again.

'That's where you're wrong, you stupid cow. There is no way this was just about you. No way on God's green earth. An Arab? With some bug-eyed English teenager? At a time like this?'

Another gasp – a burst of air so warm Lola has to stop herself leaning into it.

'And that's why we're locked in the fridge, isn't it? Because you want me to tell Andre you were with Tom. Give you a cover story he can't help believe. You know he'll stick to it if I'm the one asking. Because otherwise they'll find out that a volunteer girl – a non-Jewish one, by the way – has been letting an Arab breach the perimeter for the cheapest of cheap thrills—'

'It's not just that,' Lola whispers, but that's as far as she can make her pathetic attempts at blackmail go. The rest is frozen solid in her throat, somehow hot with tears and sub-zero with cold all at the same time. She can't threaten Sam, not even close, much less ever betray her to her parents. How could she have thought she could even hint at it? Their years of friendship, the best memories Lola has of anything, flash past just as she thinks it.

And then the door flies open.

Hebrew exclamations echo off the steel walls.

They are both ushered over to a bank of steaming ovens in a clamour of a language Lola still doesn't understand.

Lola wrings her hands as Sam stalks away, sickened at the colour flooding back into her dead-blue fingertips.

Chapter Eighteen
Thursday

Just after dawn

Jonny gazes at the sea rippling in the distance as he walks the last stretch of the coast road, the comfort of his own shadow dwindling with every inch the sun climbs into the sky. The quiet of the night hasn't lasted. There's an early headwind building in the air.

He miraculously managed to thumb a ride just before dawn as far as the last junction, but from here on up, no car was going to take him any further north without asking questions. *Why are you headed to the border? What business do you have at Beit Liora?* All questions he can't reply to if he's to get answers to his own.

Jonny thinks about the last time – the only time – he's walked up this road before, barely a week after he'd arrived in Israel itself, still addled by dreams of how his parents met, how it might have been all romance and happy-ever-afters. Just being within striking distance of the kibbutz felt so intimate it made him blush. This latest war hadn't even started, the arrangements in the peace accords were still just about holding, and still he was questioned within seconds: *Who are you, boy? What business do you have around here?* Jonny couldn't even pretend to be lost – there's only one road, and it only has one destination. So he chose to spin a story about having meant to turn inland at the earlier junction but been so distracted by the beauty of the cliffs and the possible view he might get from walking a bit further up, that he'd thought he'd see how far he could go.

It was his first introduction to how spin works on this particular shore of the Mediterranean. The fact Jonny gave away that he understood the rapid-fire Hebrew passing between the two guards that caught up with him did nothing to help his case. He didn't even have a camera looped around his neck to take all those pictures he kept blathering on about. He was lucky to get away with only being frogmarched out. Bruises were the worst of it.

He should have told the truth. Or at least, a version of it. And now he can't.

Jonny lifts his cap from his head, lets the wind blow away the sleepless night. He's just Jonny Murphy, a junior reporter at the *International Tribune* scoping out a feature on living in the shadow of a hostile border. He tries not to look at the hillside as he thinks it, shivering in spite of the rising sun. Everyone knows that paper. Everyone likes a microphone if they think they'll be listened to. And there sure as hell is no one around here that will have heard of him before.

With that, a curious mixture of relief and disappointment assails him along with the wind. Jonny jams the cap back on his head, as if that alone will push it away.

Blocked by heavy metal gates, the kibbutz driveway branches steeply off to the right of the main road, going on to form part of the community's perimeter before dead-ending a few hundred yards further ahead, at the border itself. Jonny pauses on the approach to the guard lounging in a tiny booth next to the entrance. The man's head is pitched forward, lolling slack on his neck.

Jonny blinks away the gleam of steel, menacing in the dawn light. Is the guard asleep or unconscious? A step closer and he bets on just asleep, the guard's hands are still folded across his stomach. Jonny's sigh of relief catches as he spots the border infrastructure on the horizon above. Razor-wire, gun houses, no-man's land – the thought that there's an open tunnel running under the lot sends his heartbeat accelerating up his throat, just as a stray dog appears from the brambles to startle the guard awake.

'Good morning!' Jonny finds himself practically yelping with the dog as the guard swipes it away, clocking the leather holster clipped to the man's belt. Fumbling for his cigarettes, he proffers the entire soft-pack to the guard, a fail-safe common currency, vaguely aware of the dog still pawing frantically somewhere inside the bushes.

'My name should be on your visitor list? I have an appointment with Moti Krauss.'

The guard takes the packet, coughing into it before pulling a cigarette out with his lips.

'Here, let me...' There's a click as Jonny's lighter flares. 'My name should be on your list,' he repeats, exhaling along with the guard himself. 'Jonny Murphy. I'm a reporter with the *International Tribune*.'

The guard opens his mouth to speak only to descend into a volley of coughing. Jonny waits, knowing he'll respond once he's taken a proper drag. No Israeli – nor Arab, for that matter – smokes with anything other than dedication.

'What time is it?'

Jonny congratulates himself for wearing sunglasses as well as his lucky cap, both serving to hide the relief plastered all over his face. 'Just gone half past six. He is expecting me at seven.'

The guard's cigarette crackles as he considers this, ember already almost at the filter.

'You are early.'

'Yes. I wasn't sure I'd get a ride...' Jonny tails off, cap lifting pointedly to the sky, mercifully free of any missile trails. 'But it was a quiet night.'

The guard nods, stubbing out his ember into an overflowing ashtray on the cabin's small table. Jonny spots the small bank of monitors stacked below the guardhouse window, images flickering in black and white.

'Name?'

'Jonny Murphy.'

The guard squints at a clipboard, pushing his glasses on to his head. Now Jonny can see his face; he's far younger than Jonny was expecting.

'What business do you have with Moti?'

'I'm working on a story for the *Trib* about living under fire up here.' In the context of the hillside rising beyond the kibbutz, Jonny's script feels perfectly natural. 'Must be terrifying for everyone near the border, but I can imagine when you have to make sure your crops don't fail, it's even harder.'

The man regards him with a pair of surprisingly clear eyes, considering he was asleep not five minutes earlier.

'We are bigger than just our crops. We are worth so much more than that.'

'How do you mean?' Jonny passes over his lighter again. He hadn't expected the guard to start talking, much less be relaxed enough to doze on the job. All sorts of questions flash through his head as he considers why that might be the case.

'What do you know about Beit Liora?'

'What do I know?' Jonny repeats, taken aback.

'Yes. What do you know about our kibbutz?'

Jonny reaches for his lighter rather than answer immediately.

'Open your eyes.' The guard stands as he hands it back. 'Tell me what you see.'

Jonny looks around dumbly. Gleaming steel gates, knotted brambles, tarmac so black and glossy it could be wet. White-tinged blue sky, shot through with the glare of the rising sun. The sea, whispering to the west. And the looming hillside, lumpy with rocks, patched with dry grass. The landscape suddenly seems so uncomplicated that he is instantly wrongfooted.

'That's why I'm here,' he finally answers with a half-laugh. 'Can't expect to get the lay of the land without seeing for myself.'

'Isn't it beautiful?'

Jonny has to stand aside as the man steps out of the cabin to continue, waving a hand beyond the locked gates.

'There are caves inside the cliffs, you know. Carved out by the water. Ancient holes, smooth as enamel inside, like marble, almost. You cannot swim up to them, only climb down from the clifftop. But there is a platform halfway down, big enough for a building, a restaurant, even. People would come from far and wide to see something like that. It is a miracle of the earth.'

Jonny sways as imagination gets the better of him. Did his mother know about the caves? Are they some sort of secret, romantic hiding place? A platform carved out of silken rock by water tunnelling channels in the cliffs like some undulating sea snake? He finds the soft skin inside his wrist, pinches down hard. Jonny's here for an altogether different type of tunnel.

'It sure sounds like it,' he replies, deliberately banal. 'Is tourism even a thing, this far north?'

'It should be, shouldn't it? Why not?'

Jonny studies the man as he turns to face him. He can't be more than late twenties, so must have returned to the kibbutz after conscription. Which, as Jonny understands it, is pretty unusual – he's either marrying local, or are some sort of ideological zealot – born to a founding family, perhaps? Still convinced these communities can exist as wholly socialist enterprises even within a capitalist society?

'I guess the border makes that difficult.'

'That is one way of putting it.' Jonny notes colour rising in the man's face as he scuffs a boot into the ground. 'We are so much more than just a farm. But we won't even be that for much longer if people think they are in danger up here.'

Jonny swallows down the tremor in his throat. 'And are they? What's that like?'

The man scoffs as he looks up. 'You are here to talk about bananas and avocadoes. Moti, he will tell you how important his bananas are. These are plants you have to poison if you want them to really die. Sure, you can damage a crop but it grows again in the end, it is a cycle. What matters is our hope. We cannot dream under fire. We must simply exist.'

He spits out his cigarette butt, grinding out the ember with his toe.

'Moti, he won't tell you any of this. Neither will the others, the ones who will speak to you in front of everyone else. All they care about is their farm. As if anything is ever that simple.'

'Mind if I chat with you again after I've spoken to him? I'd hate to keep him waiting,' Jonny replies lightly. Scratch the surface of any so-called utopia and its cracks appear immediately. This man isn't an ideological zealot. He's had his hope broken by war.

Which means he's got an axe to grind. And if Jonny found him before he's even passed the gate, he can bet he's going to find a whole load more like him. The dead body of a man he's never met flashes uncomfortably past his inner eye.

'Now it is time for bed,' the man grunts in reply, wincing as he arches his back. 'People like me, we only talk in the dark.'

'Glad I know where to find you, then.' Jonny takes a step forward, waiting for the nod. 'What's your name? Just in case you aren't here when I get back.'

'Rami,' the guard answers, fiddling with the holster on his belt. 'You can ask for Rami.'

He motions at the centre of the gates, pressing a button on the console just inside his cabin, separating the two panels by a few inches. Jonny's nod turns into a wince as he squeezes himself through hot metal.

Beyond the gates, the driveway shimmers, liquid-black tarmac striped up to a small courtyard edged with farming machinery. For a man who rises with the dusk, Rami was unusually talkative at dawn. Tales of wondrous grottoes snaking inside the cliffs themselves, a miracle to behold, only accessible down a perilous cliffside path? Jonny supposes it's one way of diverting him from the fact Rami's so-called day job is to stay awake all night.

Which means one set of eyes were wide open the night of the murder.

And if they weren't, then why were they closed?

Jonny gives the pitying gaze of the hillside a little shrug as he reaches the courtyard.

Chapter Nineteen
Wednesday

2:00 p.m.

Lola speeds away from the kitchen, pulling strands of hair into limp curtains around her face. Jumping into the scrub off the path, she hurries into the maze of private homes in the body of the kibbutz, before they give way to the larger housing units fringing the perimeter road. She paces between the buildings, deliberately trying to lose herself.

Who spun the cover story when Sam drank too much? And what about the shorter skirts and sleeveless tops that attracted so much parental disapproval? Apparently they were all Lola's, they were never Sam's. What about the cigarettes? And the Zippo – the chemical tang of lighter fluid steals into Lola's nose just thinking about it. They even had it engraved with her name, looping Ls, curly As. All the evidence of Sam occasionally experimenting with the smallest and most inoffensive aspects of a more secular life – Lola had absorbed it all, hadn't she? And the rumours and the whispers after the unmentionable sister disappeared? It was Lola who kept the secrets, who made up all the answers whenever anyone dared to ask a question. Sam barely had to say a word.

And was it really so unthinkable that Sam might try and make just the tiniest of adjustments so she could fit in? Just make herself that little bit less noticeable? Caught between two worlds, who wouldn't try to navigate the simplest path between them? What kind of people – no, what kind of *parents* – couldn't bring themselves even to try to understand that? Especially when they'd chosen to send her to a secular rather than religious school? Lola flicks through the memories all over again, studies their colours, recalls their sounds, turns over every last detail in order to detract from their core composition:

That no one cared what Lola did or said except someone else's parents.

And only because she was always with their daughter. Their last hope.

A rusty swing creaks in someone else's garden. A volley of Hebrew from someone else's home. Lola realises that she's drifted as far as the perimeter road – the chicken houses, the cowshed and its accompanying warehouse filled with clouds and clouds of cotton. Has she done enough for Sam over the years for her to stick by Lola now? A sudden swarm of flies buzzes discordantly past with the wind. Lola realises there's so much more at stake here than just what happens to either of them.

She darts across the perimeter road, slipping between the warehouses to the curls of barbed wire on the other side. Finally able to stop, her legs buckle, suddenly weak with vertigo as she peers out over the clifftop.

This is where Lola comes to escape. But she's never felt more trapped than she is now. She clasps a loop of razor wire, letting the metal rip into her palm. *Do you even know what you've done?* Sam's accusations rattle around in her head. Farid's gemstone eyes twinkle at her with the heady reflection of the sea.

Of course she didn't know what she'd done. She's only some silly volunteer girl, drunk in love and high on a new life. She's just a pawn in a game. If they find out, isn't that all they'll see? Isn't that all they ever see, where she's concerned? Just some silly girl who doesn't understand. A bubble of blood trickles down her wrist.

'Lola? Is that you?'

She jumps, crying out as the metal catches deeper into her palm.

'What are you doing up here?' An American accent, deep and slow.

'I could ask you the same thing,' she says shakily, pretending to be completely focused on her trapped hand. It's only Dave. It's not Oren.

'Did you slip?'

Dave's next to her now, frowning at the blood dripping down her hand.

'Yes,' she lies, wincing as she frees her palm. 'It's been a crazy morning...'

'Have you got a tissue, or anything like that?'

Dave is still focused on her hand, bending over her, tall shadow falling across her.

'I-I can just use this,' she says, jamming the loose edge of her vest into the cut. 'It's filthy anyway. I haven't had a chance to change.'

'You heard about Farid, right?' Dave pushes a big finger down on the fabric crammed into her hand. The size of Dave's hands is another standard joke. Born to work in the cowshed. But right now they feel unnervingly large.

She stares at her feet as she replies, brown with dust. 'Just so sad. Were you down in the shelters too?'

'Just came out. Why else would I still be out and about up here?'

'Of course, of course. Wow, they kept you inside for ages.'

'Don't I know it.' Dave drops her hand, stretching. 'Something about being too close to the crime scene.' He nods towards the chicken houses, further down the slope past the cowshed. 'Lucky we'd already done the milking else it would have been biblical.'

The expected laugh sticks in Lola's throat. She realises it's not just cicadas calling to her from the banana fields over the cliff.

Little Biba is still howling in the distance. But Dave doesn't seem to be able to hear anything other than himself.

'We should go get that seen to,' he continues, gesturing at her hand. 'You might need a stitch—'

'No way.' Lola starts away towards the road, willing the dog not to come bounding over, threatening to betray her connection to Farid yet again. 'On a day like today? I couldn't ask, even if I needed to.'

Dave falls in step beside her. 'I've got some stitches back at the ranch. Little sticky strip things. You know the kind? They should put them in our medical packs. I wasn't allowed to travel anywhere without them.' He runs a rueful hand along his chin. 'Four boys. My parents learned the hard way. We grew up on a farm on a prairie. Literally millions of miles from anything else.' He tips his head at the looming hillside, rolling his eyes.

'You're the youngest, right?' Lola asks, even though she already knows. She crosses back over the perimeter road, every step putting more distance between them and the chicken houses.

Dave snorts. 'The great mistake. I was seven years after number three. You'd think they'd have learned how not to have accidents by then.'

He frowns at the blood from her hand seeping through her vest. 'Press down on that, come on. What were you doing playing footsie with the barbed wire, anyway?'

Lola cries out rather than reply, makes a show as Dave pushes on her injury.

'It won't stop bleeding if you don't put pressure on it,' he chides her. 'Hurry up. I have proper first-aid stuff in our room.'

She lets him lead her down the path back to the volunteers block. She's playing to type now, she realises, sickened. Dave thinks he's looking after her. In another world Lola might have thought so too. But not anymore. Never again.

'Hey, big fella,' Tom crows from the courtyard between their rooms. 'Finally crawled out from your hole?' But his grin fades when he spots Dave holding Lola's hand.

'What happened?'

'Some razor wire collided with her fist, apparently,' Dave answers for her.

Tom's on his feet now, striding towards them. 'Where were you?'

'I was just coming back from the dining room—' Lola begins.

'Took the scenic route again, did you?' The pressure changes in her palm as Tom and Dave switch hands.

'Back in a tick,' Dave says, bounding up the steps to his room.

Tom turns back to Lola. 'I thought you went to the dining room?'

She wriggles her hand half-heartedly.

Dave is back in a flash, brandishing a bulging case. 'This'll sting a bit,' he says, reaching over with an alcohol swab.

'Look at you, mate,' Tom says, with ill-disguised irritation. 'The whole nine yards. What else have you got stashed in there? Enough to put down a horse?'

Dave doesn't reply, concentrating on his packet of sterile strip stitches. Lola watches numbly, her cut closing over as cleanly as it ripped open. She can't even feel the sting of neat alcohol.

There's a crunch of shoes on gravel just as Dave finishes up. And then Moti's heavily accented English echoes around the courtyard.

'Is everyone here? All of you?'

Lola's breath catches as she spots Sam trailing in behind Moti, eyes down, hands wringing the navy-blue apron still tied around her waist.

'Moti, mate.' Tom drops her hand to extend his own. 'How is everyone doing? Yep, we're all here, least I think we are. Just waiting for orders ... Do you need us back at work?'

Lola wills Sam to meet her eye, but there's nothing. Moti shakes Tom's outstretched hand while surveying them all.

'Where is...?' He looks between them, up and over their heads, back over his own shoulder.

'The skinny one?' Tom asks, doing the same when he notes Andre is missing.

'The greenhouse boy. Yes.'

'He's here. Hey, Andre...' Lola jumps as Johan calls from the open doorway of another bedroom. She hadn't noticed him standing there all along.

Andre shuffles out to stand alongside Jo, folding his arms across this chest.

'Shall we get going, then?' Tom asks.

Lola stares at Sam, still hunched over her apron. If this is about getting back to work then what is she doing out of the kitchen? She licks her lips, mouth suddenly so dry she can't swallow.

Moti shakes his head. 'We need to ask everyone some questions. It won't take so long, but we must do it now, before the police arrive. The emergency services will be here any minute to take care of the body.'

'Just terrible,' Jo manages to reply as they take a collective gulp. 'He was a lovely man, by all accounts.'

But Moti just looks between them, mouth set into a grim line. 'Perhaps you volunteers did not realise this. But Farid was not resident here. He lived offsite, in a village with his family.'

Moti pauses for a half-laugh. Lola feels her breath coming in little gasps.

'It is strange,' he continues. 'Suddenly we find ourselves grateful for the group that sit up late every night, singing their songs and laughing.'

'We didn't see anything, mate, I swear,' Tom counters before Moti can ask. 'You're right, we were out, making nuisances of ourselves, well after midnight. In the cold light of day it's outrageous, I agree. And I'm sure I speak for all of us when I say we are disgusted with ourselves. We're not kids and we're behaving just like them. We'd love to keep on having our campfires, but we promise you this: the noise will stop.'

'So you were out again last night.' Moti zeroes in on Tom. Lola stiffens, every fibre of her alert. 'What did you hear, besides yourselves? Or see? Farid did not come in through the gate. We would know this if he did.'

'Afraid we have to apologise again, hey,' Jo babbles. 'There was too much booze involved for us to be anything other than annoying—'

'Were you all together?' Moti cuts him off. 'All six of you?'

'Not me.' Dave puts up a hand. 'I turned in pretty early. I mean, I went to bed.'

'So you were alone?'

'I was there too,' Tom adds needlessly. Lola's heartbeat accelerates up her throat like vomit. 'That's our room.' Tom jerks his head in the direction of the doorway. 'The big fella does more reading than drinking, unlike the rest of us. He was still nose into his book by the time we all got back.'

'You.' Moti jerks a heavy head towards Andre. 'You like to walk around, at night.'

Andre puffs out his chest. 'Do I?'

Moti takes a step forward. 'Yes. What is it you see, on your long walks on the dark?'

'Other than you, occasionally, nothing.'

'Nothing? Nothing at all?'

Lola plays the question back through her head. Is that the faintest hint of a tremor in Moti's voice as he asks? What has Andre seen? And who knew he liked to walk around at night? She swallows, again and again, as she remembers that one thing he's seen is her.

But Andre doesn't skip a beat. 'That's what I said, hey. I just clear my head for the very best night's sleep available before I serve out my time in the greenhouse.'

'We both do,' adds Jo before clamping his mouth shut again.

The silence that follows is so heavy with suspicion and so unfamiliar in the narrow space that Lola can practically feel it.

Finally Moti grunts, turning on his heel and clumping off. Andre breaks ranks almost immediately, stomping through the gravel back to his room.

'Take it easy, mate,' Tom calls out to him. 'We just need to co-operate. The sooner this is figured out the safer everyone is.'

'Well you lot don't seem too fazed, hey.' Andre pauses, gaze shifting across them all, hard as flint. 'And we need to get our stories straight.'

'They don't care about us.' Tom holds up his hands. 'All we are to them is occasionally useful manpower.'

'Ja, of course they do.' Andre glares at Lola, making her shrink into herself. 'Especially when it could get some of them off the hook before the questions really get going—'

'What the hell are you talking about?' Tom's hands drop to his sides.

'You think any of us can be sure we know exactly where all six of us were all night?'

'What do you mean?' Tom's voice wavers in a way that only Lola could ever detect.

'It took you no time at all to stand up for the big fella, hey,' Andre answers bitterly.

'Huh?' Dave waves a big hand.

'Come on, bru.' Andre pauses in the doorway. 'Don't pretend like we don't all bed-hop occasionally. There's always someone copping off with someone else—'

'Stop it, man.' Jo's voice is so faint Lola can barely hear it. 'Please...'

'What is he on about?' Tom turns to Lola. Oasis sings into the silence from some distant room, the faintest of lyrics landing with inescapable clarity. *You and I are going to live forever.*

Except we're not, Lola thinks, blocking the rest of the lines out. No one is.

'Start talking, Lola,' Andre rasps. 'Or I will.'

Chapter Twenty
Thursday

7:00 a.m.

Jonny turns in a circle at the top of the kibbutz driveway, noting the idle farm floats, the breezeblock air-raid shelter, the start of a lush-looking set of orchards on the inland side. The place is deserted – standard for a kibbutz at 7:00 a.m., still in the throes of the first shift of the day before meeting for breakfast. He muses briefly on the unfamiliar details of this routine, discovered on his first visit to a kibbutz nearer Jerusalem. Rise with the sun, put in three hours before sitting down for a breakfast the size of two lunches. Put in another four hours before an actual lunch, and then the rest of the day is yours, free of questions, plans or recriminations. On the face of it, pre-dawn alarm call or not, it's a seductive way of life, even without the idyllic landscape. But to do it forever, day after day the same, the only variations being the simple ones that come with the seasons? It can't be enough for some people.

The back of his neck prickles, the crunch of gravel confirming it. Jonny adjusts his sunglasses before turning around to see who's behind him. A figure is emerging from the dark opening to the breezeblock air-raid shelter – squat, sturdy, determined.

'*Shalom*.' Jonny extends a hand, smiling as he continues in Hebrew. 'I have an appointment with Moti Krauss, do you know where I might find him?'

The figure, a man, stops in front of him without saying anything. Jonny keeps his hand in the air, cursing the sun for shining directly into his eyes. Even with the benefit of dark glasses hiding his squint, he can't read the man's face.

'Rami let you in?' A burst of static comes from the radio clipped to the man's belt, arms still firmly by his side.

Jonny nods, moving his outstretched hand to a non-existent itch on his neck as if that was what he planned to do with it all along.

'Who are you? What business do you have with Moti?'

Jonny passes over his *Trib* ID from his shirt pocket, looking past the man to the dark mouth of the bomb shelter. This time the man reaches out to take it, turning the small laminated card between his fingers, English on one side, Hebrew on the other.

'The *International Tribune*,' the man replies, this time in perfect English. 'And why would the *International Tribune* want to talk to Moti Krauss?'

'Wow, your English is really good,' Jonny answers in the crispest London accent he can muster. Another win for the sunglasses, their frames hiding his frown. Note-perfect English in the Israeli cities isn't unusual, but this far into the sticks can only mean either a family connection, an offensively expensive international education, or something entirely more classified. It's interesting that this man has chosen to reveal it immediately. 'Where'd you learn?'

'I could ask you the same thing,' the man shoots back in Hebrew.

Jonny stares at him, suddenly wrongfooted. The power has shifted in an instant – how could Jonny have thought he had any in the first place? There's a scrape and crackle of dead leaves skittering past, warm wind funnelling through the orchard.

'My mum was Israeli,' Jonny finally answers, licking his lips lamely. 'It's all we spoke when I was growing up.'

'I see.' The man studies his ID, turning it over and over in his fingers.

'So ... so you're a *Trib* reader?'

'No.' The man hands over his card, lacing his arms behind his back.

Jonny swallows. The man's posture has the effect of making his muscles bulge even more than they already were.

'What do you want with Moti?'

'We're doing a story on what it's like to live up here.' Jonny gestures at the hillside without looking at it. 'Given the rocket attacks, I mean. I spoke to Moti yesterday—'

'You spoke to him? What do you mean?'

'I called the kibbutz, set up an appointment.' Jonny squints at the man under cover of his dark lenses, thanking the god of sunglasses yet again for hiding any hint of the fact he held no such conversation, just got a name to go on, a good one too. *Safta* told him Moti founded the place.

'I was told he was the best person to speak to. When you fear for your life, not just your livelihood, by going out to work—'

'So you didn't speak to him? To Moti?'

'That's right, I didn't speak to him directly. But he's meeting me at seven...' Jonny pauses to check his watch even though he knows exactly what time it is. 'Mind telling me where I might find him? It's a bit early for breakfast in these parts, isn't it? I guess he planned to come in early from the banana fields to talk before eating.'

'Who was it that you spoke to? Who told you to talk to Moti?'

'I didn't get their name.' Jonny keeps looking at his watch. 'I promise I won't keep him for long though, if that's what you're worried about.'

Jonny can't be sure of it, but when he looks up, he thinks he sees a flicker of fear pass over the man's otherwise impassive face.

'Perhaps I can help you,' the man replies after a moment, back to speaking in perfect English. 'If it's crops you want to talk about. I manage the greenhouses. Beit Liora runs on three industries, and mine is one of them.'

A frond of cloud passes over the sun, just long enough for Jonny to confirm he's right. This man knows he didn't hold any such telephone conversation, but hasn't seen fit to throw him out yet.

'Oh, if you're sure you can spare the time, that would be fantastic,' he gushes, holding out his hand again. This time the man takes it, grip somehow warm and cool at the same time. 'What did you say your name was?'

'I didn't,' the man replies, squeezing Jonny's hand just a beat too long before letting go. 'But it's Oren. I manage the greenhouses. Olives are our main thing. But we grow all sorts.'

'Do you export the olives?' Jonny reaches for the notepad and pen stashed in his trouser pocket.

'Yes. For oil. Mainly to the United States.'

'What, from all the way up here?' Jonny feigns surprise.

'Why not?' Oren's eyes narrow. 'We are not just a subsistence farm. We can't be, in a society like ours. We have to be able to make a profit in some way.'

'So is it fair to say your export business is one thing that props up the kibbutz if your other crops were to fail ... say, because you couldn't tend to them under fire?'

Jonny looks up with a start as Oren laughs, a vein popping in his thick neck.

'Yes. Yes, I suppose that is one way of putting it.'

'It's not just olives, then? You have other options?'

Oren's mouth sets in a hard line.

'Moti is in charge of the bananas, right? You export a ton of those, too?'

'Yes,' Oren replies after a moment. 'As you can imagine, though, they bring in a fraction of the amount the Americans pay for our olives.'

'Sure can.' Jonny scribbles on his pad again, shorthand for something. 'Is that it, then? The rest of this gorgeous place is for living on?'

'I thought you wanted to talk about the challenges of life under fire. In my case, that involves putting people to work under glass when rockets could fly overhead at any time.'

'I can't imagine what that's like.' Jonny doesn't need to fake his shudder. 'Especially if the kibbutz is counting on the greenhouse so much.'

Oren's radio squawks before he can say anything else.

'You said...' Jonny flicks the pages of his notebook as if he is looking for something. 'Three industries, you said. Right? Olives, bananas, and what's the third?'

He flips his notepad to a fresh sheet of paper, waiting. A solitary leaf tips past with another gust of hot wind. He tries not to flinch as Oren suddenly grabs the radio from his belt, muttering something unintelligible into it.

'Sorry, I've already taken up too much of your time, haven't I?' Jonny makes a show of clapping his notepad closed, clicking and unclicking his biro. 'I can just wait here for Moti, if you think he won't be long coming up. Or is there somewhere you'd prefer me to sit?'

Oren looks past him down the driveway, and back again.

'I don't want to cause you any trouble,' Jonny continues, shoving his bits and pieces into his pockets. 'I'm happy in a patch of shade for a bit. If that's OK with you, of course.'

Oren turns away from him, unclasping his hands from behind his back. 'You'd better come inside,' he says from over his shoulder, gesturing towards the dark mouth of the air-raid shelter.

'Mind if I have a little walk around instead? It's such a beautiful setting, up here. If I lived here, I reckon I'd never get tired of it.'

This time there is no escaping the expression on Oren's face as he turns back to him. 'Listen to me, Jonny Murphy from the *International Tribune*.' Jonny tries not to flinch as the older man advances on him. 'I think we both know why you are here. And it has nothing to do with olives or bananas. Come with me, and I'll tell you what I know. But go walking around, and only you will be responsible for what happens next.'

'It's chickens, isn't it?' Jonny replies as lightly as he can. 'The third industry. It's your chicken houses.'

Oren spits into the dirt at his feet. 'That's right. So follow me.'

Jonny feels the chill long before he hits the shadow of the concrete shelter.

Chapter Twenty-One
Wednesday

3:00 p.m.

'You two?' Tom looks between Lola and Andre. 'You ... and him?'

'No!' Sam exclaims just as Andre laughs.

'If you knew what I knew, *mate,* it wouldn't be so hard to believe.'

'You're joking, right?' Tom's face droops as he stares at Lola, a mixture of hangover, confusion and the kind of bone-deep exhaustion that only comes from sustained, pre-dawn alarm calls.

She thinks about their stories, the ones they've shared, the ones they haven't. There's no way of knowing what each of them might be holding back. And isn't that the point of friendship? Accepting what you're told at face value, not because you have to, but because you want to? Finally she locates her voice, turns to Andre.

'You don't know anything,' Lola says, resolve strengthening with every word. 'You saw something you think you understand, except—'

'What? What did I see?'

'You were out in the dark and saw two people that you wouldn't usually put together,' Lola continues, 'and added it all up to make three.'

'But now one of them is dead,' Andre shoots back. 'Which gives us all a problem, whether the rest of you like it or not—'

'Why are you so angry, Andre?' Sam interrupts. 'Aren't we all in this together?'

'Is that really what you think?' Andre's tone softens, walking over to Sam with both hands out. Lola freezes. 'Look around you. These little houses – no, these pathetic bedrooms, this cracked-up slab of mud. It's hardly even a township – you think this is our lot? That this is our home? That all six of us aren't just *playing* at happy families? How much do we really know about each other?'

Lola gazes around the small courtyard as if she's seeing it for the first time. Four white doorways, set into each corner of a square, a slab of corrugated iron overhead linking one side with the other. She doesn't need the doors to open to visualise the grubby laminate flooring, the two coffin-width single beds and tiny shower room. A couple of shallow cupboards for possessions, little to zero privacy. Tom and Dave opposite Andre and Jo. Sam and her opposite the locked and vacant unit. The stone circle laid pointlessly in the dirt in the centre because they can't light fires there – they just create a toxic tunnel of smoke. The frayed and stained hammock at the far end on the clifftop, slung between two tired saplings above tufty, yellowing grass.

This is their only patch of real estate, in exchange for six out of seven days' back-breaking work. Little more than if they were donkeys. And they were almost all strangers, until they got here.

'You don't have to tell them, Andre.' Jo strides over from their doorway, suddenly full of purpose. 'It's no one's business but ours.'

But Andre just shoots him a look.

'I think we're at the point where everyone's business is about to become everyone else's,' Dave says, deep voice amplified by the corrugated ridges over their heads.

Lola hesitates, something tugging at her consciousness, but she can't bring it to the surface, echoes disappearing with the distant swell of the ocean.

'Lola was with Farid last night,' Andre announces. 'And not for the first time, either.'

'That's ridiculous,' Sam says, but can't meet anyone's eye, yanking at her apron instead. And now Lola is swaying on her feet, the flood of relief that Sam is taking her side so intense that she has to brace herself against the wall. 'Completely insane. And even if it were true, which it isn't, how the hell would you know?'

Andre turns the corners of his mouth at Sam. 'Why wouldn't I know, is the better question, hey. Don't you have anything to add that might help explain why I know exactly where Lola sleeps some nights?'

Sam lets out a nervous laugh. Panic kicks at Lola's chest.

'He's joking, right?' Tom pulls on Lola's elbow like a child. 'You and ... and ... Farid? You said ... you said you just went for a walk, just went for a walk to clear your head—'

'That's one hell of an accusation you're making, Andre,' Dave's disembodied voice cuts in.

'It's not an accusation, bru, it's a fact. I've seen them together at least twice before. And last night, I am absolutely sure that's where she was—'

'Wait a second.' Dave cuts him off again. 'Where she was? What do you mean? Why would you even think that? Where were you?'

Sam hangs her head. Lola's stomach churns, relief curdling to fear.

'Let's just say I know she wasn't in her bedroom. And you, big fella, know full well she wasn't in yours with him, don't you?' Andre jerks his head at Tom.

'Is it true?' Tom asks her again, his voice tiny, disbelieving. It's as if the rest of them aren't there. 'You and ... Farid, of all people? You were together last night? And you've done it before?'

Andre jumps in before Lola can even begin to collect herself. 'Ja, man. I've seen her with my own eyes. And I wouldn't care less about it if it wasn't for the fact that he's dead now.'

'What are you saying?' Sam gasps. 'You can't seriously be suggesting—'

'He would never suggest that,' Jo interrupts, stilling them all except Dave, who raises his eyes to the ceiling, as if he can find the answers there.

Lola tries to step away, even to run, but can't seem to make her body obey a single instruction. How can her brain be screaming just as her body goes deaf? Aren't they irreparably attached to each other? A sickeningly familiar bitterness courses through her. For Lola already knows the risks of freezing on the spot, and she still can't help doing it anyway.

'Here's what I don't get,' Dave says, turning to Andre. 'Even if Lola was with Farid, last night, or the night before, or the night before that. Why are you, of all people, so exercised about it?'

But before Andre can reply there's a sudden clatter as Tom kicks a rock out of the stone circle into the wall.

'What the fuck is going on?' He's shouting now, hands whirling over his head. 'Andre, are you telling me you've seen Lola with Farid? You've actually seen them together? Sneaking around after lights out? And you!' Lola shrinks as Tom whips around, bearing down on her. 'You're the reason he was here last night, and you're not even trying to deny it?'

Lola can't make a sound, she can't even cry, the disgust and betrayal on Tom's face too much to bear.

Suddenly his voice turns so soft it's almost tender, the cruellest trick of them all. 'I always thought you were something else. You know it too, Lola, you know you do. I couldn't have made it plainer – hell, maybe that's been the problem all along: I've been coming on too strong, or I've not been elusive enough, I don't know...'

'What is it you call them – sloppy seconds? Definitely not my style, bru,' Andre adds, but Tom doesn't flinch, just keeps staring at Lola with the most unbearable of expressions.

'Then what's your problem?' Dave asks. 'Why does it matter to you what Lola is doing on her own time? And don't tell me it's because you're just feeling it on Tom's behalf.'

Andre kicks at the ground before replying. 'My paperwork isn't exactly clean, hey. It's not like they scrutinise our passports for anything other than Arabic when we show up here.'

Jo lets out a nervous laugh, eyes darting. But Dave just glares at him. Andre starts shifting from foot to foot as he continues.

'I have a record back in SA, but only if you know where to look. Some fuckhead reporters thought it made for a good story once upon a time. Never mind the fact I was defending someone else a whole lot more than I was defending myself. Their version of events near on wrecked both of our lives for a while.' He nods at Jo, still quivering on the spot. 'I'll need all the help I can get hiding it now that fat fucker Moti has seen me out at night. And he knows I've seen him too.'

'A record?' Sam whispers, as if she doesn't want her question answered. 'What do you mean, a criminal record? For what?'

Andre sighs. 'Would it make you feel any better if I said it was just for tax fraud? Truth is it could be anything for all it actually matters. The point is whoever did over Farid was already on the inside, they had to have been. The place is twenty different ways of locked up day and night. So it's a kibbutznik, right? Which is a problem for the community ... therefore they need a scapegoat. We don't belong here. So who better than one of us – better still, the ex-con? Guilty until proven innocent, hey? No one is going to care about my side of the story.'

Andre pauses to jerk his head at Lola.

'Of course I don't think you had anything to do with him actually dying. But it looks as bad for you as it does for me. You're in the frame too as soon as they find out what you've been up to. We could have sorted it out between us if you'd bothered to stop and listen to me this morning. Now we're all up to our necks.'

Tom lets out an unpleasant laugh. 'No, mate. It's just you two in over your heads. And you did that to yourselves. The rest of us, we're fine. No skeletons here. We can answer a gazillion questions with a perfectly clear conscience.'

Andre snorts. 'No, man. We can't. Because the fact is that all six of us have either got motive, or not got a decent enough alibi. Some of us stand to lose more than others, hey, but still. It's that simple. Trust me, I've already been through this kind of thing once. You, for example. You've been all over her for months. Everyone's seen the two of you at it in one way or another. Now it turns out she's really been at it with the dead guy behind your back? They need to find out who did this, and we're all in the frame until we can prove we aren't.'

And Lola has it, suddenly, between her fingers. The sharpness that was needling her subconscious finds its target:

Tom's known all along that lying for her could give him motive. He just didn't have the full picture, but he didn't need it. The remotest possibility of being cast as a jealous boyfriend was enough for him to steer well clear. But now Tom's got the picture in focus, Lola doesn't stand a chance. The reality is far worse than he could have imagined.

Lola looks wildly between them, at each face etched with different stages of revelation.

Sam wouldn't have given Andre an alibi even before his latest admission.

Dave has already admitted to leaving the campfire hours before anyone else did.

And Johan – her hands fly to her mouth as the final domino falls. Jo will have been alone in his room the entire night.

There is reason to suspect all of them.

And the only way to avert it is for everyone to tell the same lie.

Chapter Twenty-Two
Thursday

7:15 a.m.

Jonny assesses Oren's broad back as he follows the older man over to the breezeblock shelter. The guy could fall anywhere in the hinterland of middle age – face perhaps weathered by the sun rather than the years, hair so closely cropped it's hard to tell whether it's thinning or not. In any other country Jonny might assume the haircut was to arrest the appearance of a monk's cap. But here, with a standing army, it could mean the opposite – that the man is still in service, or a particularly valuable reservist.

As Oren steps down into the stairwell, Jonny looks up at the hillside again. Knowing the size of the threat it hides is at least making it feel far more reasonable to head underground into reinforced concrete with only a stranger in aggressively good shape for company.

The stairwell opens out into a dank, square room. The chill should feel welcome but just feels airless, even suffocating.

'You would like some coffee,' Oren states rather than asks, heading for a small storage unit in the far corner, its surface littered with bits and pieces.

Jonny squints into the murk as a blue flame flares. A camping stove? And is that a saucepan? Some enamel cups? The thick, rich aroma of strong Arabic coffee winds through the still air in an instant. He shouldn't be surprised, he supposes. The place must be far better equipped than it looks. Other than the storage unit there seems to be an anteroom off to the side – toilets, maybe?

Jonny turns on the spot, noting the stairs rising behind him, the concrete bench seating set into another wall, the strip lighting mounted along the low ceiling.

'Sit down.' Oren motions to one of the benches, lining up two cups next to the stove. Jonny parks himself as close to the opening to the stairwell as possible without making it too obvious that he's already looking for a way out.

'Do they all look like this? The shelters, I mean?' Jonny rubs a fingertip over the bench's rough concrete surface.

'Look like what?' Oren frowns at him.

Jonny stares around the room again. What has he missed?

'Well, is this where you sleep? When things get hairy? Just, you know – lie straight down on the floor?'

'We have mattresses and sleeping bags in the shelters near the homes. And we have full trauma kits in each one. There are toilets, obviously. But no showers.' Oren jerks his head towards the doorway Jonny had spotted.

'But when you hear a siren you have to take cover as quickly as possible, right? So what if you end up in here?'

'Then you sleep on the floor, yes.' Oren turns the stove off, pouring coffee into the two cups. 'No one complains. We are survivors, not victims.'

Jonny gulps as Oren walks over with the coffee. The smell is suddenly so thick he can taste it, physical and heavy in his mouth.

'Thanks,' he says, holding the cup by its rim. Oren stands before him rather than sits, sipping from his own.

'So tell me, Jonny Murphy from the *International Tribune*, what are you really doing here?'

'Well, you were going to tell me a bit more about the third industry that props this place up. Your chicken houses.'

Oren takes another sip of coffee, his eyes never leaving Jonny's face. 'What do you know about our chicken houses?'

Jonny transfers the cup to his other hand, suddenly burning

between his fingers. 'Not a whole lot other than a dead body showed up in one sometime yesterday morning.'

Oren rocks back on his heels, raising his gaze to the ceiling. 'And why does the *International Tribune* care about that?'

Jonny gulps down some coffee, still far too hot to drink. 'You tell me. There's been over a week's worth of rockets flying around. It's not exactly a quiet time. And the man was an Arab Israeli, correct?'

Oren's sudden laugh echoes unpleasantly off the concrete walls. 'You lot are all the same, do you know that?'

'My lot?'

'Journalists. The lot of you. You hear the word Arab, and think you know what the story is before you've even asked any questions.'

Another gulp of thick coffee burns a path down Jonny's throat. 'I'm here, aren't I? If that was the case I wouldn't have bothered.'

'Yes, but why?' Oren leans towards him, hand curling into a fist around his empty cup.

'For someone who thinks we don't ask enough questions, you're not giving me much of a chance to try,' Jonny stammers, grappling for control of the conversation. 'Who died, for starters? And how do you know he was murdered?'

Jonny starts as Oren lets out a cry. Are those tears shining from the older man's eyes?

'You have no idea what you've stumbled into,' Oren says. 'Everyone thinks that it is simple – both sides hate the other and will fight to the death until one of them wins. Nothing's ever that simple though, is it?'

'Here's what I know.' Jonny grips the edge of the ledge with his free hand. 'An Arab-Israeli kibbutz worker has shown up dead in a community that may as well sit on the border. This is a community that lives in constant fear of—'

'No!' Oren shouts. 'No. We do not live in fear. We never have.'

'I'm sorry, I didn't mean to put words into your mouth,' Jonny mumbles, but the older man can't hear him.

'Farid exemplified this. He may not have lived here, but the kibbutz was his home. He worked harder than us all to manage the chicken houses—'

'Was Farid the man who died—?' Jonny tries to interrupt.

'But there are still some who would have you believe that his motivation was far different to just wanting to do the best job he could, for himself, for us, and for his own family.'

'Was Farid the man who died?' Jonny asks again.

'Yes.' Finally Oren turns back to him, face crumpled with regret. 'Farid was murdered. You are right, he was an Arab Israeli. A Druze, to be precise. He was the only Arab in charge of a division. What does that tell you?'

'He must have been very good at his job.'

'Not just that.' Oren's eyes blaze at him. 'What do you think it takes to put an Arab, an Israeli citizen or not, in charge of an industry that could potentially bankrupt the entire community if it failed? Someone who doesn't even live here? That was Farid. That was the kind of man he was to us.'

'How do you know he was murdered?'

Oren pauses then, long enough for Jonny to see a tear settle into the lines around his eyes.

'There is no other explanation.'

Jonny stares back, watches the man compose himself.

'How so? You mean it wasn't obvious?'

'Not in the way you would think.'

'You mean there were no obvious signs of struggle?'

'Not exactly, no.'

'So what happened? Where was he found?'

Oren unlaces his hands, lets his arms drop by his sides, cup dangling from a set of fingers.

'We think he died just after dawn yesterday morning. By the

time he was found, work had already started in some places – we were already in the greenhouse, and the trucks were out in the banana fields. We found him after he didn't come in for breakfast. He was just sprawled in the sawdust in the main chicken house.'

'It's still possible that he could have just dropped dead, isn't it? Unusual but not impossible?'

Oren spreads his hands. 'He is young – was young, I mean. Not even thirty.' Sighing, he steps over to Jonny and takes a seat further down the bench.

Jonny pauses, finally able to see the top of Oren's head, hair far thinner on the crown. The man must be older than he'd first thought. 'I'm still not clear how you know he was murdered.'

Oren fiddles with the sharp edge of the bench. 'Have you ever been inside an industrial chicken house? Or had any experience with what happens when chickens are fed?'

'I can't say I have, no.'

'Chickens aren't the sort of animals who know when they are full. They are the closest existing relative we know to the T-Rex. If you give them lemons, they don't just make lemonade, they get drunk.'

Jonny snorts, filing away the extent to which Oren has mastered the English language. It is better than fluent. It is practically native.

'They made mincemeat out of Farid. And the even sadder part is he would have been so proud of them. Farid cared for the chickens. It wasn't just about what they provided. Farid gave them the best, to get the best out of them. He would have expected chickens of his to make a feast of warm flesh, of course he would—' Oren's voice cracks. 'He was facing upwards, but he no longer had a face. Every inch of him that was uncovered was pecked open. They'd taken his skin off, plucked his eyes out. There were flesh wounds absolutely everywhere.'

Jonny swallows down the dregs of his coffee, cold and gritty.

'So when we rolled him over, there was no mistaking it. His

whole back was completely clean, save for the puncture mark on his neck. It was clear as if someone had drawn it on. He must have been injected with something.'

'I guess a post-mortem will confirm all of this and more.' Jonny toys with his empty cup. 'The police must be all over that?'

'That is up to his family. Not to us. It is clear to us why this happened.'

'And why is that? Why would anyone want to kill a man like Farid? By your account, he had no enemies. He was a pillar of the community, even more so because he wasn't actually part of it. So why would anyone want to kill him? What were his secrets?'

Jonny flinches as Oren stands, stalking over to the far wall.

'The thing is,' Jonny continues, simultaneously trying to work out how many steps it will take for him to reach the stairwell if needed. 'If he really was murdered, someone must have hated him enough to do it. You don't just cut a man down without a reason. So you can see why the most obvious explanation might send a newspaper up here to check it out?'

Oren's shoulders rise and fall with the depth of his sigh. Jonny stands up, quietly as possible, so he can run if he needs to.

'I think you'd better join us,' Oren says, without turning around.

And before Jonny can ask what he means, a figure emerges from where he thought there were only toilets, long shadow falling on the ground between them.

Chapter Twenty-Three
Wednesday

3:30 p.m.

Lola is running. She knows they are all shouting after her, but she has nothing left to say. How can she take any more questions when she doesn't know the answers herself? Her mind is burning, every memory tainted, every belief founded on lies. And what is it she's even trying to preserve? These friends-that-became-family who it turns out she hardly knows at all? Her reputation? Her dignity? Her freedom? If Lola is forced to stop and think about it all for one more second she feels like her head might explode.

What could she possibly say to Tom? That she knew full well how much he liked her, but every time she entertained the idea he became too possessive and controlling? That she deserved more than a relationship based on just being grateful someone wanted her?

And is that why she fell for Farid? Because a man like that could never be too possessive and controlling? Because he was just so thrillingly different? OK, so Lola didn't think it through. But who does, in the first, second, even third flush of attraction? Why should Lola be punished for thinking the best of people rather than the worst?

And what about Andre? Isn't he just a man as thrillingly different as Farid? What might Sam say if Lola asked her as pointedly as that? Isn't it that Sam finally feels in a safe enough place to follow her heart rather than her head – as what safer place could there be where Sam's family was concerned than in the Holy Land itself?

A sudden gust of wind off the sea blows hair into her eyes. For Lola is already on the clifftop, almost as close as she can get to the edge without falling. A spot where, for the last six months, she's only ever felt like she might fly if she jumped. But now she feels trapped – worse, almost buried by a pile of lies, excuses and clueless miscalculation.

To Lola, the promise of finally belonging has felt so exhilarating that it's blinded her to so many other things that have been staring her in the face all along.

These people aren't her family.

This place isn't her home.

Lola doesn't get to belong to something just because she wants to.

She finds the sharp gap in the wire fence, deliberately grazes herself on her way through. The thickets of plants close around her almost immediately. This is the only place she can hide.

Lola tunnels in deeper, tries to focus on matters she knows she can control. This steep slope gets the most light of any on the kibbutz, each row of banana plants lower than the next, able to photosynthesise the moment the sun breaks over the hills in the east. The plants are at their most aggressive here. She pictures them fanned out like an army around her. Lola's position is a matter of both luck and judgment. She takes comfort in this.

She begins to traverse the hillside, allows one question into her mind at a time. Do all the volunteers have enough at stake to stick by the same lie? The songs they all sing, the stories they all tell, suddenly rattle around Lola's mind in chorus – a circus merry-go-round, every revolution a little more out of tune.

Tom isn't here to find himself. He's here to find someone else.

Andre is running from something, and only Johan knows what it is.

Sam is trying to mend fences she never built in the first place.

And she realises the only stories she ever hears from Dave are from the books he's always reading.

The reality is that whatever Lola thinks she knows about them all, even about Sam, about the truth hovering just beyond the edges of those shiny happy family photos, there's no way she can be sure that she really does.

Lola turns a hairpin corner, one cheek starting to burn. What did Farid see in her that made him pick her out? What made him think she'd do it if he asked? Is she sure it isn't what they all see – the gullibility she is always trying to hide? She didn't even know what it meant, to be gullible, when she first heard herself described her that way. Did it mean naïve? That she gave no thought to ulterior motives? Doesn't that just mean she trusts people, that she believes they'd rather do her good than harm? Even now Lola sees it differently. Being gullible is just hope in disguise.

She kicks at the undergrowth. This burden of hope is hardly Lola's fault. It's just what happens when no one cares as much as they are supposed to. Her mum is just too busy with Richard, with Holly – her real child. The one with two real parents. The one who Lola's hand-me-downs aren't good enough for, because they've been handed down from someone else already. The one who's turned their family even from odd, like a full stop at the end of a sentence that Lola still can't bring herself to read.

And what has Richard ever actually done wrong, anyway? What's he ever actually physically *done*? They're only looks, aren't they? Suggestive of nothing other than – *Good morning Lola, did you sleep well?* Shouldn't Lola be pleased he's buying her new things, even if it's only ever silky, sexy underwear? Shouldn't she be happy that someone has started thinking about what she needs? Isn't attention what she craves?

Lola remembers how it felt when people started to notice her – that day when her body no longer felt like her own, felt like someone other than her was suddenly living in it, reshaping its angles into curves. Suddenly Lola had a means to be seen, when all she had felt before was transparent. Suddenly there were people upon people – men, mostly – who were really interested in her. And just as suddenly she would realise, too late, that interest was actually the ravenous gaze of a half-starved wild animal.

Another corner, her face blistering with heat even without the sun on one side. Lola's in the school bathroom now, where all the worst rumours are spread, not just by the writing on the wall. The one where whispers become facts that even lies can't challenge. Where girls who go with boys just because they feel seen are slags. Where girls that go with girls can never tell. Where even changing the writing on the wall doesn't change the story. Lola swallows, but the acid keeps rising. What other choices do girls like her have? When the right choices – the loyal friendships, the good grades, the obedient behaviour – just make them more invisible?

The slope levels off with another turn. She still has a choice, Lola reminds herself. She can choose to admit to the mechanics of everything. She can choose to be the person she knows she is, the one who can only ever seem to see adventure and opportunity, even when the red flags are so bright they may as well be bleeding. She's surely young enough, can play dumb enough, that no one could possibly suspect her of actually doing anything more than that? She can plead her innocence, because everything about her suggests she's just that.

Lola sways slightly as she considers this, the chill of full shade falling over her with the final corner at the bottom of the slope. Fouad and Issam will still blame her, even if there are others that don't. Farid was their family, not hers, not even close.

That's the revelation that pulls her up short, stiffening into the crack of another twig.

For she is no longer moving. It didn't come from beneath her feet.

Chapter Twenty-Four
Thursday

7:30 a.m.

The figure, another man, stops next to Oren to survey Jonny from a distance. Jonny immediately regrets moving so close to the stairwell, the light from the electric strips overhead falling at the most inconvenient of angles, illuminating precisely nothing on the stranger's face other than the fact he has one. No one speaks, the silence so immense it feels as heavy as the concrete enclosure.

Jonny finds himself counting, slow and deliberate – some ancient mental trick that used to help him tune out anything going on around him that he didn't understand. Except this time a new revelation lands with every digit. Oren must have known this other person was already in here – there's no other way in apart from down the stairs, is there? He resists the urge to look around, even as a pulse in his neck starts to twitch. Who in their right mind hangs out in a fortified underground bunker if they don't have to? The counting speeds up as Jonny's mind races – the fact the place is littered with bunkers brings the whole notion of 'right mind' into question, doesn't it? Jonny is somewhere between twenty and thirty when he realises a whole lot more planning seems to have gone into intercepting his arrival on Beit Liora than just running into him in the courtyard. And he's a whole lot more counting away from figuring out exactly how and why.

He flinches as Oren finally turns around. For some reason the fact Jonny can now see both men's faces makes the whole tableau feel even more intimidating. He makes himself swallow rather than speak, organising the questions inside his head.

Oren breaks ranks first, trudging past the other man to flick the camping stove back on. Jonny flinches again as it hisses.

'You can sit down again, you know.' Oren taps more coffee into the pot. 'No one is going to hurt you.'

The stranger stays standing to regard Jonny. Eye to eye, they're the same height, give or take an inch or two to allow for perspective. Unremarkable shirt and shorts, traces of dirt streaked across his front. Not as suntanned as you'd expect for a kibbutznik – so does this stranger work indoors? He hardly looks fresh enough to have come straight from folding kilos of clean laundry?

Jonny takes a deep breath as the heady aroma of coffee hits him again, this time laced with something else.

'You got a restaurant back there?' Jonny keeps his voice level. 'Or is it just coffee?'

Oren frowns at the coffee pot. The stranger acts like no one has said anything at all.

Jonny takes another deep breath. There's something acrid underneath the coffee, pungent and sour.

'Who's your friend?'

Again, no answer – just another hiss as Oren turns off the flame, pouring the liquid into a fresh enamel cup. Jonny fights himself as the counting starts again. It's like a reflex, he can never seem to control it. And right now he needs every single one of his senses primed and alert, not distracted like some confused child.

'Thought you'd never ask,' the stranger finally replies, his accent unmistakable as Oren passes him the cup, blowing on the surface of the liquid as he gazes steadily at Jonny. 'And no, there's not a restaurant back there. I should be so lucky.'

Adrenaline blasts up Jonny's back, damp patches spreading through the cotton under his armpits. 'So who are you? And what are you doing down here?'

'He's a volunteer,' Oren says, moving out from behind the storage unit to take up position next to the stranger. Jonny blanches at the word, yet another inconvenient mental reflex taking flight. A young, beautiful woman twirling hair around her finger at a mysterious, exciting man from a far off land. This is where his parents met. This is how it started.

'What do you mean, he's a volunteer?' Jonny asks, dumbly, as if there is a world in which he doesn't know exactly what it means.

'We have eight beds available on the kibbutz,' Oren explains, as if suddenly they're talking about a lifestyle feature. 'Anyone can apply to come and live here, so long as they work here. People from all over the world are drawn to our way of life. And we welcome keen, young blood. There is always more work we could be doing if we had more people.'

Something snaps inside Jonny as the stranger keeps sipping, staring at him. Jonny was the big cat around here to start with, and now he feels like the mouse – worse, like the claws have already got him, but has no idea when or how.

'So what's a volunteer doing hiding in a bomb shelter at first light if there's all this work to be done? Hanging around, listening to private conversations? Are you running a command-and-control centre back there? Mining for gold?'

The stranger's face darkens.

'Why don't you sit down again, Jonny Murphy from the *International Tribune*,' Oren says meaningfully. 'We know you have a lot of questions, and we're here to answer them.'

'I'm OK here, thanks,' Jonny replies, the sweat suddenly pouring down his back. 'In fact, I think it's high time I went back outside. I wouldn't want to keep Moti waiting.'

'Take a seat, Jonny.' The stranger steps towards him. 'If you want to get out of here, you're going to have to help us out first.'

A sequence of images plays through Jonny's mind – the steep, stone steps behind him, the fortified metal gates at the bottom of the driveway, the guardhouse with its bank of monitors flickering in black and white. Running would get him precisely nowhere … He sighs as he looks up, only to find the pimpled concrete ceiling. Somehow Jonny's managed to dig himself so far in over his head that he never even spotted it closing over. He tenses every muscle as he sits, kidding himself that he's still coiled and ready for action.

'You're English, right?'

Jonny nods, eyeing the stranger's hands still in the air as he asks.

'So you'll be familiar with some of our politics, then.'

'Politics?' Jonny repeats, allowing himself a little mental snort. 'Whose in particular? There's a whole lot of different kinds in play round here. And I don't even know your name.'

The stranger advances a step.

'You can call me Big Bird. Or Geronimo. Take your pick. Both fit.'

'Geronimo,' Jonny murmurs to himself, trying and failing to place the actual name, better still, its significance. But he draws a blank.

'Like your style.' The stranger laughs. 'Fine. So I'm Geronimo. And I hear you're a journalist.'

Jonny brightens, if only for a second. 'Yes. I'm a junior reporter at the *International Tribune*.'

'Ah, the *Trib*.' Geronimo gives Oren a little nod. 'A fine editorial news outfit, to be sure. So I imagine you'll also be familiar with the one hundred million dollars that the international community pledged not just three weeks ago to the Israeli administration in exchange for – what did they call it? Ah yes, human intelligence gathering.'

Jonny's jaw slackens. He read about the windfall, of course he did. The *Trib* covered it at length. The total pledge was actually in excess of three hundred million – a hundred for so-called anti-terror activities and the rest for some new-fangled missile-interception system. It was a massive political and financial coup for the Israelis, and the timing couldn't have been any more prescient. The rocket attacks from Lebanon had started days later, as if the couple of deadly suicide bombings a few weeks earlier weren't already enough.

'I thought...' Jonny licks his lips, tries again. 'I thought you were a volunteer?'

'That I am,' Geronimo says, folding his arms across his chest. 'I've been working here for over six months now.'

'Do the rest of the volunteers call you Geronimo too? Or are you just Big Bird to them?'

'Smart.' Jonny quails under the larger man's stare, anything but approving. 'No. They don't. And I'm not. If you get me.'

'Volunteering's not the only job you're doing around here, is it?' Jonny asks in a small voice, as it if will diminish the answer.

The two men regard him with a curious mix of admiration and pity.

'Right again, Jonny-boy. It is not. That's about all I'm going to tell you on this particular topic, though. For now, anyway.'

And with that Geronimo steps fully out of the shadows. Jonny tries to assess him dispassionately. He can't be much older than Jonny himself – late twenties, maybe? Is it even believable that someone would volunteer as late as that? That someone was still at such a loss about what to do with their life, they pitched up at a kibbutz for a few months of wondering? Would it really wash, turning up and saying they'd come to put in the hard yards for nothing more than a room with a view?

But then Oren comes into focus too. And Jonny's heart kicks at his chest. Of course it wouldn't wash, but that doesn't matter if founder members of the place are in on the secret too. It's just another quid pro quo. So what is Geronimo really doing on the kibbutz? Not volunteering in exchange for bed and board, that's for sure. Oren's perfect English suddenly chimes in Jonny's head, along with a whole bunch of other questions he won't get any answers to. A strange expression crosses Oren's face – as jarring as it is unreadable.

'You know I'm a journalist,' Jonny says, as if it will somehow reassert his authority over a situation he knows he lost control of a long time ago. 'And suddenly I find myself in a room with, what, a spy? And his informant? Human intelligence gathering in the flesh?' He shifts his gaze to Oren. 'Presumably none of this is on the record, is it?'

'Right again.' Geronimo digs dirt out from under his fingernails, one after the other. 'And presumably you understand that I'm doing you a favour. If I told you any more—'

'Yeah.' Jonny cuts him off rather than say it out loud. 'I still don't get it, though. You know I'm a journalist but you're telling me anyway. You must have a whole lot at stake. A whole lot more than a dead guy in a chicken house.'

'That's why we need your help, my friend.'

Jonny winces at the word.

'What do you know about why Farid was killed?'

'Me?'

'Yes, Jonny-boy. I need to know what you know, if you get me.'

Jonny folds his arms, more in self-preservation than anything else. 'Not a whole lot other than he was. And that the chickens turned him into mincemeat.'

'Do you really think you are a position to keeping claiming you rocked up here on a wing and a prayer? Does a newspaper like the *International Tribune* routinely send cub reporters to check out random deaths in largely closed communities?'

Jonny casts around for Allen inside his head, but there's nothing. Every late night telling war stories around a shisha pipe, every impatient, rapid-fire conversation justifying her latest deployment. Nothing, not even the slightest nugget that could give him a strategy out of this.

'Well, it's not exactly calm around here,' he continues lamely.

'Anything to do with bodies on the border is a story at the moment.'

Jonny shivers reflexively as Geronimo steps towards him, shadow falling over his head.

'I'm only going to ask you one more time. After that you're going to tell me, whether you like it or not. Make no mistake about that.'

The pause that follows weighs heavy as the concrete itself.

'What do you know about why Farid was killed?'

'Was he—' Jonny's breath catches in his throat before he can finish. He takes a deep breath, has to start again. 'Had he found out about some sort of tunnel? Running under the border?'

Geronimo's arms tighten around his chest. 'Had he? Are you asking me or telling me?'

Jonny continues, emboldened by something he can't identify. 'Well you asked me what I knew. And so far all I have is a tip, because I've only got as far as the air-raid shelter in the courtyard.'

'So you have a tip,' Geronimo repeats, thoughtfully. 'From whom?'

Jonny swallows, coffee grounds still lodged in his throat. 'You know ... you know I can't tell you that.'

'I'd have thought it was more than obvious by now that you are going to have to tell me everything.'

Jonny tries not to flinch as Geronimo advances, instead looking past him to Oren, still planted in his original position. That curious expression is still spread across his face. If Jonny didn't know better he'd say it even contained a bit of fear.

'Had he? Had the dead guy seriously found a tunnel under the border?'

The air leaves Jonny lungs, suddenly and completely, as a rough hand wraps around his throat.

'When I let you go,' Geronimo hisses, 'I expect to hear two things. First, the gasp of someone who understands that they've been granted another breath because I'm a merciful kind of guy, followed just as quickly by the sounds of someone who knows this breath could be their last if they do not use it to answer my questions as fulsomely as fucking possible.'

Jonny feels his eyes bulge as his vision darkens at the edges, pixelating and pixelating until the stranger finally lets go, and a gush of fetid air floods back into his body.

'I'll let you have your little cough and splutter, too.' Geronimo's face is still inches away from Jonny's as he gulps. 'So you better make it good.'

'I got—' Jonny has to stop, clear his throat again.

Out of the corner of a blurry eye, he notes veins popping improbably large from Oren's neck. The older man is scared. Jonny is sure of it. When he finally feels ready to reply, he starts gabbling like a maniac.

'I got a tip from a former intelligence officer that a body had been found here. An Arab Israeli worker turning up dead on a kibbutz that may as well form part of the border itself was enough to set up a meeting. I know Arab Israelis hold full citizenship, but let's face it, plenty of other citizens don't see them as equals... I'm not saying that's how I feel personally, you understand, I'm just saying that there are all sorts of tensions at play here – and especially at a time like this, right? The rocket attacks aren't exactly easy to live with. I bet you'd be the first to tell me that too, what with all the rushing around having to sleep in bunkers at a second's notice and whatnot. Anyway, she told me about the tunnel when I met her. How this man was a traitor, basically. That not only had he found out about it, but he'd told the wrong side about it.'

'Wrong side...' Geronimo repeats meditatively. 'And how exactly does a cub reporter like you come by a source like that?'

Jonny shrugs, still staring at Oren. 'I suppose now you'll want her name, too.'

Geronimo laughs, high and mad. 'Well, at least I know you really are a cub reporter.'

Now it's flush spreading up Jonny's sore neck, instead of relief. Of course any intelligence officer has at least ten different names. Jonny should have known when this man chose to introduce himself with a choice of two. And they weren't even proper fucking names.

'Here's the thing, though, Jonny Murphy from the *International Tribune*,' Geronimo continues. 'Now we've been properly introduced, I expect you think you have the full picture. Especially if your last chapter and verse was anything to go by. You think it's perfectly obvious why this man was murdered. Better, you're sure who delivered the lethal injection. It wasn't what you were necessarily expecting, but it doesn't matter, because it's even better. What a story, huh? And now your main concern – other than getting out of this hole before you piss yourself, or worse – is that you'll never be able to tell anyone about it. You'll have to sit on the scoop of a lifetime. You've found covert intelligence operating in plain sight on top of a massive secret buried under one of the hottest borders in the world. You'll have to pretend you haven't got a clue, because of course if you don't do exactly as you are told from here on in you won't even get a chance to pretend.'

Jonny's neck pinches again as he looks up. 'What are you saying? That it's none of those things?'

Geronimo nods as he spreads his hands again, flexing his knuckles into the fetid air.

'That's right, my friend. That's right. We had nothing to do with this particular occurrence. I need to know exactly who did. And since we have to skin this cat in short fucking order, you best listen very carefully to what I want you to do next.'

Chapter Twenty Five
Wednesday

4:00 p.m.

Lola tenses between the plants. A sudden gust of wind off the sea whips their leaves into hysteria. She takes her chance and climbs on to a long-dead stump, just wide enough for both her feet. Any noise from here on it won't be hers – is that another twig snapping somewhere further down the row? She holds her breath as the leaves still. The edge of a red plastic sandal confirms it, paused just within her peripheral vision.

Lola lets her breath come in little gasps, sipping just enough oxygen that she doesn't pass out. It's not Fouad, it's not Issam. They wear boots – they all do; no one can work in the fields without. She bites her lip, noting her own feet, tottering in flip flops on the black stump. Of course she hadn't had time to put her own boots back on, much less collect her trauma kit before she ran. Why is Lola even surprised she forgot to protect herself?

Another red sandal appears in a sharp volley of snapping twigs, the person it belongs to moving at increasing speed. Now they're clumping past her hiding place, it feels impossible she won't be seen. Banana plants aren't bushes, their leaves are as slender as they are long. Lola dare not even gasp as the sandals disappear in the other direction, cracks and snaps receding with every step.

Lola's mind spins. Who is down here too? And why? This field is the most northerly section of kibbutz land, she's sure of it, and the only area on the side of the cliffs, inhospitable to everything except plants that thrive in relentless sunshine. There are more banana fields, spread both below the spot where she is, and again further down along the coast. Is that where this person is headed? There's the path down to the beach, right off the very bottom edge, but that's not accessible from this particular field. Unless ... She peers in the direction the sandals disappeared, as if she will see an opening she knows isn't there. Instead she recoils as their owner comes into view from between the plants a little further down the row.

'You are here,' Moti observes, as if they've been in conversation the entire time. Lola lets out all her breath in one go, sagging on her spot on the stump. Well, of course Moti is down here. It's a perfectly regular development. He's in charge of the banana fields. Farid wasn't his brother. He's getting back to work. And that's why she's down here too. Everything is exactly as it should be, apart from the shoes they're both wearing, his red ones stepping heavily towards her.

'And you are hiding. Why? You did your job.'

'I thought I should get back to work.' Lola stumbles off the stump, a new kaleidoscope of light and shade falling over her face. 'I figured no one would be around to drive the floats so I came down this way. It's really easy from the volunteers' block.'

She's in full shadow now, Moti moving even closer. A little yip tells her Biba is somewhere close by in the plants. Her forehead creases before she can stop it.

'You did your job,' he repeats. 'So there is nothing left for you to do today.'

'My job?' Lola's voice catches at the sight of the machete hanging from Moti's belt. It's not unusual in the fields. It's all that works to fell a full-grown bunch of bananas. And yet the purple pendulum banana flowers, the precursor to the actual fruit, are swaying all around them.

'It was you who kept letting him in, yes?'

She stares at her feet, hears rather than sees Moti lift and drop his hands in triumph.

'So, then. You did your job.'

Lola blanches, shaking her head as if it will make the pieces starting to fall into place land differently. So Moti knew about her and Farid? Why hasn't he said anything before now? And what does he mean by job, if not what she does in his precious banana fields every day? But all each shake does is bring another glimmer of sharp, silver blade into view.

'I don't understand,' she mumbles. 'How do you know ... I mean, do you know what happened to him? Why did he die?'

'It is better you do not know why. You would not understand, anyway.'

Now it's resentment boiling through Lola. For why *wouldn't* she understand? She's a volunteer. She's up at dawn, working like a donkey, committed as every last one of them, but with zero ties to show for it ... Her blood, sweat and tears are propping this place up too, and for what?

'Well, I know he didn't deserve it, no way. Anything but, judging by the way you all behaved around him.'

Moti just looks like he's laughing when she finally meets his eye. 'Is that what you think they will say about you, when they find out? That you do not deserve to be punished?'

Lola feels the blood drain away from her face. 'What do you mean?'

And there it is, the smile that always comes next, the ugliest of leers spreading slowly through Moti's thick, white beard.

'You are safe here, do not worry.' He waves a meaty hand at the banana plants. 'That is why I came to find you. I knew you would run to the fields. I suppose it is good that you are hiding. Especially if you are alone.'

Moti's brow furrows as he squints over her shoulder. She's missed her chance to move. He's suddenly so close to Lola that she can smell the sweat coming off him in waves.

'I'm not ... I'm not hiding,' she stammers. 'You told us ... I mean, you always tell us ... you always just tell us to get back to work.'

Moti snorts, looking her up and down. 'This is how you come to work? In sandals? Without your medical pack?'

Lola's empty pocket suddenly feels as if it were laden with stones, the allergy bracelet on her wrist weighing like a handcuff without its accompanying antidote by her side.

'This is why you can never tell, with people like you. With girls like you.'

'Girls like me.' Whispers, not words. What would Moti know about girls like her? But now Lola can't get even any more whispers out.

A rough hand lands on Lola's neck, cupping her face, like she knew it would. For she's been here before – a different field, a smoother hand, an equally malign set of intentions. Another false promise, another twisted lie. From the moment Lola saw him, her body knew, if not her brain. Moti followed her for his own purposes. No one else's. And this horrible, degrading, shameful thing is about to happen in this beautiful place, surrounded by these wild and fierce plants, the perfect environment she literally helped create herself is about to turn against her too.

'I just know what they say.' His breath lands hot on Lola's face. 'And I don't believe all of it. No, I think you are a good girl, even if you are sad. You are a good girl. You make the right choices.'

The hand, it's in Lola's hair now, stroking strands away from her face.

'And you do have a choice,' Moti continues. 'But I cannot help you if you tell everyone. That is why I am here. To protect you from what you do not understand. You need me. What will happen if anyone else finds out what you have been doing? Your friends, they can't protect you. They are worth nothing, out here. Fouad, Issam...' He pauses to spit. It lands just shy of her toes.

'They will blame you. Without me, there is no way out. I am the only one who can save you. If you make the right choice.'

A thumb lands on the corner of Lola's mouth, pushes between her lips. She wills herself to bite down, but her jaw just hangs, slack and terrified. Is it possible the dog is still snuffling somewhere nearby in the trees? Biba loves her as much as Farid – there's no scent on Moti that she'll trust. And she won't be able to watch someone else she loves get hurt.

'Without me, you have no options. You can say you had nothing to do with it, but I know the truth. He was only inside the kibbutz because of you, and look what happened. Who do you think they will believe?'

'You were part of this,' Lola stammers, willing that Biba hear her, even though all that's coming out is a lisp. 'You ... you must have seen us together. So you're just as suspicious.'

With that Moti snaps Lola's mouth shut, pinching her lips together between his thumb and forefinger. Blood trickles down her throat.

'Only Farid can prove this. Only Farid can prove anything one way or the other. Shall we go and ask him, yes? Would you like to see what the chickens did to his face, to his body?'

One hand stays clamped around Lola's mouth while the other reaches into her vest, pulling her breast out of her bra and up over the low neckline – there's her nipple, already pimpled and hard, already ready for it. And Lola's cry is completely stifled. She's a blank: nothing is happening to her. It's happening to someone else.

'I see why he picked you.' Moti shoves a hand into her pants. 'We all see it, you know that. You know this power you have over all of us. And you like it. This ... this power. This power that makes men do whatever you want. This is what makes you happy. What you do to men. I am only doing this because you make me, you understand? It is you who makes me this person.'

A scream builds in Lola's throat but emerges with only the tiniest of squeaks. Moti is still speaking, but it's Hebrew now, or is it Arabic? She doesn't understand it, doesn't understand it at all. She sees herself from above, face like a duck with its misshapen mouth, shorts pooled around her ankles as alien body parts drive deep inside her most private of places. There's no escaping the chorus suddenly roaring inside her head, pain should be exploding all over her except it's not, she can't feel a thing except her lips, they're still bulging and bulging between a filthy finger and thumb, and there's just heat, the boiling heat of the sun, and this other body bearing down on her so heavy and thick she'll surely suffocate before she feels anything else ... yes, that's it, that's what's going to happen, for there's no air, no oxygen at all, there's just burning heat, sharp between her fingers, silver-slick and steel...

A blade.

The machete.

It's in her hand.

Lola's mind and body finally fire in perfect synchronicity, emptying of every sensation, every silent scream, every action except one.

This one. This sharp, determined, decisive flick of her wrist.

The knife slides pure and clean into a bare roll of hairy fat like it's a sheath.

The heavy, thick body simply falls away, toppling on to the blade, embedding it to the hilt.

Moti slumps, but can't drag her down with him. Nothing can. It's just fat, flesh, and blood, slippery and thick, pulsing away from him as rhythmically as a heartbeat.

Chapter Twenty-Six
Thursday

7:45 a.m.

'I don't understand,' Jonny manages to choke out, gawping at the two men, hand curled protectively around his sore neck. 'You expect me to believe it wasn't you that killed him? Isn't that exactly what you'd do if you were a covert intelligence officer who found an Arab using a tunnel running under the border between Israel and Lebanon?'

'Careful, now,' Geronimo answers, flexing his own hands with a grin. 'There are certain things you can't forget once you know them. And it would be a problem for my professional reputation if I left anything to chance. So I'd say you don't want me to slip up for a second, do you?'

'What's that supposed to mean?'

'That if I told you I'd have to kill you. Come on, Jonny-boy. You're a journalist. You must know all the cliches. Don't tell me you haven't seen this movie before.'

Jonny kicks at the concrete, immediate stab of pain in his toe a reminder of how solid it is. He considers the reality of his situation, nothing in sight to soften the blow. No one is going to just wander down here and get him out of this hole. Even if it wasn't already perfectly obvious there are other forces in control of this situation, the fact people have had to sleep in these bunkers as recently as last week is hardly going to encourage random appearances when they have no reason to be underground. He suddenly finds himself willing for a siren, for an immediate, indisputable threat that might send people rushing to his side.

'I don't understand,' he repeats. 'What is it you need me to do? What could someone like me possibly do that would help people like you?'

'Now we're in business.' Geronimo bares a set of perfect white teeth. 'And I'll let you have that, if only because telling you what kind of person I really am is most definitely not something you want me to do. There's only one ending to that story. Instead, let me paint you a picture. There's certain bits I won't colour in, so don't ask me about them. Remember, my man, it's for your own protection. So let's start with a simple picture. It should be easy enough for you to understand.'

Geronimo starts to pace, back and forth, from wall to opposite wall.

'This is a picture of the countryside. A green and pleasant land, if you like – yes?' He chuckles to himself. 'And how do people typically make a living in the countryside?'

Jonny stares as Geronimo pauses, meditatively examining another fingernail.

'Come on, Jonny. Don't tell me you've never heard this hymn before.'

'Well it wasn't farmers who built Jerusalem,' Jonny mumbles.

'Bingo, my man.' Geronimo claps, even as his eyes narrow. 'They farm it. That's what you meant, isn't it? So cover this picture of the countryside in farms. Paint 'em however you like. But remember this.' Geronimo waves his hands at the blank wall. 'These farms are all separated by fences. And of course the farmers all disagree about where the fences should be. Doesn't matter what's written in some ancient deed, or half-baked agricultural register. This is about money and power. Each square metre of soil is more of it, as far as they're concerned. And that's where this pretty picture gets complicated.'

Jonny notes Oren wince as Geronimo brushes past him. The older man is trying less and less hard to hide it. But Geronimo continues undaunted.

'The farmers, they're wily old folk. They have to be, making a living from something so unpredictable. You can't just up and move a fence. You can't just plough on – literally – and rely on fighting back if you get challenged. Think about it on that level for just a second. You're one farmer, and I'm another. You want to go ten rounds in the ring with me every few months? Yep, I thought not. So what do you do? You have to use a little imagination.'

'Imagination?' Jonny echoes, instantly regretting it as Geronimo rounds on him.

'Yes, my man. Imagination. How about you use a little of your own right now?' He taps the side of his head. 'Dig around in there for a minute. We're still farmers, you and I. We're on opposite sides of the fence. How do you make sure you always have the upper hand? By anticipating my every move, right? By knowing all my secrets.'

Jonny's mind races. Geronimo is a spy. Oren too, at least in some shape or form. But Jonny's just a journalist. Doesn't that make him more threat than asset here? He opens his mouth only to snap it closed again.

'Exactly right.' Geronimo gives him a triumphant nod. 'You're smart, huh. You've already got a few ideas. But you can't tell me what they are as then you'd blow your advantage. Especially since farming is an enterprise that has been evolving since the dawn of time. Experienced farmers know *alllll* the tricks. So you have to get really inventive. Lay a few unexpected traps to protect all the cards you've got. But you can't give me specifics. As then they wouldn't be traps at all.'

'What do mean?' Jonny whispers, he can't help himself.

'Careful, Jonny.' Geronimo's voice is somehow amplified by the open stairwell behind him. 'The more indirect I am, the better position you're in.'

'So you've ... you've laid a trap,' Jonny continues hesitantly. 'Right? A few traps, even. Like you said. Because land is the prize around here, that's for sure. Before someone died you thought you knew all the secrets, now it turns out you don't. And you can't ask too many questions yourself as then it would give away what you knew in the first place. It would also risk blowing some of your traps. Not least give away who you really are, and what you're really doing here—'

'Right.' Geronimo cuts him off. 'But here *you* are, asking all sorts of questions. Good ones too. As anyone might expect of a journalist of your calibre. Me – I'm just a volunteer. People might start to wonder why I cared so much. People might start lying to me, trying to catch me out. Suspicion is a fact in a place as tight as this. I can't afford to cast suspicion on myself. Don't forget, I'm still the one with the advantage right now, and that's worth far more than just fucking money and power. Lives depend on it. Human lives. Like yours, for example.'

Jonny feels his breath coming in little gasps. 'So ... you need me to find out what you can't?' He tries not to pant. 'To work out what's really happened? I don't understand. Why can't he do it?' He gestures at Oren with a shaky hand, tries to pinpoint exactly what the older man is afraid of.

'Smart again.' Another triumphant nod from Geronimo. 'You'd think, huh? But can you imagine what would happen if other founder members of this place discovered one of their own had known about this all along? What did I tell you about suspicion around here? It doesn't take much. Plus, the old man has more pressing matters to attend to.'

Like what? Jonny wants to ask, but knows he's out of chances. The dead guy mattered. The dead guy was doing something that mattered. The spy didn't kill him and needs to find out who did, without blowing his own cover. Right on cue the fall guy has strolled in, as desperate as he is dumb. Even better, the fall guy is a journalist, both expected and paid to ask questions. Geronimo needs someone to do his dirty work, and who better than someone who might already have some of the answers? Not the look Jonny has been going for, but he supposes he'll have to take it.

The fact that Jonny is actually paid to *tell* people about the answers to his fucking questions sits uncomfortably in his chest, expanding with every passing second. How did Allen put it, back when Jonny first walked into the newsroom, box-fresh cap on his head, pristine notebook in hand? Journalists are paid to bear witness. To hold power to account. To give voice to the voiceless. To shine a light into the darkest of corners regardless of what they find. Sure, Allen went on to snort at the cliche of it all, but the facts of the matter never wavered. This job means everything to Jonny. Is he honestly going to have to leave the facts of this particular matter in the dark?

But Jonny says none of this. Instead he just gives a meek nod of his own.

'Listen, I'm doing you a favour,' Geronimo adds. 'All we've done is talk about paintings, acted out a little role play. Farmyards, white picket fences, that sort of thing. I didn't give you anything to incriminate yourself with. You don't know the full story, you'll never know the full story. I want you to remember that, Jonny Murphy from the *International Tribune*. Because this little conversation of ours could have ended very badly for you. It still could, by the way. If you're not as careful as me. Don't go getting carried away, now. This discovery of yours isn't a scoop. It will never be a scoop.'

Geronimo shakes a final finger at Jonny, his hand blotched an angry red. Jonny swallows hard, realising how hard they must have been clenched behind Geronimo's back.

'He sounds like he was quite a guy,' Jonny says, turning to Oren. 'Can you tell me a little more about him? I'm in a better position to ask other people questions if you're able to give me a bit more background.'

'Good point,' Geronimo replies instead. 'I can tell we're in safe hands, old man. Go on, you can answer him.'

So Oren's taking orders? The two men aren't working together? Fragments of theories pass through the back alleys of Jonny's mind, forming and reforming as they collide.

'Farid and his brother have worked here for more than ten years,' Oren replies gruffly. 'Fouad was still a child when he brought him here. They live in the nearby Druze village with the rest of their families – Issam is a cousin, he works here too, both in the banana fields with Moti. Farid pretty much built the chicken houses from the ground up – not the warehouses themselves, but the industry. We didn't have chickens before he arrived. Only turkeys, even when it was obvious that turkeys are only good for one thing—'

Geronimo interrupts with a snort. 'Sad, really.'

'What is?' Jonny can't help but ask.

'Americans are coming over here in their droves to settle on any hillside they can find. And still Thanksgiving hasn't caught on. Christmas, now I can kind of understand that. But has anyone in Bethlehem, even now, ever seen a turkey?'

'I guess not,' Jonny answers, mulling over something quite different. 'The allegation I mentioned earlier, though – that Farid was using a tunnel under the border to compromise Israel's position. I must say, I'm confused—'

'I'd back out of this alleyway if I were you, Jonny,' Geronimo interrupts.

'It doesn't fit with the kind of man you just described.'

'No, it doesn't,' Oren replies before the larger man can.

Jonny tries to ignore those hands again, suddenly out and under examination, finger by finger, in an increasingly un-meditative way. He tries a different tack.

'I should tell you that my news editor is expecting to hear from me by lunchtime. And then again at nightfall. If I don't call in, we've got a team close by in Haifa that she'll send straight up the road to looking for me—'

'Thanks for that, son.' Geronimo's smile stops halfway out of his mouth. 'Now I know where to set up the roadblocks if I need to.'

Jonny rubs his grazed knuckles against the concrete, makes them bleed.

'Can I at least go and get on with it now, then? Since the rest of my questions aren't going to get you any answers if I ask them down here?'

'I'd stop that, if I were you.' Geronimo nods at Jonny's hand. 'This is going to move a whole lot more slowly if you've got to do it carrying any injuries.'

Jonny squeezes his bleeding hand with the other, tries to steady his breathing.

'Go with him.' Geronimo waves at Oren. 'I know you won't do it if you're together.'

Do what? More half-formed theories skitter around in Jonny's head as the older man nods. Suddenly Oren is at his side, yanking him on to his feet.

Jonny's heart flutters an uncontrollable staccato. Just because Oren is scared, doesn't make him an ally. He shrugs against the older man's grip as they start the climb up the steps.

What would happen if Jonny just bolted? He would only need to make it as far as the border guards to raise the alarm. He slows on his way up the steep steps, picturing the thicket of brambles choked around the main gates. Could Jonny make it? And what would happen if he did? The pull of Beit Liora, as silent as it is primal, tugs at him just as the sunlight strikes their faces, dazzling him blind immediately.

And then it hits him.

These two men must know he won't make a run for it.

Because any sane person would leg it immediately. Somehow, these two men know Jonny's got enough of a stake of his own up here not to run. They must do. They can't afford for him to go missing, as that might blow their cover. So what else do they know? And why? Jonny rubs his eyes but can't get rid of the glare. The realisation that there are people within his literal grasp who must know something about his past is practically rooting him to the tarmac. That's what these two men are counting on.

And Jonny? He considers the driveway, shimmering beyond the locked gates as seductively as the missing pieces themselves. Gotcha, he wants to say. Except he can't.

The only chance Jonny's got now is to find out who killed Farid and why.

But can he find out more about himself in the process?

Beyond the gates, the tarmac dulls to implacable black as a cloud scuds over the sun.

Chapter Twenty-Seven
Wednesday

5:00 p.m.

It starts to hit Lola in bits. A whirlpool of images and sensations glancing off the sides of her consciousness.

A body, empty of both action and intent, beached in a curious heap at her feet.

Cuts, bruises and blood, so much blood – all over her, all over absolutely everything, puddles not even close to seeping away into the dirt.

A knife – huge, almost cartoonish. Lola had never seen one so big until she came to the kibbutz. And now it's in her hand, dripping with fat, flesh and more blood, viscous red liquid undulating on its surface.

A familiar pair of shorts, laced around her ankles, torn and sodden – violated.

A naked breast – hers? Thrust unnaturally over the stained neckline of her vest.

And pain, a blaze of it, flaming between her legs as old wounds bleed into new.

But this time, there's something else.

Something so unfamiliar, Lola has to feel her way around it, test its limits, try it on for size.

Power.

She stares at the body at her feet – Moti, a founder member of the kibbutz, blood still leaching from his side, wounded at her hand. The thrum of cicadas, clamouring from the banana plants, rises in a chorus of knowing. A bird now, a parakeet – its vulgar-green flash unmistakable between the darker foliage – chirps directly at her, reversing the direction of the whirlpool, bringing past to present in her mind.

For Lola has found herself in this position before.

But she wasn't holding a knife.

There she is, starting work experience at a TV production company, organised for her by a rich school dad. There he is, lavish with attention, promises, little token gifts – a longed-for charm bracelet, a matching pair of earrings. There's his second wife, Saskia, a week off their honeymoon, perky at the reception desk, all crisp white shirt, a neon foil to her impossibly tanned chest. Her eyebrows always seemed permanently raised – plucked into deliberately high arches or because she knew what her husband was suggesting to Lola, behind her back?

Rich School Dad is kissing Lola now, the most gentlemanly of brushes on the lips, behind the closed door of his big Soho office. Now it's the Groucho club, a cold green bottle, a gilded gold label, he's pouring actual champagne down her throat. Is that popping cork a bugle heralding some magical elixir from a far-off land? No, it's just the clank of gates, heavy wrought iron and black, unclicking padlock upon padlock that all open with the same key. One of those over-grown garden squares that pockmark central London, thick with high hedges to screen prying eyes, free only to those who can afford it.

The spring sunshine dims behind Lola in the same way it did then, all too quickly. Just as what she thought was desire curdled to fear. She should have known when she saw the single key that no one else would have it too.

And wasn't it just simpler for Lola to go along with it? And a whole lot simpler to forget about it afterwards? You wanted this too, Lola, Rich School Dad had said, that handsome head cocked rakishly to one side. Those shoes, that skirt, that top. What was it all for, if not this?

Not this.

Not this time.

Not ever again.

Last time, Lola reeled. She heard a noise, a sort of whimpering, only realised where it was coming from when she finally cried out. She wanted to sob, but there wasn't enough space. It felt like someone had tied bands around her chest. Nothing had hurt her there, but it was curiously the only part of her body she could feel – tight with pressure, suffocating with strain. For a moment, her mind was a blank too, more than numb, just wiped vacant and empty. Until it filled with a series of sensations and images that she could never shake, flashing back every time Richard walked past with a leer, even though she never told anyone what had happened, not even Sam.

This time there is no reeling.

Nor collapsing in horror at a dead body at her feet.

No uncontrollable trembling of the bloody knife in her hand.

Lola allows that unfamiliar sensation to crystallise, harden and solidify. To take root and expand the tight space in her chest.

She looks up, finds the parakeet still staring, cocking its head imperiously before flying away.

Lola grips the knife, breathing hard. Moti. A founder member of the kibbutz. He could still be alive. Lola could still help him, if she moves fast enough. She's even got a medical pack at her disposal – Moti's bulging leather case is still sticking out of his pocket. She reflexively reaches out to grab it for herself before she's fully realised what she is doing. The next chapter flashes before her eyes: there she is, crying as she stumbles out of this field and into the next, back across the main road into the soft soil of the orchards. Can she walk? What does it matter, she can crawl … There she is again, tear-streaked, clothes torn and bloodstained, screaming for reinforcements as she limps past the avocado trees. There she is, as Moti comes around.

And then what happens? Did Lola find him, fallen on the blade of his machete? A freak accident of his own making? Is Lola's yet another story of bad luck rather than terrible judgement? What of the pain between her legs, burning hotter and harder with every minute? How does she explain that away? How does he explain it? Why would he even have to? Lola clutches the unfamiliar medical pack as she considers this, knife wavering in her other hand.

For the truth is, her biological stamp is all over Moti. Another flare of pain confirms the worst of it, plays out a different sequence in Lola's mind. There she is, almost as injured as him, stumbling towards salvation, towards medical assistance, towards absolution by a different name. Self-defence, it was all she could do, he was attacking her, she had to find a way to stop him. The parakeet is back, swooping low over her head, circling with her thoughts. She's all over Moti. Her injuries are consistent with the evidence.

But then Lola sees the others. The others at the edge of this story. How can Lola be sure how they will answer the same questions? There's the history she's given herself – both Tom and Farid. There's Andre, smirking as he confirms it. There's Sam, pale green and shaking under oath. There's the police cell, the police doctor, the clipboards and the forms, all in a language she doesn't understand. She looks to the parakeet, for its darting bright flash amid the darker canopy. But only the limits of the sky hover in the gaps overhead, tinged purple and pink as the sun speeds to dusk.

There is no certainty it will go Lola's way. Any of it.

And it should. It must.

Lola looks it in the eye, this thing she knows she has done, and that sensation, now as inescapable as it was unfamiliar, blooms through her body, binds to her bones, takes up permanent residence in her skeleton. A different ending to her story starts to take shape in her mind as she shoves Moti's medical pack deep into her own pocket.

For this time, Lola herself is different too.

She draws a final fingertip across the knife, writes her name in the blood.

Then plunges the blade back into the body's gaping, open wound as far as it will go.

Chapter Twenty-Eight
Thursday

8:00 a.m.

'So, Jonny Murphy. Where do you want to start?'

The question sounds as benign as if it's about redecorating. What difference does it make which blank wall gets it first? Jonny massages his arm, freed of the older man's grip as soon as they left the shadow of the stairwell.

'This is crazy,' he mutters, flipping his sunglasses back down on to his face from the top of his head. Even with the protection of tinted lenses, all he can picture is the open hole on the other side of the hillside looming over them.

'C'mon, Jonny. You've got a job to do. And a cub reporter can't risk calling in with nothing. I'm here to help. There's no one who knows Beit Liora better than me.'

Oren's expression has settled into a mask, the soldier going through the motions. But Jonny is certain there's no void behind it. Why is Oren so sure he won't just bolt for the gate? His hands itch to grab the older man and shake the reason out of him.

'Is this the only way in?' Jonny jerks his head at the driveway.

'For vehicles, yes.'

'So you can get in and out on foot from other places? Where?'

'Not exactly. I wouldn't recommend trying, if that's what you mean.'

Jonny sighs so deeply it hits the inside of his glasses. 'You know, you'll get your answers a whole lot faster if you don't blow hot air at me.'

Oren's mask slips into a frown, if only for a second.

'There are certain spots on the kibbutz where it is possible, yes. But only if you have help. And only if you know how.'

'Now we're talking,' Jonny mutters, wiping droplets of condensation off his glasses with a fingertip. 'OK. How about you show me around. Give me the brief walking tour. I'll ask you first if I want to talk to someone.'

'Be my guest,' Oren replies without smiling, motioning Jonny to follow as he starts to walk. Crossing the turning circle, he takes the path leading down towards the kibbutz buildings.

Jonny falls in step beside him, his heart fluttering with the crunch of gravel underfoot. These may not be the terms he expected, but he's finally going to get inside Beit Liora. He's going to get a proper look around. Whatever complexion it takes in reality can't damage the overall picture. He's never had one to start with. He feels his breath coming in little gasps as the blank wall starts to colour at the edges.

'How old is the kibbutz?'

'Soon it will be fifty years. It is one of the oldest in the country.'

'You mean since the creation of the State of Israel.'

Oren pauses. Jonny watches his eyes narrow.

'That is correct. It was established after 1948. It is not one of the original ones.'

'Original ones?'

'The very first. They were built around the Kinneret. Not up here on the border.'

Jonny grunts as if it is genuinely surprising. No one pitching up on a wing and a prayer in the so-called land of milk and honey was going to set up a communal farm right on some unforgiving clifftop with a hostile enemy yards away. Not when there were the shores of the freshwater Lake Kinneret, safely inland and at the apex of the fertile Jordan Valley.

His hand drifts up to his sore neck. Even if he hadn't been

trapped underground for the last hour by a different hostile enemy, the strategic concerns that must have underpinned the creation of Beit Liora suddenly couldn't be more obvious. Still, Jonny ploughs on. These questions aren't just about answering someone else's.

'How did it, you know, come into being? Beit Liora itself?'

'The same way they all have. A big enough group of people who all believed in the same thing planted the flag and took ownership. When enough people stake their lives on the success of a project – growing enough not to starve, building enough to fight exposure, farming enough for backup – it's really not that complicated. Build it and they will come.'

Oren pauses again as a small dog skitters across their path. Jonny drops to his knees without thinking, reaching for her. He is surprised to find Oren squatting too, hand out, muttering sweet nothings in Arabic.

'Is this your kibbutz dog?' Jonny smiles as he asks, the idea of a family dog instantly enveloping. It was when the Hammersons brought home a rescue dog that those words Jonny read off the pages sticking out of the buff file started to make better sense. That rescue dog was as loving as it was old and tired. Much like the Hammersons themselves. But this hound is agitated rather than soothed by Jonny's caresses, wildly licking her lips and panting.

'She's a stray,' Oren mumbles between entreaties. 'Was a stray, at least. Until Farid took care of her. She has her uses.'

Jonny's mind barrels backward as he reflexively tries to calm the dog, all his usual childhood tricks failing. She must have some bloodhound in her, he thinks. Only the right scent will calm her down. Unease rapidly dilutes the fledgling warmth in Jonny's chest. Pure-bred bloodhounds can scent a trail for well over a week – a trace trail at that. It's why Jonny fell so hard for his own – zero chance of abandonment. He even named her Hero. But no tracking dog, mongrel or not, plans for what happens when a trail is gone forever. Jonny looks past the dog, down the path, remembering the body of the only human she trusted must still be sprawled in the dirt somewhere.

'Didn't that raise a few eyebrows? It's not exactly common to have domestic dogs around here, is it?'

But Oren just stands and starts to walk again. Jonny reluctantly leaves the hound alone, even though it couldn't be more obvious that she is distressed. He jogs to catch up, thinking about how unwelcome dogs usually are in the Middle East, unless handled by soldiers in combat. Search-and-rescue dogs. Cadaver dogs. Trained to smell death.

'These are our administrative buildings.' Oren waves at the low buildings starting to dot either side of the path. 'Telephones for local and international calls, the fax machine, our medical centre. Paperwork. That kind of thing.'

'Can I use one of those phones before we move on?' Jonny asks, even though he knows what the answer will be. He thinks of Allen, immediately feels her at his back.

'Not unless the person on the other end can tell us who killed Farid.'

Jonny sighs as Oren steps up the pace, eyeing the radio clipped to the back of his belt. Just because it's silent doesn't mean it isn't listening.

'Medical centre, you said?' A whiff of antiseptic makes Jonny's grazed knuckles sting all over again.

'Yes. Everyone in this country has medical training—'

'In trauma injuries, huh.'

'Right again, Jonny. What's your point?'

'You seem to think Farid was killed by some kind of lethal injection. Knowing what kind of kit you've got in there, and whether any is missing, would be a good place to start.'

'Smart.' Oren stops and turns. 'But we don't have time for that now.'

'You think there's somewhere more important to start than the murder weapon?'

'What difference does it make if a syringe is missing? It won't tell us who stole it.'

Jonny kicks at the gravel. 'And I suppose you're about to tell me everyone has a trauma kit of their own out here.'

'Correct again.' Oren starts to walk again, slower this time. 'Those who need to carry them at all times. Noradrenaline for anaphylaxis. Insulin for diabetes. Immaculate identity tags – we even colour code the cases so there can be no mistakes. No one can afford to be without the basics here. We are always on the defensive.'

'Sure you are,' Jonny mumbles. 'Except now. You need someone else to do your defensive work for you.'

'Don't pretend it isn't yours too.' Oren's voice hardens. 'We all need to find out what happened to Farid, including you. It's the only way you get out of here.'

'Don't I know it.' Jonny's mind races, suddenly full of the many different ways to kill people with a single needle.

Oren slows as they pass a larger, two-storey building with a big staircase leading up to a double set of plate-glass doors.

'This is the dining room. Everyone will come in for breakfast in fifteen minutes.'

It must be gone eight, Jonny thinks, forcing himself to concentrate on the mechanics, rather than get carried away with fanciful imaginings of his parents meeting over eggs. Maybe that's how it happened, he wonders. Did Patrick Murphy, the mysterious and exciting volunteer from the Emerald Isle, simply pass the farmgirl a fork? He gulps at the thought of the volunteers, then again at the inexorable movement of a clock ticking closer to a conclusion he'd rather not imagine.

'Let's stop here then. If everyone I want to talk to is about to arrive...'

'And you think the stories you'll get in front of everyone else are the ones to believe?'

Oren walks on. Jonny eyes the shapes moving behind the plate-glass doors, still closed at the top of the stairs, before following. All meals together, every day, seven days a week, fifty-two weeks a year. Do they have allotted seats? Did his mother have a favourite table, a chair? What about on special occasions, or birthdays? Would there be tablecloths, or more decorative china? He has to jog to keep up with Oren, suddenly moving more quickly down the path. They're cutting across a small green field now, plastic children's play equipment laid out at awkward angles.

'Hang on.' He pants as he catches the older man up. 'I want to talk to the volunteers first. Can't we intercept them at breakfast? I've changed my mind about looking around. It's pretty obvious the person who killed Farid was already here...'

He trails off as Oren leads them into the maze of individual cabins starting at the far end of the field.

'These are the private residences,' Oren says, waving a hand in the air.

'Does every family have one of their own?' Jonny can't help but ask, even though it's irrelevant to the task in hand. He's dreamt of life on a kibbutz. Of community at every turn. An instant family around every corner.

'Yes. They are allocated according to size – however many children there are, and so on. Of course, the children all sleep together in the children's houses, but it is important they have a spot with their parents too, even though they almost never use it.'

'How do you mean?' Jonny lifts his shirt away from his skin to let in the sea breeze. The wind has a sudden and welcome edge to it now they are in an open space.

'It's the best fun in the world,' Oren says, speeding up past the cabins either side. 'Every night is a sleepover. Why stay with your parents when you can stay up with your friends?'

'Wait a second...' Jonny jogs. 'Please.'

Oren turns just as he catches up, the path dead-ending on to a thin but tarmacked track cutting the kibbutz off from the very top of the cliff.

'Wait,' he repeats, reaching for the older man's shoulder. 'Can we stop here for minute?'

'There's nothing here of any use to you,' Oren says without looking at him.

'How do you know?' Jonny wills the older man to catch his eye. He's asking two questions right now. Which will Oren answer? The sun is hard on one side of his face now, burning like a slap.

'There's only one question you need to be concerning yourself with right now, and I highly doubt you'll find the answer anywhere inside these cabins. You already have your answers where I am concerned. Where we are concerned.'

'We? Do you mean...?'

Jonny's teeth clang in his jaw as Oren spins round and advances on him, the shade of his shadow never more unwelcome.

'Careful, Jonny. Careful. You haven't met the volunteers yet, remember. You haven't met anyone except Rami, and me.'

Jonny nods extra vigorously at the mention of Rami. Someone else who should definitely have some answers; and if not ... well that's a clue too. Still he can't shake the feeling, growing in certainty with every nod, that Oren knows far more about Jonny himself than he's letting on. He's just waiting for the right moment to give it away.

Jonny sizes up the older man for at least the eightieth time. He'd seen a flicker of fear, back in the shelter, he's sure of it. A flicker of more than just discomfort at what was going on. He doesn't need to understand it to exploit it.

'Is Rami the only night watchman on the kibbutz?'

Oren starts walking, seemingly satisfied with the question for now. 'Officially, yes. We have other means, of course. But he is the kibbutznik who mans the main guardhouse.'

Jonny commits the geography of their location to memory – the banana plants lining one edge of the road, sloping steeply downwards towards the precipice edge of the cliff; the cabins giving way to more capacious low-rise buildings; the warehouses up ahead of them as the road slopes more and more steeply towards the hillside at the far end.

'Seems like a harsh job for someone to have to do full-time. Don't you rotate it between you, or anything like that?'

'We used to, before Rami returned from military service.'

'So what changed?'

'Just that. He was happy with the job. And he is very good at it.'

The banana plants on the cliff side of the road give way to a series of wire fences as the drop down to the sea becomes more and more pronounced.

'Is that usual? For kibbutz kids to come straight back after military service and just set up shop where they grew up?'

Oren pauses, turning to face the sea. 'Does this look usual to you?'

Jonny follows his gaze, noting the pearlescent gleam of the water, the endless blue of the sky, the sudden, intractable bulk of the hillside rearing up in front of them. The intransigence of the landscape should feel reassuring, but all he can think about is what's running underneath.

'I guess not.'

'Well, then.'

Jonny's calves sting with the gradient of the slope as they start to walk again.

'Everyone's committed, I get that. It's blood-and-sand stuff. Fine. Except I'm getting the guided tour because someone has shown up dead in a way none of you were expecting. So Rami can't be all that good at his job, can he?'

Oren slows as they reach the cluster of warehouse buildings. 'You want to talk to Rami?'

'Of course I do,' Jonny replies, an unmistakable farmyard smell suddenly pungent on the air. 'As well as the other volunteers. They can't all have the same story as the one I've already met.'

Oren leads them off the road back on to gravel, and into the small courtyard around which the warehouses are arranged. Jonny can hear the birds squawking as they stop in the middle of the courtyard.

'That is chicken house number one.' Oren gestures at the warehouse furthest away from them. 'Where we found Farid.'

Jonny stiffens, even though the scene before him looks, on the face of it, completely unremarkable. Four warehouses arranged in a semi-circle around the courtyard. Beyond their far walls, a sheer drop, protected by a double wire fence. The perimeter road itself curves round to the right, running parallel to the line of the hillside itself. They're right on the edge of the border, but only students of both history and geography would know that. And there's a bit of hazard tape hanging off the side of the far warehouse, flapping feebly in the wind.

'Can we go inside?'

'We can, but there's nothing to see.'

'Isn't it still a crime scene?'

Finally the older man turns to face him. 'I thought you wanted to go inside?'

'Of course I do,' Jonny replies. 'I'm just surprised I can. Since in any other country – even any other place in this country – it would still be a crime scene. If someone had been found murdered in there a day earlier.'

Oren scuffs at the gravel underfoot, seemingly at a loss for words for a moment.

'The chickens have made that part difficult,' he says eventually.

'I bet.' Jonny peers into the darkened mouths of the other

warehouses. 'These ones look pretty empty, though. Why can't you just stick them all somewhere else? Are you telling me your chickens are as fussy as the rest of you about their real estate?'

Oren lets out a wry laugh. Jonny jumps as a heavy hand claps him on the back.

'Can we walk around the back, at least?'

'That we can,' Oren replies, removing his hand. 'Watch your step, though. We're on the very edge of the cliff.'

Don't I know it, Jonny thinks to himself, as he picks his way around the edge of the condemned chicken house, still full of birds chattering away to each other. Oren's decided to walk behind him now, as if he needed the threat to be any clearer. Jonny runs a hand along the slatted wooden wall, ignoring the splinters threatening his palm, the length of one warehouse, then another, pulling to a stop somewhere around the back of the third as what is most definitely remarkable about this otherwise unremarkable tableau finally hits him.

'Wait a second. Where the hell is everyone?' He jumps as he turns to find Oren so close behind him they're almost touching.

'They're all heading to breakfast. Everyone stops for the full hour. Remember, we've all usually been at work since dawn.'

Oren's radio squawks, a burst of something unintelligible. Jonny stares out to sea, rubbing his hand against the wood. Suddenly, all he can hear is the other man's breathing. On the other side of the wall, even the birds seem to be holding theirs.

'Who was that?' Jonny jerks his head at Oren's radio. 'Five minutes? What does that mean?'

He shrinks against the wall as Oren silently shoulders past, noting nothing but open air beyond the wire fence to his other side. The older man stops and turns a couple of paces ahead, holding out a meaty hand.

'You're not going to fall, OK? I promise you. Come on.'

Jonny sags against the wooden wall, vertigo licking at his legs.

'You have to trust me.' Oren steps back towards him, grabbing his free hand.

'Oh, sure, because you've made that part so easy,' Jonny mumbles, willing that his skeleton obey him, legs buckling with every glance at the open air, even if criss-crossed by chicken wire. 'It's not like you've already detained me against my will, underground, and only let me go to ask questions you can't ask yourself.'

Oren's large, warm hand closes around his.

Jonny's mind spins with his legs. 'Where are you taking me?'

'Somewhere you can ask all those questions in private.'

Jonny sways as he eyes the wire fence ahead, registers the ragged opening his body had sensed long before his mind caught up. Beyond, even the sky itself feels shallow, backlit with the white heat of a relentlessly rising sun.

Those wondrous grottoes, he thinks, an altogether different set of images supplanting the pearlescent marble caves he'd conjured in his mind. Rami's miracle of the earth. Only accessible down a perilous cliffside path.

It really exists.

Except it's not much of a path at all.

It's the entrance to a tunnel.

Chapter Twenty-Nine
Wednesday

5:30 p.m.

Lola is moving with even more purpose now. It seems impossible she's physically able to, but she is, popping her breast back into her bra, pulling her shorts and pants back on. She reaches high into the canopy, running her fingers through the closest leaves, selecting just the right ones for her particular purpose – not too mature that they will splinter and crack under pressure, not too immature that they won't bend in the right direction. A sharp few crackles later and Lola feels armed, able to hobble over to the body.

The body, she repeats to herself silently. Lola will not use its name from here on in. It doesn't deserve a name. It's no more than an inanimate object. One she's got to move out of her way.

She drops to her knees – it's easier to crawl, the undergrowth suddenly as forgiving as a comfort blanket, soft with blood slowly percolating away. Unrolling one giant banana leaf across the body to shield it from any more of her biological footprint, Lola drapes herself over it to reach the parts that need to be cleaned.

First, the handle – sticking out of the fatal wound like it's the open end of fish head. Funny, Lola muses, grasping the wood with the ribbed side of her second leaf, scrubbing into every groove and splinter. You can always find a catch with a good enough hook. You don't even have to cast your net particularly wide. She scrubs harder, digging fingernails into the smooth side of the leaf, deepening her purchase on the handle below.

Is that what Moti thought? That he was out fishing? Hunting? Prowling around until he spotted something worth snagging? Or just something? Anything? Is that what all predators think, when they walk around, clocking up their hours, rounding out their time? Do they all just assume everything and everyone they see is on offer just because they want them to be? Perhaps it's not that they act like they have a right to whatever they want, but like whatever they want owes them pleasure.

Beneath the leaf, the handle twists as she rubs it to contaminate every last fibre of potential evidence. She knows it's squelching, rotating through fat, through innards, but all she can hear are the cicadas, a keening buzz of judgement. She doesn't need to tell herself they're on her side. For it doesn't matter to her anymore. The only person Lola needs on her side now is herself.

Sitting up, she eyes the rest of the body under the banana leaf. Its front side is uppermost, and Lola knows there's inescapable evidence all over it – blood, sweat, muscle fibres, tears – no, not tears. No more tears. There's no room for any more pain, frustration and betrayal in these fields. With that she drapes herself back on top, using her weight as a full-length scour, rolling and pushing and shoving in order that the thick ribs on the underside of the leaf contaminate the evidence as much as possible. The body is still soft enough to move like dough, a giant flabby roll bending to her every move. Funny again, Lola thinks, digging her knees into the lifeless crotch underneath. It's not muscle memory after all, is it? Muscles will do whatever you want them to, in the end. Wriggling as far over the body as the edge of the leaf will allow, Lola heaves it back on to itself in one fluid motion, embedding the handle of the knife into the soft earth below.

'He fell on it,' Lola mutters, sitting back on her knees to assess her scene. And why wouldn't he? That's what it looks like. Moti fell on the machete. He literally fell on his own sword – look, the wound is right above where it hung. He was reaching – see, here are the leaves he tore down as he stumbled. And he fell, right into the blade in his other hand. No, it's no longer wrapped around it because he had enough in him to struggle and it moved, but then blood loss took hold and he lost consciousness.

What was Moti doing alone in the banana fields at this time of day? Who cares? Isn't he in charge of the entire plantation? Accountable for both profit and loss? What about any trace evidence of Lola … Well, she works here, too. Surely there's evidence of Fouad, of Issam, of all of them down here if anyone bothers to look hard enough. Lola rubs her second leaf between her hands, staining her fingers green, cocks her head and casts a more sceptical eye on the angles of various body parts, the near-impossibility of what she is suggesting.

For Rich School Dad had said similarly ridiculous things too, hadn't he? Lola's bruises – well, they were easily explained away. She had ridden her bicycle to the Tube station that day; certain saddles can do that to you. Her cuts and scratches – don't plenty of girls do that to themselves, just to make sure they get noticed if they want to be? It's hardly self-harm when it brings about more care, is it? The rash all over Lola's neck, her face – some plant she must have been allergic to, simple. After all, they were in a private garden, one she'd happily followed him into, by the way. And girls bleed every month, don't they? Especially mature ones like her.

Lola squeezes her thighs together, rips at the leaf in her hands. Never mind the internal injuries. The tear in her most private of places. The infections that set in after she couldn't get it treated immediately. She could hardly rush to a doctor. What if they were male too? Asked the wrong questions? Worse, didn't ask any at all? And they're not exactly injuries if they don't need hospital treatment, are they, Lola? They're just evidence of a good time – a great time. One that she willingly participated in – enjoyed, even. One that she invited, just by being herself.

Lola rocks back and forth on her heels, noting the green patches amid the bloodstains and scratches all over her hands and arms, as livid now as they were then. A ragged patchwork of rust-red brown and green – she snorts as she realises it looks like deliberate camouflage. But for what or whom? Lola already knows it doesn't matter if the story doesn't make sense. It only matters if there's anyone listening who cares enough to question it.

The pain flares again as she thinks about Farid. Another body within twenty-four hours will make plenty of people care. Another unexplained death at an already tense time in a place never far from all-out war. And in a community founded on the strength of its collective – yep, there'll definitely be people listening who care enough.

And then Lola sees it. The scene's last remaining prop. It's been there all the time, swaying just beyond the corner of her eye.

The purple pendulum banana flower overhead, with its tell-tale speckles of blight.

Everyone laughed when Lola called it that – an English word for an English disease, taught only in English schools, in her beloved geography lessons. Lola doesn't even know what it's called out here, only that its caused by aphids.

But whatever it's called, it's only cure is the same the world over.

Total destruction.

Lola finds herself almost salivating as she squints at the speckled flower, notes the mottled stripes on the leaves on the rest of the afflicted plant, the already misshapen beginnings of the fruit forming on the stem above the flower itself.

For this is the host plant, as surely as its green is striped with blue and black.

Moti will have slipped as he tried to cut it down.

The explanation presents itself with the same clarity as it did the first time she saw the blight for herself. There is no one on the kibbutz that doesn't recognise, and more importantly fear, a mortal threat to a crop. And know what must be done about it immediately. A community founded on the strength of its collective won't question anything about that.

Lola leans back on the plant's trunk, eyeing the striped canopy above. She lets the sun into her eyes until she can see spots, and still, they are there. Stripes, speckles, bulges, deformities.

Some protection afforded to her at last. Her plants have not let her down. Plants never could, she thinks. They are only born to grow.

Lola takes one last look at her tableau before twisting round on her heels and crawling away, down the lane in the direction of the sea.

Chapter Thirty
Thursday

8:30 a.m.

Whatever breath Jonny managed to gasp in the seconds before Oren squeezed through the gap in the wire fence catches in his throat as the older man disappears from view almost immediately. Jonny commands himself to run, to bolt away as quickly as humanly possible, but all that happens is he stumbles, knees buckling further as a hand wraps around his ankle – Oren's, anchoring him firmly to the tiny lip of ground left before the fence gives way.

Jonny wills himself not to topple forward as he looks down and sees the older man standing almost directly below him, banana plants level with his head.

'It looks worse than it is,' Oren remarks, as if following him through the gap is as simple as climbing down a ladder. 'There are notches in the rock directly below you, OK? But I have to let go of your ankle to make room for you. Climb down two notches, and you'll be on the same level as me.'

Jonny tries to squint at the ground below Oren's feet without leaning any further forward. The path, or whatever Oren is standing on, seems to be directly cut out of the cliff face, a narrow ledge's worth, as smooth as it is sharp.

'I'm not going to let go until you tell me you are ready,' Oren continues. 'I know you can do it, or else I'd never have climbed down. If you fall on top of me, we're both toast.'

Jonny concentrates on the fact something sturdy is most

definitely wrapped around his ankle, Oren's grip reassuring until he realises it also means he can't back away, the sanctity of the slatted wooden back wall of the warehouse only a few feet behind him.

'The longer you stand there the more disorientated you are going to be.'

'Who says I'm disorientated,' Jonny mumbles, wobbling at the limitless glare ahead.

'Come on, Jonny.' Oren's grip tightens on his ankle. 'Time is not on our side—'

'Whose side is that?' Jonny stumbles, even with his ankle tethered, showering dirt over the edge of the cliff. 'No one here seems to be on mine.'

'The sooner you find out who did this, the quicker we can shore up our position.'

'And you think taking me into the tunnel itself is going to help matters? Just, you know, casually walking me over to the other side?'

Instantly Jonny is gulping all over again at the thought of exactly why it will. Nothing like tuning a threat to its maximum to focus the mind. Somehow Jonny feels worse than if there was a loaded gun pointed at his temple. Oren gives his leg a little shake by way of an answer, sending Jonny down on to his haunches.

'See?' There is an unmistakable twinkle in Oren's eyes as the older man looks up at him. 'I told you. I won't let you go until you are ready. We can only do this together.'

Jonny forces down a couple of deep breaths, the mental image of a loaded gun morphing into his limp body arcing gracefully into the endless sky, notepad full of questions and answers spilling uselessly from his cargo pants, brains mulching up against his shattered skeleton a couple of seconds later, somewhere on the rocks far below ... *The remains of Jonny Murphy, a junior reporter at the* International Tribune, *have been found off the coast below*

Kibbutz Beit Liora, a day after he left Jerusalem to follow up on recent rocket attacks in northern Israel. Would he even get a full write-up, much less a headline? Not a chance.

And of course this is the thought that finally compels his body to follow instructions, not the image of the sea toying with various parts of his body until they either disappeared or someone cared enough to claim them for their own.

'Two notches, you said?'

'That's right. You can't miss them. If you know they are there.'

Two notches, Jonny repeats to himself, turning around as Oren loosens the grip on his ankle. Grabbing a tree root in one hand and some chicken wire in the other, he stretches out a leg, Oren's hand moving from his ankle to his heel, planting his foot firmly on a ledge of rock below the gap before letting go.

Closing his eyes, Jonny lets the length of the root slide through his fingers as he climbs down, one notch, then two. He finds a surprisingly wide and firm section of ground under his feet at the end.

Jonny turns on the spot. Oren is smiling as he lounges against the cliff.

'What did I tell you?'

Jonny stares at the section of cliff he has just scaled. The notches are actual footholds, carved very deliberately into the rock. Wide and deep, big enough for two pairs of feet at a time. The path itself gives way to enough earth to house a full row of banana plants, seeded to grow deliberately along the outer edge, as tall as a full-grown man. Anyone looking from the cliff wouldn't have a clue they were there.

Vertigo licks at Jonny's legs again as he realises the only thing able to actually do that would be a bird. Or a very low flying plane.

'They look a whole lot stronger than they are.' Oren jerks his head at the banana plants. 'Best to lean against the cliff as you follow me.'

Jonny swallows, realising Oren is doing anything but lounging even though his grin is growing wider by the second.

'Has … has this path always been here? And where … where does it end?' He doesn't even try to hide the tremor in his voice. What's the point? As far as Jonny can tell, the only way out is down. Scaling the cliff face in the opposite direction would require more than just a leg-up. At least Oren wasn't lying when he said they could only do it together. The thought nags at him, an incomplete sentence, the missing piece hovering just beyond his reach.

'There's only a short stretch like this. Then it turns inside. You'll find it much easier, don't worry. It's no more than two minutes.'

But Jonny doesn't move, the smooth rock cool and reassuring against his back, the sun still a few hours away from cresting the top of the cliff.

'Fear won't get you anywhere, Jonny,' Oren shouts over a sudden swell and crash from the sea below. 'At best, it'll get you injured. At worst you'll die never knowing the answers to any of your questions, and what they'd have meant to you.'

'Why don't you just fucking tell me, then?' Jonny shouts back. 'Save us both the trouble of killing ourselves out here? If we can only do this together then what made you trust me enough to try? Don't pretend you didn't have any choice. A guy like you always has a choice.'

Another crash drowns out Oren's reply, the wind whipping the sea into a sudden frenzy. Jonny feels like they're just skimming the surface of this territory, interlopers passing time until the water takes it back. He licks salt off his lips.

'And now I don't have a fucking choice. I'm suddenly stuck on the side of a cliff with nothing but banana plants to break my fall because of a dead guy in a chicken house that means absolutely nothing to me other than the fact he died here, in this fucking place that I have to find a way to understand, because if I don't, I'll never understand anything about my life or where I came from or why certain things happened the way they did…'

Oren's fingers are wrapped around his wrist now, both their arms no longer plastered against the cliff, leaving them dangerously unsupported.

'This ends only one way if you don't calm down,' the older man shouts over the cry of the sea. 'You want to try climbing back up that cliff? Because that's the only way we'll have if we don't move with the tide.'

Jonny totters in position as Oren drops his wrist, finally able to laminate himself back against the cliff face.

'I don't believe you,' he hisses. 'We're not going inside this fucking mountain to drown. Whatever tide we're dealing with, it's got to come in and out long enough for us to do our business, else we wouldn't be bothering at all. I don't need to be detained underground by some guy calling himself Geronimo to figure that out for myself.'

'You're right, of course, Jonny Murphy from the *International Tribune*. And you're right that a guy like me always has a choice. I chose you, believe it or not, as ridiculous as that may sound out here. And unless you want me to grab you again, you need to follow me and you need to do it now.'

And just as the waves calm, Jonny hears it, the unmistakable crack in the older man's voice. He dare not turn his head lest vertigo overwhelms him, but it's there, he's as sure of it as he is of the cracks his fingers are desperately scrabbling against in the rock face supporting them both.

Who is this man to him? And how did he figure it out in the space of an hour in an air-raid shelter with some guy called Geronimo?

Slowly but surely, Jonny is able to inch his way along the path, eyes level with the tops of the banana trees as he moves. From time to time, he feels the older man's fingertips wait to brush his before taking another step. The sea quiets, murmuring its encouragement.

Chapter Thirty-One
Wednesday

6:00 p.m.

The pain is giving way to a curious numbness now Lola is crawling along the ground. Just one more knee in front of the other will get her closer to the opening that cuts straight down to the water, to the strip of sand only available at certain times of the day and night. The tides don't worry Lola, she knows that particular strip of sand's secrets – the pockets in the rock that are always exposed, however enthusiastically the waves greet unexpected visitors.

She speeds up round the final corner, forgetting herself at the sight of the sea, a patch of violet at the far end of the lane. By now the plants are uncultivated and wild, it feels like an embrace of the most tangled and messy kind, enough to propel Lola upright between the trees, growing so close together that they can support her if she needs it. And now she's there, on the sand, the tide on her side too, the tiny secret cove at the foot of the cliff opening to curl around her like a shell, hard against her back.

Lola braces herself for her last steps.

For those will take her directly into saltwater, the only weapon she's got left in her arsenal that can wipe any last trace evidence away.

Because any infection could be more than just painful. It could be incriminating.

Still Lola cries out as she immerses herself, the saltwater working as medicinally as nature intended.

By the time she is done, it is dark. So dark that she doesn't notice the shadow morphing and shifting on the sand in front of her until it becomes the shape of a person.

The shape of a man.

Instantly Lola is alert. Every fibre of her body is thrumming, wired to survival. For of course it wasn't her and Farid's own little secret, was it? Of course it wasn't a magical, enchanted cove, hidden to all except lovers.

The man is directly in front of her now, barefoot, wearing just a vest and shorts. She eyeballs him just as he eyeballs her – mouth open, whites flashing as he blinks and blinks and blinks. Is it just sand or disbelief? The pearlescent snakeskin of the cliff face looks on impassively, the little grottoes Lola knows it hides invisible in the dark.

And here it is, the question she always knew would come from anyone who ever found anyone else down here.

But it's in English, not Hebrew.

This man must already know who she is.

A marble of panic rolls in Lola's chest. Does this man also know what she has done? She considers her banana plants, a tangled black mass in the gloom next to the exposed cliff.

The man asks again. 'How did you know about this place?'

Lola thinks fast. 'I could ask you the same thing. Especially since you already seem to know enough about me to speak English.'

The man takes a step back. Lola can see enough to note unmistakable surprise on his face. What was he expecting her to say? She wobbles into standing, brushes down her shorts, wonders if she'll have to explain the bloodstains away.

'How did you get down here?' he asks. 'You're one of the volunteers, right?'

Lola frowns, salt falling whisper-light from her face. 'So you're from the kibbutz too?'

But the man doesn't reply. Lola checks over her shoulder – only the sea, still far enough out that she has time, turning from black to pearl with the moonrise. And when she turns, she finds the man doing exactly the same thing, just in the opposite direction.

'You've still got time, don't worry,' he says. 'Before the tide comes in, I mean.'

Relief, but only for a second. The moon is throwing a new light on the man's face, crystallising a few of his features. Where has she seen him before? What does he do on the kibbutz? And how does he know who she is? Lola winces as she shuffles on the spot.

'Are you alright?' the man asks.

Lola waves the question away. 'I just wasn't expecting to find anyone else down here.'

'Neither was I. I've never seen anyone down here before. Not for years, anyway.'

He takes a few steps backward, away from the incoming shoreline. Lola can hear the water rippling behind her, urging that she follow.

'Are you sure you're alright?'

'It's just the sand.' Lola feigns a stumble, legs stinging with every movement. The saltwater has run deep. 'There's not a lot of it around where I grew up.'

'And where's that?'

'London. Well, just outside, but everyone says London. Everywhere close by is faceless and nameless otherwise.'

The stranger pauses. 'And that's why you've come out here?'

Lola opens her mouth, closes it again, considers the hundreds of different things she could say in response. But none of them should make sense to anyone else, much less a total stranger on a secret, invisible beach. Except this particular stranger has somehow divined exactly why she's out here from little more than ghosts and shadows. She peers at him.

'Don't beat yourself up about it,' he continues after a brittle little laugh. 'It's not like you're the only one. The volunteers are the same every year. They come out here to try living on the edge for a bit. Most of them fall off. When this is all you've known, it's as interesting in reverse. That faceless, nameless place you come from is a whole lot more exciting when all you've known is the sharp edge. And yes...' The man pauses to kick at the sand. 'I'm from here. I'm a child of Beit Liora – hah! Not that it's amounted to much.'

Lola checks over her shoulder again. There's no way of reversing the tide.

'Don't worry about that,' he says as she turns back. 'There's still time.'

But the sand is hard below her sandals, a warning from the water. She's edging away from him now, an incoming wave knocking her further off balance. And even if it really is only stretching out to break her fall, the unwelcome touch of yet another hand just prompts Lola to collapse, trembling legs finally refusing to comply. The stranger mutters in Hebrew. She can't understand a word. All she can do is let him drag her the few remaining steps of sand back to the cliff face.

Lola struggles, trying to brace herself against the cool rock, vision swimming in the dark. There's only one way out, and it's dwindling with every second.

'Look, you'd better go,' the man says. 'Take it slow, if you're dehydrated. But you'd better go now. You want to be up the slope before the tide catches you. You know that, right? You've been down here before?'

'I'm ... I'm not usually here this late.' She curses herself for stammering. 'The dark is so intense out here. There's no city lights close by, like at home.'

'On a night like tonight, all you need is the moon.'

Lola is suddenly rigid. Water licks at her sandals, cold and threatening. For she's heard that before too, of course she has. Moonlight – so spellbinding that people will do anything in its thrall. So enchanting it can make even the most misguided of ideas feel like fairy-tale endings.

Except the last time Lola was out with the moonbeams, someone died. The cold, calculating eye of the moon saw everything and did nothing. She pulls herself straight.

'Don't you need to leave soon too? We're safer together.'

The stranger's outline stiffens. 'Didn't you say you work in the bananas? You'll be fine if you already know the terrain.'

The inanimate object inside Lola's head reanimates with a little twitch. She's not going to give this stranger the opportunity to follow her unnoticed.

'I can wait for you, if you don't mind?'

'Well, I do mind.' Lola senses rather than sees him step away from her, the lightest brush of air on her bare skin. She lets a little quaver into her voice now. 'You have to leave now too, though, don't you? The tide is on the march—'

'No.'

A cloud scuds over the moon, veiling its light. Lola hesitates.

'I don't understand. We both have to leave, and we both have to leave now—'

'No, we don't.'

But the water is insisting differently, little pools of it collecting in Lola's sandals. And then a hand, so cool and dry it could belong to a ghost, is closing around hers.

'It's this way if you want to come with me. Go back through the bananas if you want, I don't care. But if you want to stay together, then don't let go. You won't find your way without me.'

'There's another way out?' Lola whispers, heart thudding.

'Sort of, yes. Are you coming?'

Lola flails. Blinded by impenetrable dark, she has only nature left to guide her. Isn't she being tugged in the wrong direction?

But her banana plants stay quiet as the stranger's grip tightens, black water lapping at her heels.

Chapter Thirty-Two
Thursday

9:00 a.m.

Every inch forward brings with it a new obstacle. Some unexpected ridge in the ledge underfoot, some extra-sharp-edged crack in the cliff face. Jonny's surrounded by air, air and more air, but he can't properly inhale any of it, because to breathe for more than a nanosecond might risk unbalancing them both. There is no choice other than to move in lockstep, approaching every obstacle exactly as Oren does. They have to follow a single compass. There's no space for even the slightest recalibration. The only thought propelling him forward is the fact that Oren is deliberately taking the same risks as Jonny. And if Jonny slips over the edge before he finds out why – he catches himself before he shudders, for that will just increase the risk of it happening.

The path edges steeply downward, still hidden by the line of banana plants. The cliff itself bulges in an outward curve, so there must be coves at the foot to its either side – no, don't look down, Jonny! He focuses instead on the thickets of plants tracking their journey. Some leaves are torn and jagged in places. Why? Has some other idiot been tricked far enough down this stupid path by their robust appearance only to discover that against gravity they are worth nothing more than tissue paper? The cliff face starts to curve even more sharply, Jonny has to bend himself backward now, chest puffing out with the strain. Ha! Is this another trick of the land? Reminding them all that in any contest, the elements will always triumph in the end?

'We are almost there,' Oren shouts over the sea churning against the rocks below.

They're at the apex of the curve now, they must be, Jonny thinks, even with the plants partially shading them, the exposure is almost unbearable. He can't bend any further backward without wobbling, and suddenly there is nothing to grip on to, not even a hairline crack, the cliff face pounded smooth as marble by a gazillion years of storms – out of nowhere Jonny's sunglasses topple from their sweaty confines on the top of his head right on to the bridge of his nose. He shouts frantically to Oren, suddenly as dizzy as he was at the top of the cliff, except now one false move could send him into the swan dive his body is already preparing for, arms outstretched backward around the swell of the rock, face with nowhere to turn other than out into the endless sky enveloping them on three sides.

'Close your eyes!' Oren shouts, fingertips brushing his. 'You don't need to see. Just concentrate on what you can feel. This is my hand, against yours. You can feel me right here beside you. You don't need to look at me to know that I'm here. There is solid rock under your feet, against your back...'

And as rapidly as the panic rises, it falls, the path just beyond the apex of the curve widening into a platform, almost a cove within the rock, cast instantly in shadow by the overhang above, the sun still mercifully in the east behind them. Oren tugs Jonny away from the shallow edge.

As Jonny opens his eyes, he collapses, instantly registering that there is suddenly enough space to back away from the false promises of the banana plants and sit, safely, encircled in a pocket of rock. A warm hand comes to rest on his shoulder.

'Good job.' Oren's hand moves to Jonny's hair, by now completely plastered to his head with sweat – no wonder his glasses hadn't stood a chance. Glasses ... Jonny removes them, folding them into his shirt pocket before rubbing his eyes as their new location comes into focus. His vision can barely adjust to the enormity of the cave he's now looking at. Much less register the depth of the black holes narrowing at the back.

'No, don't look.' Jonny only realises he was leaning forward to peer outside again as Oren pins him back against the wall. 'You need to get your sea legs back.'

'Sea legs...' Jonny mumbles to himself, letting his head loll. That's one way of putting it. He swears repeatedly under his breath.

'Drink, come on.' Oren shakes a plastic water canteen under his nose. Jonny takes it dumbly, never mind where it's come from. Can Oren really have been carrying that this entire time? The water, cool and refreshing, snaps his senses a little closer to their rightful places.

'Good.' Oren nods as Jonny hands back the canteen. 'Ready to stand up?'

Jonny takes in the full dimensions of their location as he straightens. It is so astounding it feels like it must be an illusion, except he knows it is as solid and real as the rock beneath his feet. They are standing in a hole in the cliff so wide and deep it is amplifying the sound of the sea. Yet they are almost completely hidden from external view – in a political location that couldn't be more scrutinised.

'I know,' Oren remarks, even though Jonny hasn't said anything, just reached immediately for his notebook and pencil, still mercifully in his pocket.

Fumbling with the cover, Jonny is sketching before he's even fully flipped it open, forcing himself to picture every torrid step of their journey in order to commit it to paper. A couple of boxes to mark the chicken houses at the top of the cliff, a line for the path cut steeply down the side of an outward curve until ... The pencil stills as Jonny looks up, dumbfounded all over again by both the improbability of their physical location and the enormity of its political significance.

'I know.' The older man takes a drink for himself, tipping his head right back to catch the last dregs from the canteen.

Jonny grips his pencil afresh, even though it is more than obvious he'll need more than just a new piece of paper to map out the entirety of what he can see.

They've alighted on a platform of some kind. Initially Jonny thought it was longer than it was deep, but even though his eyes are adjusting to the murk he can't identify any far walls at the back. The ceiling overhead is high, they aren't having to stoop at all, and the walls are a startling white, smooth and polished by years of pummelling from the elements. He turns to look inside again, noting how the white walls give way to grey until the black takes over. They must extend far further than he'd originally thought, or else they'd still be white – perhaps it's just a trick of the light, when the sun crests the hill won't the place be in its full beam? He looks back at his pencil drawing, so insufficient for what he now sees before him, except this one salient fact: the dark at the back must be heading north, straight north. The sun probably never reaches right inside the opening. Jonny scratches out a little compass at the top of his pathetic sketch before finally asking.

'What is this place?'

'It's probably easier if I just show you.'

'No.' Jonny holds up a hand, pencil clattering to the floor. 'I've had enough of being shown without knowing first, thanks.'

He stoops to retrieve his pencil, noting again the smoothness of the rock underfoot, running a finger over its surface.

'This can't be man-made,' Jonny mumbles. 'Not a chance. It's like he said. The sea's done this. Over however many million years—'

'Like who said?'

This time Jonny doesn't flinch as Oren steps towards him. 'You know I can't tell you that.'

Oren frowns. 'Aren't we far enough past the journalist protecting his sources by now?'

Jonny folds his arms, protectively tucking his notebook underneath. A little too self-importantly, but still. He's got no leverage left other than his professional principles. His arms tighten around himself, fending off the facts of the matter: that he's basically stuck inside a cliff with the worst of all enemies on the other side and no one other than an unpredictable stranger to help him.

'It's a bit of a worry for you if we are. I'd have thought you'd want to be protected like the rest of them.'

But Oren laughs, a musical little jingle now they're enveloped in fucking marble.

Jonny tries to continue as belligerently as he started. 'So are you going to tell me what this place is or not?'

'It's a miracle,' the older man replies. 'Isn't it?'

'Certainly seems like it.' Jonny unfolds his arms, flips open his notebook again. 'Although I expect your next point to be that it's a miracle of the Israelis' own making.'

Jonny squints towards the still-invisible back walls again. If he didn't know better he would say the blackness is more intense in some spots than others – are those openings to different passageways, perhaps? He suddenly becomes aware of a soft rushing sound, a tinkle somewhere in the background. And there Jonny's legs go again, panic like a hand wrapped around his throat.

'Wait a second.' He props himself against rock. 'Do you hear that? That noise? What is that?'

Oren snorts. 'The water level is predictable, Jonny. We know exactly when it rises, when it falls. And it hasn't come up this high for thousands of years. The question is who else knows these secrets. Before Farid was killed we thought we knew exactly who did.'

Jonny licks his lips, looking back out to sea. Considering the wide-open sky is suddenly far more appealing than the murky depths of the cliff. He tastes salt, sour and acrid inside his mouth.

'Have you got any more water?'

Oren wordlessly hands him another canteen, it's as if he's producing them from inside the cliff. The sweet, fresh water reminds Jonny he's still not at the full mercy of the elements just yet. He drains the canteen in a few gulps.

'OK,' he mumbles, screwing on the lid. 'OK. Fine. Let's go.'

Oren nods as he takes the empty canteen, tucking it into the cargo pocket below his belt. Jonny notes the radio, still clipped above. Will it work all the way out here? He's beyond surprised as a torch emerges from Oren's other pocket.

'What else have you got in there?' Instantly Jonny regrets asking. He doesn't want to know about the weapons inevitably stashed somewhere he can't see.

'Everything we need to stay safe in here, don't worry, Jonny. Like I told you, we can only do this together. Come on.'

Jonny's eyes have to adjust all over again to the beam of the torch, cutting a path through the dark ahead. There are passageways, he can see them clearly now, three openings in total, all abyss-like without the beam of a torch, branching away from the platform into the depths of the cliff. There are a few other pockets in the rock too, quite beautiful really, like windows set into walls, the ones with the right aspect must light up as the sun sets ... He shakes his head as violently as he can. There Jonny's imagination goes again. Now is not the time for stupid flights of fancy. Allen's voice chimes in his head alongside his own.

Allen. Jonny pulls up with a start. 'What time is it?'

Oren turns around, torchlight dazzling as it beams into Jonny's face. 'Doesn't an intrepid journalist like you wear a watch?'

'It ... it fell off,' Jonny answers lamely, trying to dodge the torch beam. 'And, like I told you, we've all got a problem if I don't call into the newsroom on time.'

Oren turns away, taking the passageway in the middle.

Jonny calls after him. 'I suppose you've got a phone stashed down here too?'

But his questions echo unanswered off the darkened walls.

Jonny curses softly to himself. Leverage. Just when he thinks he has some, it evaporates. And he was never even wearing a fucking watch.

'We think these were created many hundreds of years ago,' Oren says after a few paces, waving the torch beam so Jonny can see from wall to wall. 'The rock is soft in places, two different layers of chalk, soft enough that the water penetrated over time, forming these passageways and grottoes within the cliffs themselves.'

Jonny brushes a hand along the wall, relieved to find it cool and dry. The passageway is sloping lower now, and starting to curve back on itself.

'Do all the tunnels lead to different places? Or do they connect to each other?'

Jonny glances overhead as he asks, flinching at the ceiling's proximity, wondering suddenly how stable the rock can be if it's so full of holes. Oren doesn't answer, picking up speed as the gradient steepens further downwards.

'When did you discover them?' Jonny tries again, running his hand along the wall. Still cold. Still dry. Not as smooth as it was.

'Many years ago now. They are still a closely held secret. Only a handful of people know they exist. We had to bore a new tunnel to the main complex once our divers had discovered where some of the holes lead.'

Jonny's next question dies on his lips as he skids on a pool of water, righting himself just as the passageway opens out into a cave.

'Jesus Christ,' he mutters, eyes flicking nervously between the puddle somewhere behind him and the new space he's arrived in.

'He's not a lot of use to you out here, I'm afraid.' Oren reaches up to tether his torch to some hidden clasp in the rock overhead. Jonny blinks into yet more unfamiliar light, somewhere between grey and yellow, as Oren twiddles the rim of the torch to widen the beam. They're in a bulge in the passageway more than large enough to be described as a cave, a rough oval shape with a few ledges poking out from the walls. The passageway looks as if it continues at the far end. And there's that rushing sound again, closer, more of a jangle than a tinkle this time.

'Right, that's it,' Jonny says, flinching at the sound of his own voice, strangely amplified in the confined space. 'You want me to figure out who killed Farid? To work out how far your stupid intelligence operation is blown? How about you tell me first how the hell you knew I would go along with coming down here with you. Because most other people might have picked throwing themselves into the banana plants if they hadn't already tried bolting down the driveway.'

Jonny curses himself as he says it. Because it is true. Jonny has willingly put himself in this godforsaken position all because of some loose thread fluttering deep in his own mind. What's to say he's going to like what finally pins it down?

Oren turns to him, torchlight throwing twisted shadows across his face. 'What would you know about strategic intelligence, Jonny Murphy from the *International Tribune*?'

'Nothing.' Oren's eyes narrow but the fear is still there. Jonny continues, emboldened. 'But that doesn't exactly answer my question, does it? And don't pretend you know everything there is to know about strategic intelligence either. You're still working out how big of a mess you've made of this operation, and that's only because of what's happened to Farid. And now...'

Jonny gasps. He sees it now. Safta's words come back to him with the echo of rushing water. These tunnels should have been sealed off years ago. And what had Geronimo said, back in the bomb shelter?

'He knew you wouldn't do it if we were together,' Jonny mutters to himself.

'What?' Oren takes another step forward.

'How about you tell me? What are we really doing down here, old man?' Jonny tries to keep the tremor from his voice. 'You and Geronimo – or whoever he really is – can't be the only two people left who know about this tunnel. Fine, there may only be a few of you, but it's an intelligence operation of gigantic proportions, it has to be. There's even a foreign agent working on it – with the stupidest fucking code name I've ever heard. So who else knows? And how do *they* feel about the fact you've been compromised?'

A hand closes around Jonny's throat.

'We don't have time for this,' Oren hisses.

'Too fucking right we don't,' Jonny rasps, concentrating on the fact that if he can still speak, he can most definitely breathe. 'So here's what I think. You're finally supposed to be sealing them, aren't you? All these tunnels. And fast. Those are your orders. That's what Geronimo doesn't want you to do yet. They probably should have been dead-ended hours ago. But you don't want to if you don't have to, huh? Why blow years of intel if Farid was just done over by a jealous lover? That's the only reason you need to find out exactly who killed him. You've gone rogue, and now the only way to turn it around is to make it count. Even standing down here, with no protection at all, you're still convinced the intelligence might be worth it.'

Oren's grip tightens, but the fear is still flickering in his eyes, Jonny is sure of it.

'And that's why you've dragged me down here too, isn't it?' Jonny feels his eyes bulging but keeps croaking on. 'So I've got no way of going rogue myself. Of calling this in despite all your threats and dropping you in even deeper shit than you already are.'

'No.' Oren drops him, the older man's face crumpling like a paper bag.

'What do you mean, no?'

'Shhhhhht.' Oren waves a hand at him, leaning towards the far wall, to the abyss in the gloom. Jonny cocks his head, adrenaline tingling up his back. The jangle in the distance is rising to almost a clatter, echoing from some far point inside the cliff. There's another burst of noise now, Oren's radio, improbably squawking at his belt.

'That's impossible,' Jonny whispers, hands clenching into fists by his sides.

Oren lifts a finger to his lips, still tensed in the direction of the far wall. Another clatter now, a definite sound of movement, rather than susurration of rising water. Jonny starts to pant – his airways constricting all over again as his prospects narrow down to either a charging battalion of heavily armed terrorists or a remorseless wall of seawater.

Until he sees the face on the shape emerging from the gloom.

Chapter Thirty-Three
Wednesday

8:00 p.m.

By now the dark is so intense it has an almost physical quality. Lola can see nothing other than the occasional shimmer of moonshine off the sea. They're moving away from the banana plants now, ankle deep in water, following the smooth line of the cliff. Every soft splash reminds Lola that in a matter of moments the water could be over her head, and all she's got as an anchor is sand beneath her feet. Ahead, the stranger turns, somehow into the cliff, into an opening that Lola can't see, only sense, as the dark swallows them up almost immediately.

'Careful here,' the stranger murmurs, his voice echoing awkwardly back at her. 'It can be really slippery in places.'

Lola plants her feet as deliberately as her body will let her. The ground is sloping steeply upward with every step. They're out of the water in a matter of seconds, but Lola knows this tide, it rises high and fast. In a freak storm it would be impossible to outrun even if the gradient to this slope was almost vertical. She cocks her head, straining for the ocean's song – still whispering, no freak storm whipping overhead. The air feels oddly fresh on her face as they climb – the passageway must be wide and high, in parallel with the banana field she knows opens out somewhere to its other side.

That's the miracle of the invisible cove, Farid had said. A trick of water, sand and rock, all acting together as nature's lock, opening and closing only to those who know its secret.

Actually the trick was all yours, she replies silently, reflexively squeezing the hand in hers. The stranger's grip tenses back – it's as if he can sense what she is thinking. Lola remembers he thought it was his own little secret too.

The walls feel tighter and closer now. She still can't see them, but the sound of their feet on rock is harsher, more amplified than it was. And just as she opens her mouth to ask where they are headed, they are there.

Inside a cave of some kind, carved deep within the rock.

Lola blinks into the alien-yellow light illuminating the space around them.

A mattress and blankets. A pair of boots, neatly paired against the wall. A large jerry can full of water. A small silver camping stove.

The stranger drops her hand to turn and face her. Lola feels her jaw slacken as she stares.

Where is the light coming from? What is all this stuff doing in here? And what is the black shape curled on the ground next to the shoes?

'I got the feeling you might not want to go straight back to the kibbutz.' Now the stranger's mumbling, staring at the floor. 'But I can take you all the way up if you want. It's not much further.'

Lola takes in the mattress and blankets again as if they are figments of her imagination.

'I know it looks a little odd.' He fiddles a bare toe into a crack on the rock floor. 'But it works for me. When you have to stay awake all night, it's the best way to get enough sleep during the day. I couldn't survive if I had to do it on the kibbutz.'

'You can't...' Lola's voice dies away again as she gazes around the cave, a pocket of shelter it feels like even the elements can't reach.

'I have a room on the kibbutz too – well, a bathroom, mainly. I sleep down here most of the time. And I get to wake up to the sunset, bathe in the sea by myself every day.'

Lola turns on the spot. The cave is fitted out with everything for an overnight stay. The mattress actually looks comfortable, there are even pillows – the volunteers should be so lucky. She registers the camping stove again, the set of enamel mugs, the individually wrapped packets of coffee, tea and sugar.

And there's that black shape again, the solid, unmistakable curves of a pistol.

The stranger squats, flicking the camping stove alight.

'Coffee?'

Lola shakes her head dumbly at him, but he just smiles, turning up the flame.

'Tea, sorry. I should have guessed.'

'Tea,' she murmurs, gazing up at the light tethered to the ceiling. It must be a battery-operated lamp.

'I don't have the English kind, though. You'll be used to that by now, I'm sure. Those Lipton tea bags never quite cut it, do they?'

'How do you...' Again she has to stop. 'You're going to make me tea?'

Water streams from his jerry can into a small copper pot. He sets it on the blue flame to boil before motioning to a cushion propped against the opposite wall.

'I'm happy to take you all the way back up if you prefer. I have to go myself, soon, anyway.'

But Lola can't just prop herself painlessly against the cushion. She can't just plonk herself down and take tea with a stranger on a promise anymore, much less next to a gun on the floor. The stranger's brow furrows as she stays standing, but he doesn't say anything else, just fiddles with his stove, turning up the flame under the pot.

An enamel cup fills with tea. The cave fills with the smell of mint. The air turns so sweet with the sugar he's ladling into the cup too that Lola can almost taste it in the steam curling off the top.

'The sugar will do you good,' he observes, stirring.

Lola stares at the tea leaves swirling in the cup. Is she trapped all over again? And she's done it to herself, she's let this stranger lead her into this hole. She lets the pain bite, remembers why it's there, tries to channel her anger, only for the strangest sensation to break out all over her instead – a curious warmth rather than cold sweat. The cave shimmers in her peripheral vision – a bed, a stove, some clothes, other living essentials. It's not a trap. It's a refuge. For someone just like her.

First the steaming cup, then the stranger comes back into focus. A small smile turns the corners of his mouth as she accepts it from his outstretched hand.

'Coffee for me,' he says after a moment. 'Even when you sleep as well as I do, staying awake through a quiet night can be a challenge.'

And Lola realises what he must do on the kibbutz, just as the pungent smell of coffee trumps the sharpness of mint, air suddenly thick with it, suddenly a little harder to breathe.

She may have never laid eyes on him before, but Lola knows exactly who he is now.

Rami. The night watchman. The man who no one ever sees unless he wants them to.

The tea leaves tremble as Lola fiddles with her cup. What has Rami seen? What does he do with those dead hours while the rest of the kibbutz sleeps? Farid's face flashes into her mind so hard it sends pain through her temples, right as the sugar in her tea charges right to her limits. Lola tries to plant herself steady, but it's too much for her legs, shaking uncontrollably, sugar rush almost narcotic.

Rami sips slowly from his coffee, eyes never leaving her face.

'This is the last time I'm going to ask you if you're alright. I haven't seen anyone in that cove for years, much less a girl writhing around even though she's still in the shallows.'

Now there's water in her eyes, trembling as she tries not to blink, because to blink will make her cry. 'I could ask you the same thing,' she mutters, looking up at the rocky ceiling, letting gravity do its work on her nascent tears, push them back behind her eyeballs. 'It's not exactly normal to make yourself at home inside a cave.'

Rami sighs, long and deep. 'Let's just say when you disgrace your family as far as I have, even running away doesn't cut it. Letting everyone pretend it never happened, no, that would be too easy. Letting everyone pretend I was dead—well, then there might be mourning, and they can't have that either. Not the devastated, emotional kind of mourning, anyway.'

'So this is your punishment?' A solitary tear escapes as Lola looks around the cave. 'You've been banished down here? Why?'

'Not exactly.' Rami pauses for a meditative sip. 'I mean, yes, I have been banished to overnight watchman for the rest of my days. I am a pariah. But I choose to sleep down here. It's something I can do on my own terms.'

'But why?' Lola wonders again. Can Rami have done anything nearly as terrible as she has? He answers with a curt little tap of his cup on the stone floor.

'You wouldn't understand. None of you would. Those faceless and nameless places you've all come from? Nothing there will have prepared you for what it's really like out here. We have to fight for our homes, for every inch of ground. We have to spill blood to hold on to it, sometimes deliberately. And mistakes cost far more than you could ever imagine.'

Lola eyes him drain the rest of his coffee. 'So that's what happened?'

Another harsh tap of enamel on rock. 'What do you care? People die all the time around here, and it doesn't seem to matter to any of you.'

'That's not true.' Lola shifts awkwardly from foot to foot, flinching.

Rami lets out a brittle little laugh. 'Well, I suppose it isn't – where you're personally concerned, anyway.'

Lola freezes. Farid's face is suddenly all she can see, his touch all she can feel. She hates herself in the same moment for remembering it as a caress.

'Don't worry,' Rami continues, quietly. 'It's the same story every year with the volunteers. There are at least three break-ups to every romance. It's standard. It's believable.'

Believable, Lola wonders, flinching as Rami leans over – is he reaching for the pistol? He pauses with his arm still mid-air, expression darkening.

'If I was going to hurt you, why would I bother bringing you down here?' Lola holds her breath, but his hand just flicks overhead. 'This cave is the closest thing I've got to a home in the world. You seemed like someone who might appreciate its protection as much as I do. That's all.'

He reaches for her empty cup. Lola lets it drop from her fingers. She feels the beginnings of pity as she gazes at Rami, at this man who has been judged to have done something so traitorous that he can only exist in the shadows.

Until he swaps the cup for the pistol on the floor.

'I need to go and get changed now. Make yourself comfortable. I promise nothing can disturb you, not even the sea. It's impossible.'

Lola flinches. Rami is standing now, pistol in his hand, waving it around in the air.

'The last time the water got this far inside the cliff was literally a million years ago. And the people who know about these holes won't come by tonight, trust me. I can show you the way out too if you like, before I go. But if I were you, I'd hang out where no one else can bother you. On a kibbutz, there's nowhere to do that other than underground. There's someone in every field, even if you can't see them. There's always someone watching, whether they'll admit it or not.'

Now the gun is pointing towards the mouth of a tunnel in the opposite wall.

'No more than ten minutes this way and you're out. There's one turn to the right. You can't really miss it if you keep touching the wall. I'll leave this for you in any case.'

And just like that, the pistol is pressed into her hand.

Heavy, solid, implacable. Lola gasps at the weight of it.

'You won't need it,' Rami says. 'But it might help you give yourself a break.'

The ridged black handle blurs as she stares past the gun at him patting a pillow with his empty hand.

'Sleep it off. Everything might look different once you have.'

Chapter Thirty-Four
Thursday

9:30 a.m.

The dazzling torchlight throws Jonny for a second, clicking off almost immediately that its beam enters the cave itself. He only realises there is more than one person shuffling behind it when they start stumbling around in the shadows.

'Oren? Is that you? What are you doing down here?' A girl's voice, English, quavering as she asks.

The torch goes on again in time for Jonny to do a quick count – a girl and four men, all demonstrably non-native, one man shrugging his shoulders with the most curious expression etched all over his face. If Jonny didn't know better he'd say it was dumbfounded surprise.

'Have you seen Lola? We can't find her anywhere!' The panic is rising in the girl's voice as she continues, wringing her hands.

Oren blanches. The beam shines around the confines of the cave as Geronimo waves it around, lingering on Jonny a beat too long for someone feigning total surprise.

Understanding begins to dawn. Western accents, all speaking English – these must be more volunteers, Jonny thinks. They don't know who one of their number really is; and he doesn't want them to know either. And in case shining a literal spotlight away from himself wasn't already enough, Geronimo flicks the beam into Jonny's eyes for another beat too long for comfort.

Jonny has to look away in spite of himself, cursing the larger man all over again. Why doesn't Jonny have a torch too? Why doesn't he have the million and one other things that could have been more useful to him over the last few hours than just the pair of sunglasses folded lamely in his top pocket? He is suddenly gripped by the urge to snap his stupid fucking sunglasses into teeny, tiny pieces. He should have known when he'd smugly congratulated himself for wearing them earlier.

Oren steps forward, brow furrowed. 'What do you mean? Where *is* Lola?'

'Nobody knows,' the girl wails, clawing at her face. 'And now—'

'Slow down,' Geronimo interrupts, resting a hand on the girl's shoulder. 'Just breathe, come on. In, out, in, out...'

But the girl just cries out and falls to her knees. And now it's Geronimo stepping forward. Jonny tenses, hands curling into fists at his sides as he tries to put it together.

'There's no easy way to say this, Oren. I'm sorry,' Geronimo begins, again swinging the torch beam directly into Jonny's eyes. 'But we found Moti in the banana fields on our way down here. We were looking for Lola...'

'In here?' Oren shakes his head.

'That's what I asked,' another man mumbles.

Geronimo shoves him before continuing: 'I remembered what you'd once told me about these caves,' he says meaningfully. 'So we came down here to check. Lola knows the banana fields better than any of us, hey. But I'm afraid there must have been some sort of accident.'

'Accident?' The question is out before Jonny can stop it. On cue, the torch beam swings directly into his eyes.

Jonny tries to dodge the beam as a different man asks, 'Who the hell are you?'

'This is Jonny,' Oren answers. 'He's a journalist at the *International Tribune*. You know, the paper we get just so you lot can read the English translation?'

Jonny shakes his head, but before he can say anything the girl starts wailing again.

'Oren, please! Something terrible has happened.'

Oren turns to Geronimo. 'What is she talking about?'

'It's Moti,' Geronimo replies, training his torch on the floor so no one can see his expression properly. 'Like I said, there must have been some sort of accident.'

'We couldn't help him,' the girl sobs. 'We tried, but it must have happened a while ago, he was already cold.'

'Cold? What do you mean?' Oren asks.

'He's dead, Oren. I'm sorry you're having to find out from a load of panicked volunteers, but there's no doubt about it.' Geronimo's voice rings round the cave with a heavy air of finality.

Jonny watches Oren's head turn on his neck, looking robotically at the bedraggled group in front of them. This isn't what he expected. Jonny is sure of it. The wobble in the set of his broad shoulders, the parroting of questions. Jonny may have only met Oren a few hours earlier, but Jonny's watched his every move. Oren isn't good enough at feinting and diving to fake shock.

There Jonny's stomach churns with a sudden wave of adrenaline. Safta had told Jonny to ask for Moti at the gate. She can't have been expecting this to happen either. Oren and Geronimo – or whoever he really is – were already struggling to bring this situation back under some form of control. And now someone else has died. Not just any someone else, either. A founder member of the kibbutz itself.

Two bodies in twenty-four hours. And where is Jonny? Standing directly in the subterranean line of fire. His legs twitch with the urge to bolt away headfirst into the dark.

'You found Moti? Dead? In the banana fields?' There is more than a note of panic in Oren's voice as he asks.

'I'm so sorry,' the girl gibbers. 'When we found him, we thought you might already know. That maybe that was why we haven't seen you this morning—'

'I'd already told everyone that you wanted to speak to us in private,' Geronimo interrupts. 'We were trying to find Lola first.'

Jonny tries to put it together again, but just comes up with a bigger puzzle. A few moments ago he'd thought he had it – that once Farid's body was discovered, Oren and Geronimo were told to block these tunnels and shut their intelligence operation down. That Jonny was only down in the tunnel with Oren so he couldn't leak his information. But Jonny's been surer and surer for a while that Oren and Geronimo are at odds themselves. So what do they have to gain by bringing a bunch more westerners into the line of fire?

An altogether darker thought crosses Jonny's mind then, but is shaken loose by a sudden animal yelp echoing around the cave.

'How the fuck did that dog get down here?'

Jonny flinches as one of the men aims a kick at the hound skittering out behind them, clearly as terrified as she is desperate to find a scent she can trust. Farid's dog, he thinks. The stray that Farid took care of. And she's still searching for a familiar scent down these slippery, dark passageways. The man continues to question Oren instead.

'Are you sure?' Oren looks up as if no one else has spoken. 'Are you sure that Moti ... that Moti is...'

The torchlight quivers as Geronimo nods his head. 'There's no doubt about it.'

'Look, Oren.' Another man steps forward. 'Are you OK to walk? We'll show you, come on. Then we can call whoever you need us to.'

'How did this happen?' Jonny tenses as Oren addresses Geronimo directly.

'I don't know,' Geronimo replies slowly, as if he's weighing every word. 'It was impossible to really tell without disturbing the body. He was just slumped on the ground.'

'I'm so sorry for your loss,' Jonny hears someone say. 'This must be a terrible, terrible shock. Is there anything that I can do to help?'

It's only when all heads swivel in his direction that Jonny realises it was him.

'Thank you,' Geronimo replies after a moment. 'You're ... wait, did you say he was a journalist?' The beam flicks to Oren.

'Yes,' the older man whispers. 'Yes.'

'A journalist?' The torch beam twitches as a different man addresses Jonny. 'What the hell are you doing here? Is it because of Farid?'

'I'm afraid I really don't know what you are talking about,' Jonny says, surprising himself with the ease of his response. 'But something tragic has obviously happened here, and I certainly don't wish to intrude on private grief.'

The solution presents itself as Jonny says it. There's a way out, and it's down that opposite tunnel. It can't be far, because there's no way anyone, called Geronimo or not, could have got this many people down a pitch-dark passageway having just chanced upon a corpse. All Jonny has to do is cut his losses and leg it. It's time to leave his unanswered questions behind.

'If you're sure there's nothing I can do to help then I'll get out of your way. We can continue another time...'

Jonny is already at the tunnel opening by the time the torch finds him again, but this time his back is turned. Still, the barely concealed threat that comes next is enough to bring him to a stop.

'You've got a job to do too, though, right?' Geronimo asks lightly. 'Why would a journalist be here otherwise? What did you say your name was again?'

'I do,' Jonny replies without turning around. 'You're kind to ask. But please, don't worry about it, not at a time like this. You've obviously got far bigger things to worry about.'

'Exactly right,' someone else says. 'Does anyone have any water? Oren, look, just drink this, rest up a second.'

'I wish you all the best,' Jonny murmurs, plunging into the dark ahead, stumbling instantly as the light disappears. The thought he's leaving the rest of them inside the cliff, knowing what could be approaching from the other side, nags at him, but only for a second.

Chapter Thirty-Five
Thursday

9:30 a.m.

Lola wakes with a start. Equally instantly she realises she must have been asleep for hours. Her head is pounding, her throat so dry she can hear her breath. She rolls on to her back, reaches a leaden arm to the side of her face, completely numb from resting on Rami's pillow. Enough memories fall back into her mind to piece it together. It doesn't take long. Not another movement until she's checked the pistol is still where she left it, resting undisturbed between the pillow and the stone wall. She reaches out a hand, yellow light overhead casting more alien shadows in the gloom. But the hand flies to her mouth as she registers the similarly alien numbers on her digital watch.

Someone must have found the second body by now. The floats will have rolled out to the banana fields more than four hours ago.

More memories clatter back into Lola's head. She feels for the pistol, touches her new-found piece of steel. Surely the rest of the volunteers must be looking for Lola too. Or at least, raised the fact they don't know where she is? Her heart kicks at her chest. What if her disappearance has done the exact opposite of what she wanted – sent people into every corner of the kibbutz to try and find her? The body might have stayed undiscovered for longer if she'd shown up for work on time. She could have sent the floats in a different direction on the off chance they'd been heading for the lower fields, and there's no way they would be, because those lower fields aren't a priority, they're far too exposed to saltwater, that's what Moti has always said ... Her cry wins out, even as she clutches at the steel between her fingers, the inanimate object taking back its name again.

Moti. He's dead. He won't have come home – the alarm will have been raised hours ago. Does he have a wife and kids? Doesn't everyone on the kibbutz? Isn't that the whole point of the place – happy families in technicolour? The feeling slowly starts to return to the side of her head as she rubs it, considers the equation, scratching at her scalp with her fingernails.

Perhaps it is better this way round. Perhaps the fact Lola is missing works in her favour. They'll be worried about her, not suspicious. Two bodies in twenty-four hours. They can't find her. They'll be worried she's going to be the third. When she walks out of here, she'll even have an alibi. She was with Rami. What better alibi than the night watchman?

This is the thought that propels Lola to sitting, only to realise too late it wasn't a ginger enough movement for her lower body, especially not on a mattress supported by solid rock. There's a sickening squelch, and she simultaneously realises she has been bleeding through the night. But her gasp of horror stills in her throat as she hears it.

Hears them.

Voices – low and indistinct, humming from somewhere else inside the cliff.

The unmistakable sound of people approaching.

Lola grabs the pistol. Panic overrides pain as she stands, cocking her head. There's the sound again, little peaks and troughs of it. The people must be moving. Are they coming closer? Or is this another trick of the cave? Couldn't the sounds be echoes off the water as it rises and falls with the tide?

The image of a wave rushing into the cliff suddenly floods her brain, blood trickling inescapably down her legs. Rami said it was impossible, and water doesn't talk. Suddenly Lola feels like she's already drowning, air leaving her lungs at the picture of the water chasing through the rock, filling every tunnel, pooling in every cave. She freezes on the balls of her feet, looking wildly round the cave as if she might find some new fissure in the rock that she could push open, slither through into the outside world where the sun is shining, the birds are singing, a new day is well under way and ready to welcome her, because why wouldn't it be? Why should Lola be punished for defending herself?

There's that sound again, a spike of it – two voices, male and angry. She instinctively turns away from it, towards the tunnel opening she came through last night, trying to remember what Farid had told her about when the tide would reveal the sand.

As the sound fades, she turns back again without thinking ... and he's there.

Another stranger.

Another man.

In her cave.

An unpleasant bolt of noise ricochets off stone – is it a laugh? Lola considers the pistol, the reassuring weight in her hand – can she aim it? But just as she thinks it, she doesn't have to, noise trailing off as the man holds up his hands, says something to her in Hebrew.

Lola keeps the pistol low as she surveys him: young, unremarkable, more surprised than threatening. She's certainly never seen him before. More Hebrew now, but this time some words Lola understands. He's asking if she's OK. Can't he see she's the one with the gun in her hand? But all she can do next is shrug, as what follows makes no sense at all.

'Wait a second – are you English?'

Lola freezes, shoulders still halfway to her ears. Her initial impression of this stranger instantly crystallises into something more familiar.

'Well, I suppose I shouldn't be surprised,' the man mutters, hands still in the air. 'And I suppose you're going to tell me you're another one of the volunteers.'

But before Lola has a second to do or say anything else, a cannonball of tumbling fur careers out of the passageway behind him. Biba, whimpering inconsolably, absolutely frantic, velvet nose frenzied at her bare flesh.

Lola feels the primal rush of love jostle with an equally intense revelation. What can possibly have scared Biba enough to propel her into a pitch-dark labyrinth in search of her scent? And how can Lola realistically deny any connection to her while she's clamouring at Lola so hard she may as well be trying to climb inside her body?

And the man suddenly only has eyes for the dog, even as a trickle of blood reaches all the way down to Lola's ankle.

'Who...?' But she has to stop, Biba barking just at the sound of Lola's voice, *bang-bang-bang*, like a pop gun.

'Is this your dog?' the man asks.

Lola shakes her head, remembers she's the one holding a real gun. Keeping her voice low so Biba doesn't startle, she tries again. 'You've met the rest of the volunteers? Who are you?'

'Me?' Surprise creases the man's otherwise nondescript face. 'Christ, I cannot fucking believe I am having this conversation.'

But his snort dies away as Lola tenses, gaze flicking at the pistol in her hand.

'I'm a journalist,' the man continues warily. 'I live in Jerusalem. Which, judging by everything that has happened to me so far this morning, is definitely where I probably should have stayed, instead of coming up here to have my arse handed to me for the eightieth time.'

Lola's grip tightens around the ridged black handle in her palm. Why has a journalist arrived on the kibbutz? One that speaks as perfect Hebrew as he does English? What does he know? And who is he going to tell?

'What's happened this morning?' she asks.

'You don't know?'

Lola gestures at the bed rather than say anything that might incriminate her, but realises too late she's just pointing out its bloodstains.

And it's the bloodhound who knows before Lola does, Biba growling immediately that the man steps forward, tail rigid in the air. On cue the stranger freezes, eyeing the gun, the blood, the tunnel openings.

'I'm fine,' Lola says quietly. 'This happens to women every month.' She waves a dismissive hand, deliberately chooses the one with the gun in it. 'I guess your mum never explained that, huh.'

But it's like the words land more physically than the gun. The man recoils, tottering on his feet. Lola keeps the pistol aloft as she digs around with her free hand for the unfamiliar medical pack mercifully still stuffed deep in her pocket. Gauze, a simple bandage— that's all she needs.

'Do you...?' the man hesitates further as Biba lunges for the trauma kit immediately, salivating over the distinctive leather case. 'Look, are you sure you aren't hurt?'

'I don't need an audience.' Lola scrabbles with the case one-handed – she's got no choice, she needs to stem the bleeding but can't bring herself to put the gun down. 'And I need to get going. I've massively overslept.'

'Going? Where? Like that?'

'I've missed an entire shift.' Lola raises her voice as if it will disguise the fact she can't move without wincing. The dog's got her teeth into the case now – Lola's having to fight to keep hold of it.

Lola wavers, if only for a second. She's got a gun in her hand. She shouldn't have to fight to keep control of this situation, of any situation. There's no aggression coming from this stranger, hands still held above his head, a curious mixture of panic and relief wiped across his face.

'So you know how to get out of here? Because we need to move, and pronto. If you can.'

He takes another step towards her, the dog is still too busy chewing the medical pack to notice.

'It's that way, isn't it?' Lola jerks the gun at the dark opening the man came through, but this time he doesn't flinch, not even close.

'You mean you don't know?'

A sudden burst of noise answers for her. Lola's arm flies up, gun hand trained instinctively towards the commotion, only to drop again almost immediately.

'Rami,' she whispers, pistol clattering away. She's lost her grip in the shock, it's already too late to hide anything else.

Another step closer and the overhead light illuminates the full horror of his stricken expression. Lola reaches out to catch him but the stranger gets there first. Rami crumples to his knees, cries reverberating around the cave like sirens.

Chapter Thirty-Six
Thursday

Now

For a face he's only seen once before, Jonny figures out who is emerging from the tunnel pretty quickly. And the night watchman has the look of someone who has been up for far longer than just one night. He reaches out reflexively as Rami falls, the familiar weight of dealing with someone in agonised shock an immediate pressure on his shoulders, pinning him in position. It's an automatic response, he knows that – a learned behaviour, doctors called it, those many years ago after his mother died, because it was laid down while his childhood brain was still developing, an unexpected pathway that no child would ever choose unless they were forced to travel it again and again. The freeze setting, rather than fight or flight.

Rami's cries, the dog's barks – Jonny's heard those before too. They land like he's deaf, because he is – another learned behaviour, to find something else to listen to when the rest of the noise is too loud. So he knows he's humming too. It just happens, it's his own personal distraction, tuning out the storm. He blinks away the child bent over its mother, suddenly all he can see in a cave full of yellow shadows.

'What's happened?' the girl whispers, tightening her arms around herself.

Jonny twitches as he gazes at the terrified hound fleeing into the gaping tunnel. Never has an abyss seemed more inviting.

'You have to find out who did this,' Rami says urgently, in an unexpectedly clear voice. 'Hey. I'm talking to you.' He grabs at Jonny's ankle.

'Are you alright?' Jonny replies automatically, still staring into the abyss. He doesn't need to hum anymore, but he's not quite ready to re-enter reality.

'Rami…' the girl whispers. 'You're … you're scaring me. What's going on?'

'You have to find out what happened,' Rami repeats, levering himself up off the floor via one of Jonny's legs.

Jonny flinches at a stranger's touch, both relieved and furious at the same time. Where would he rather be? Stuck in the pain of the past, or trapped inside this fucking hole?

'And when you do, you have to tell everyone. You're a journalist, that's what you people do. Because someone murdered him—'

Another cry this time, higher – the girl? Now she's the one on her knees.

'What are you talking about?' Jonny curses himself for asking. Why does he always want to know why? Even when he's got more than enough answers to make him stop asking for good?

'My father.' Rami cries out again. 'Someone has killed my father. And you need to find out what happened, because no one else will bother. They'll want to bury it like everything else around here.'

'I don't understand,' Jonny whispers.

'You know what I'm talking about! I overheard the lot of you. In the other cave. Talking about finding the body. So I went to see for myself. He's still there. I need you to see it too. Because then you won't be able to turn away.'

'Moti's your father?' The girl's voice quavers. 'I-I thought…'

She trails off, reaching for her pistol. Jonny stares. She can't seem to close her hand around it this time. Something altogether different snags inside Jonny's mind, a loose thread catching a current of memory.

Rami answers bitterly. 'Oh, we hated each other. Well, he certainly hated me. In a country like this, who wouldn't hate a military disgrace? Blood is worth nothing when it comes to all that. Even after everything I told him about this place, it still wasn't enough. And now—'

'This place?' Jonny interrupts. 'You mean these tunnels? So you knew about them? The truth about them, I mean?'

'Yes. I found out what they were being used for. And what some people were trying to do with them. My father founded this kibbutz. I had to tell him.'

'What happened when you did?' The thread is tightening in Jonny's mind now, drawn to its opposite end.

'Well, he didn't forgive me, if that's what you mean. Hah! Who could?'

'What do you mean, who? Forgive you for what?'

Rami rounds on Jonny. 'Do you think I want to run night patrol around here for the rest of time? Sleep in this fucking tomb forever? I'm only in here because I let my unit down in the worst possible way. Kids died because of me! And he couldn't take it, oh no. In this country, it turns out the military trumps even a father's own flesh and blood. I had to be dragged back here to serve guard duty just so he wouldn't be ostracised from a place he founded himself. Everyone had to see and feel my punishment. When you lay a cornerstone you have to see it through, right? If you came from here, you'd understand. When a nation is only as strong as its military supremacy, mistakes don't just disappear unless they're deliberately covered up.'

'You thought once you'd done it for long enough, he'd forgive you?'

'Especially once I'd told him about this.'

'This?' Jonny gestures around the cave. 'This ... wait, what did you call it...? This miracle of the earth you told me about too?'

'You told me you were a journalist.' Rami's face hardens. 'I knew exactly why you were here. Why would any reporter from an international newspaper come sniffing around a random dead body on a kibbutz? It had to be far bigger than just that. And I knew how big ... So I gave you enough to go on to get started. I wanted you to find these tunnels, to understand what we were up against. No one else was going to send you in the right direction.'

'But you'd told your dad,' Jonny says slowly, returning to the thread still loose in his mind. 'So wouldn't he have told me, too?'

'No.' Rami's head drops then. 'And I think you might already know why.'

And Jonny sees it all, instantly, laid out before him as unmistakably as the landscape spreading away from the top of the cliff.

The disgraced soldier and his humiliated father.

That soldier's desperate need for rehabilitation.

And the scapegoat. The outsider at the end of a tunnel.

The thought of Farid is what snaps Jonny back to the present.

'We've got to move.' Jonny starts towards the tunnel opening, beckoning to them both. 'We've got to get out of here.'

Rami's face brightens. He scrambles to his feet.

'Yes. And there's a quicker way.'

'That's backward, isn't it?' Jonny pauses as Rami steps towards the opposite passageway.

'Trust me. I know what I'm doing. I know exactly where all the tunnels lead.'

Jonny shifts from foot to foot, itching to get going while Rami holds his hand out to the girl. But she stays rooted to her knees. A frown crosses Rami's face as she stutters.

'Are we ... are we going back into the banana fields?' She fumbles the leather case in her hands back into her pocket.

'Anywhere but here,' Jonny snaps at Rami, suddenly frozen on his feet, staring at the girl's empty, wringing hands. 'We can't afford to stay a minute longer...'

The hairs rise on the back of Jonny's neck as her eyes widen, looking past him.

'Well, well, well,' a voice drawls from behind him in melodious American English. 'How very convenient.'

Jonny turns on the spot to find a slow smile spreading across a now sickeningly familiar face.

'Dave,' the girl gasps from behind him. 'What are you doing down here?'

Geronimo pauses, looking between them all.

'Like your man says. He knows exactly where these tunnels lead. I was always going to catch up with you, Jonny. It's just a tidy little bonus, Lola, to find you loitering down in here too.'

Chapter Thirty-Seven

Now

The relief Lola finally feels stirring at the sight of a familiar face stalls the second she sees the journalist tense, his body language re-tuning to unmistakably aggressive. She assesses Dave, considers all the physical tics he usually uses to put people at ease – hunching to make himself seem smaller, spreading his arms wide to detract from the size of his hands. But they're all landing so far off key she can practically hear them. There's still blood streaked all over her, and he hasn't given it a second look.

Lola eyes the pistol, suddenly well beyond her reach. Has someone deliberately kicked it out of her way? Was it Rami, when he saw her scrabbling with the last of the evidence? Or was it Dave? How does he know about these caves? Why is he down here too?

Now the journalist is turning to her, outstretched hand trembling.

'Not so fast, Jonny.' Dave's hands move to his hips.

'I don't understand,' Lola whispers, questions scudding through her mind, answers hovering just beyond her reach. 'How do you—?'

But Dave just cuts her off. No thoughtful pleasantries. No country-and-western charm. 'You don't have to. All you need to do now is exactly as I tell you.'

The radio at his belt squawks; this time the Hebrew is clear enough for Lola to hear it. But the only words she understands are the curses exploding from the other two men – shrill, disbelieving and horrified, their echoes repeating before they can die away.

'What's happened?' Lola has to ask again and again over the radio, bursts of sound coming every few seconds. The answer strips Dave's deep voice of the last of its familiarity.

'The Israelis just dropped a bomb into a U.N. shelter full of women and children. Over a hundred of them, to be precise. Just across the border, barely a few miles from here. By mistake, apparently. Rocket attacks can do that to a fella, huh.'

Time seems to slow around Lola. All her questions become disembodied, coalescing together inside her head. She watches, transfixed, as Dave takes a rucksack off his shoulders. Out of it come some small black canisters, a packet of some sort of powder, a large roll of copper wire.

'What are you doing?' Rami asks, tense and coiled to her other side. Lola feels the nudge, trying to snag her attention. 'Isn't he a volunteer?'

'As far as you're concerned, I still am,' Dave snaps, looking up. 'You know where these tunnels lead too, huh? Don't gawp at me, I heard everything you just said. So you're going to help me, and you know you are. You've still got a chance to be a good soldier—'

Lola feels her jaw slacken. To her other side, the journalist lets more Hebrew curses fly. But the English that comes next isn't anything Lola could ever have imagined.

'You're finally going to rig the place? All these tunnels? You're actually going to trip-wire the lot while we're all still down here?'

'Over a hundred dead women and children is going to make some folks very fucking angry indeed, Jonny-boy. And some of those people are armed and waiting less than a mile that-away.' Dave points into the abyss behind him. 'What else would you have me do? I'm just following orders.'

'That is bullshit!' the journalist howls. 'They'd have been dead-ended hours ago if you were happy to follow orders. You're only doing it now because you absolutely have to. Revenge is about to come charging down here, if it isn't already on the march.'

'Over a hundred dead women and children.' Dave brandishes the end of a copper wire at Rami with increasing agitation. 'They were taking cover from the latest salvo in a U.N. compound, and *bam*. If you know these tunnels, my man, then you know what needs to be done, and pronto.'

The journalist elbows himself between them, talking fast. Jonny, Lola registers dumbly, brain moving like treacle.

'You need to let us get out of here first. You gave me the job in the first place, and I've still got plenty of work to do—'

'The loose ends are all that matter now,' Dave snaps.

'My father is not a loose end,' Rami hisses back immediately. 'Whoever killed him isn't going to get away with it. Not for as long as I'm still alive—'

'And that's exactly why you're going to show me around every last inch of these tunnels,' Dave cuts him off, uncoiling to his full height. 'Show me anything I don't already know. Vengeance of a different kind, is all. Make sure he didn't die in vain, huh?'

And the inescapable reality of what Lola has done finally empties her mind of absolutely everything except what is happening around her.

'Dave, please!' she cries. 'What are you doing?'

'Don't ask him,' Jonny says urgently. 'That bag is full of explosives. We just need to get out of here, and fast. We already know too much.'

'About what?' Lola looks wildly between them. 'Dave works in the *refet*. I work in the bananas. We've been living here together for more than six months—'

'Wait a second.' Jonny cuts her off. 'What about Oren? And all the others? How do you know they are already safely outside? You can't risk—'

'Afraid I can, Jonny-boy. I have to. You know it, too. And besides. They got in. They'll get out. They aren't all as stupid as they look.'

Lola's crying now, breath coming in little gasps. Now it's Rami swearing again before continuing in breathless English and waving at Dave.

'You're part of this too? You're just posing as a volunteer? Manipulating all that dreamy-eyed stuff for … for … what? Doing someone else's dirty work?'

But Dave doesn't answer, hoisting up the roll of wire.

'Holy shit,' Jonny whispers. 'That's why you tricked the rest of the volunteers into coming down here too, isn't it?'

'What?' Lola gibbers. 'The others? Is that who you meant?'

But Dave just shoulders her aside. 'Don't fuck with what you don't understand, Jonny.'

'Oh, I understand perfectly well!' Jonny screams back. 'You've been buying time on these tunnels for so long that what's a little more bait between friends, huh? *That's* why we're all down here. If a bunch of terrorists had come screaming down this tunnel, you were actually going to try bartering with the lives of a few western citizens first? As if that would have made any fucking difference. We're a human shield. And now you have to cover the place in trip-wires anyway…'

'Inhuman, more like,' Rami snarls, stepping forward, but Dave gets there first, huge hand landing squarely in the centre of Rami's chest.

'A hundred dead women and children is the inhuman part, my man. That's the side you're on, isn't it? And how do you propose defending yourself against the consequences now? I'm down here doing *your* dirty work.'

The pause that follows is so loaded with tension that Lola finds herself wondering if the air itself is crackling. Is that the noise of footsteps rising and falling in the abyss opposite? Instantly she realises what she can hear. A rushing sound, rising and falling, echoing and rebounding between the caves and grottoes she now knows pockmark the entire cliff.

The unmistakable percussion of water.

'The tide!' Lola screams, her own panic mirrored on Rami's face. 'The water's rising.'

But Dave just keeps bearing down on him, face dark with fury. 'You're going to help me, and you're going to do it right now. Unless you're prepared to drown down here.'

'There's no time,' Rami shouts, gesturing wildly at the opposite tunnel. 'No one knows these tunnels like I do. We have to run...'

He fades as someone yanks Lola away, the dark abyss of the opposite tunnel suddenly flickering with torchlight ... but whose? Dave is bellowing now, there's the unmistakable clamour of a scuffle. She trips, screaming as she lands hard on the rock below. They're dragging her now, there are hands under Lola's armpits – Rami and Jonny, it must be, it's only Hebrew darting overhead – and suddenly she's up, over a shoulder, head hanging off her neck as she's draped upside down. Lola's at the end of the line, dangling like a rag doll, able to see nothing other than the dark receding behind them. Her hands find flesh, but there's nothing left of her fingernails to land even a scratch as the pair of boots below her thunder ahead, away from the distinct sounds of water slapping stone ever closer in the dark.

And so Lola hangs, limp and pathetic, as whatever tunnel they're in starts to climb, so steeply it feels impossible, until suddenly they're out into a burst of air so fresh and sharp she can taste the salt as she gasps.

Chapter Thirty-Eight

Jonny's lungs feel like they will burst if he gulps any harder, dropping to his knees on the smooth stone of the platform. The girl flops off his neck on to the rock beside him, crying out as her body connects with the hard surface. He gazes around the platform, in the permanent shadow of straight north, breathing steadying with every glance, before it hits him.

They're not alone. But Rami and Dave are nowhere to be seen.

He blinks at the figure rounding the corner of the path on to the platform, tiny precision movements so taut she looks like she might snap, except—

'Safta?'

Another step, and she's there, directly opposite, there's no doubt about it.

'You came,' Jonny murmurs, sweaty palms scrabbling for purchase on the smooth rock to push him to his feet.

The words chime back at him off the surrounding stone walls, the sweetest echo he's ever heard.

'You came!' He's finally steady now, cheeks exploding with smile. It really is her, wiry, determined and right in front of him. He hears himself again, so intoxicated at the sight of her it takes him an extra beat to realise it's not an echo at all.

Jonny follows his grandmother's gaze to the other end of the platform. For Oren is standing just shy of the mouth of the far tunnel, his silhouette practically glimmering with disbelief against the dark inside.

'Of course I did. What choice did I have?' she spits.

'You came,' Oren repeats, stepping towards them. 'After all this time, you finally—'

'Stop.' She holds up a hand. 'I told you this would happen. I warned all of you—'

'Safta?' Now it's the voice of a little boy, an echo from the past. But she doesn't look at Jonny, just keeps her hand in the air.

'You're a good boy. I know this now. Go on, back up to the kibbutz. Do as I say, and no harm will come to anyone else...'

'Anyone else?' Another echo, another note of panic. 'What do you mean?'

'Please...' Oren steps towards her, arms outstretched. 'Please don't do this—'

'We have to!' Jonny flinches as his grandmother screeches. 'And it is all your fault. I told you these tunnels could never be used in an intelligence operation. It was always going to be too big of a risk. And guess what? I was right. It's all blown up in your stupid face!'

Jonny turns to face Oren. The only possible explanation as to why these two particular people don't seem to be strangers to one another starts to dawn with the light slowly but inexorably illuminating the pocket of rock above Oren's head.

'And you...' She waves at Jonny, still without looking at him. 'My long-lost grandson, arriving to haunt me after all these years, trying to do the right thing by my country. I told you these people were idiots.'

'All you said was we could never do it.' Oren takes another step towards her, face hardening. 'You don't know the half of it. You've no idea what Farid was capable of. What he managed to do for our country before he was killed.'

'Exactly.' A bony hand closes around Jonny's arm. She's next to him now, except not in the way Jonny wants, not even close.

'I told you it would be a suicide mission, and that's not even the worst of it. You sent the man to his death. These are the citizens this country asks the most of, and you did it anyway. It was always going to happen. Even if the Hezbollah believed a Druze could switch sides, do you think the loonies over here would ever believe an Arab if they caught him doing such a thing? Someone dumb enough was always going to find out.'

Jonny can barely get his voice above a whisper as the final piece of the puzzle clatters into place. 'Farid was a double agent?'

Oren starts to nod, only for his expression to dissolve to panic at a sudden scrabble behind them. Jonny turns just in time to see the girl disappearing around the curve of the platform, on to the path. Finally his grandmother's attention turns to him, tugging at his arm.

'Go now,' she says urgently, stepping between him and Oren. 'Follow her, go on.'

'But you came,' Jonny says piteously, grasping her back so tightly she should flinch. except she doesn't, she doesn't move at all. 'Didn't you come for me? Aren't I the reason you're here?'

'No,' she replies stonily. 'I did not.'

'Do as she says, Jonny.' Oren's face turns completely blank as the sun crests the lip of the rock overhead.

'But why?' Jonny cries, nine years old again, trying to make sense of a pain he still doesn't understand. 'Why else would you come back here? After all this time?'

'Because this stupid fool and his cronies don't have the guts to do what needs to be done!'

'It's happening already.' Oren so close now he's almost on top of them. 'We're rigging the only tunnel that matters as we speak.'

Jonny looks wildly around the platform as if Rami and Dave will materialise out of thin air.

'It's not good enough just to rig it,' his grandmother hisses. 'Not now. Not after what's just happened on the other side. It needs to be foolproof. You can't take any more stupid risks. We need to collapse them all. We need to make them disappear.'

'They'll be out any second, I'm sure of it.' Oren twists round towards the mouth of the tunnel he came from. 'Please, Noa. No more innocents can die today.'

'Innocents? Have you forgotten what that word really means? None of us are innocent. We will never be innocent. The bodies of innocent women and children are still smoking less than twenty miles away!'

'Who are you?' Jonny screams at Oren, desperation bursting from him like vomit. 'How the hell do you know her name?'

'Who do you think he is?' his grandmother screams back. 'Only her father could be as stupid as her. She didn't get it from me!'

Jonny's head moves on his neck as if by itself, staring at one face, then the other.

These are his mother's parents.

He's finally found them – but is on the edge of losing them both all over again.

Oren must have suspected Jonny from the start because of the information he had. For how else would someone like Jonny have come by a classified intelligence leak as explosive as that? All the conversations they've had since flash through Jonny's head with an intensity that's almost painful. *What would you know about strategic intelligence, Jonny Murphy from the* International Tribune? Jonny stares at the older man's face – his *grandfather's* face – and makes sudden, nauseating sense of all the emotions he's watched flicker across it in the last few hours. Oren must hardly have been able to believe it – maybe he didn't even *want* to believe it. Not least because Geronimo has been pressuring him to use Jonny and the cover of his job in the most kamikaze way imaginable.

And now Jonny's grandmother is here too. Confirming it for good, only to leave them hanging on the precipice all over again.

Jonny's legs buckle, the initial shot of heady, distilled happiness fermenting to the most unimaginable kind of disappointment.

'Go now, Jonny.' Oren this time, beseeching him. 'Go back up to the kibbutz. You'll be safe there. I'll come back for you, I promise.'

'Like hell you will!' His grandmother releases Jonny to claw at Oren. 'Not if we do the job properly.'

'Stop!' Jonny cries as they tussle. 'You don't have to do this, Safta. I know who killed Farid. Please, just let me tell you everything...'

'As if it could ever be as simple as working out who killed Farid.'

Jonny reaches for Oren frantically. 'Your medical pack. Show it to me. Quick.'

Oren pins his grandmother with one hand, fumbling in his pocket with the other. Jonny's fingers slip as he unzips the case, registers the identity tag – the blood group, the allergy information, the clinical details as immaculate as Oren had said they would be. Then he feverishly checks off the contents neatly labelled and stored in its compact, uniform mesh pockets.

'I don't care who killed him,' she hisses. 'The fact that he died at all is enough. Another innocent life ... He should never have died in the first place.'

'Wait,' Jonny says as he reaches into his own pocket, pulls out the case he'd slipped from the girl's pocket as she dangled over his shoulder. Oren's grip slackens on his grandmother as he realises what he is doing, computes the significance of the object in his hands – inescapably red, no possible other colour it could be.

'Where did you get that?'

But Jonny ignores him, feverishly turning vials over so he can read their labels, prove it to himself once and for all, even though its identity tag has already told him all he needed to know.

'Look.' Jonny's voice quavers as he plucks at his grandmother. 'Safta, please, just look at the evidence.'

'Where did you get that?' Oren asks again, harsher this time.

'It doesn't matter,' Jonny gabbles. 'All that matters is what's inside, I mean, what's missing.'

Safta's eyes glitter as Oren drops her, reaching for the case and its contents.

'This is...'

'Moti's.' Jonny braces himself against the cliff face with a clammy hand. 'You said it yourself. No one can afford to be without the basics here. You are always on the defensive. Noradrenaline for anaphylaxis, insulin for diabetics. You even colour code the cases.'

'But how did you—?'

'You know how.' The steel is all Jonny's as he cuts Oren off again, the image of his mother hitting him so forcefully between the eyes that he has to screw them shut. 'She was a diabetic too, don't tell me you've forgotten that.'

Jonny doesn't need to say anything else. The realisation dawns on Oren so physically that he crumples to the floor, back sliding down the stone face of the cliff behind him.

'Moti killed Farid?'

'Unless you can explain why a diabetic is carrying around a medical case missing all its insulin at a time they could get stuck underground for hours, even days at a time, then yes. You'd never have let *her* do that. You said it yourself too. A puncture wound. An overdose. Undetectable to all but those who know how to inflict silent, invisible and deadly injury.'

'It doesn't matter anymore,' his grandmother says, whirling around in the mouth of the tunnel. 'I don't care who did it. He's the idiot still trying to prove himself right, not me. The tunnels have to go. The risk is still too great.'

Jonny screams as she unzips her jacket, blinking at the shapes laced around her waist, an impossible combination of knots that can't be undone because ... He freezes, dumbstruck, as he realises what they are.

She's wearing a belt made of explosives.

'Don't cry for me, boy.' His grandmother's eyes glitter as she gabbles feverishly, tightening knots, straightening cables. 'I was born to do this. I won't see my country betrayed any longer.'

Jonny falls to his knees, can only whisper. 'No, Safta. Please...'

'And don't you dare come after me, you stupid old fool.' She turns to Oren. 'Nothing can mess this up. Nothing...'

Her shouts die away into the call of the gulls overhead as she disappears into the dark.

And what's left of Jonny's legs gives out, except Oren's hands are under his armpits, refusing to let him go.

'There's more than one way out, Jonny.' Oren's hand is under his chin now, propping his face straight, willing him to return his gaze. 'I promise you. I'll save her, and I'll come back for you. Now I've found you both, I won't lose you again. But you need to go, and go now. Every second counts. Can you do this?'

His eyes find Jonny's, clear and hazel, a gaze suddenly as familiar as his own heartbeat.

'Go,' he repeats, lessening his grip, testing whether Jonny can stand on his own.

And just as Jonny balances, Oren turns, swallowed almost immediately by the cliffs.

Jonny staggers, crying out, for only the gulls to answer him.

He's alone again. And it's as if no one else was ever beside him.

Chapter Thirty-Nine

Sam cries out as Lola stumbles into the courtyard, soaked to the bone with sweat. The sun is approaching its apex, they couldn't be more exposed, but Lola is shivering as they collapse into each other, the familiar bumps and curves of her best friend's body the only thing not to feel alien. Her mind is still whirling with dark caves, dead bodies, coils and coils of copper wire. She's dimly aware of Andre at Sam's side, and the hovering shadows of others.

'Lola ... oh, my God. What's happened to you?' Sam pulls away, only to grab her again, burying her face in Lola's shoulder.

'How did you get out?' Lola whimpers into her hair, breathing in the familiar scent of Sam's Impulse body spray so deeply she tastes chemicals in her mouth.

'We just ran back the way we came ... Wait.' Sam cups her face, relief creasing to horror as she takes in the bruises and scratches all over Lola's body, the marks blackening her shorts and legs. 'You *were* down in the caves too? That's where you've been all along?'

Lola tries to brush it off, but the smell of chicken shit wafting from between the warehouses knots her throat. She thinks about losing so much more than she came here trying to find. Sam pulls her back into another hug, murmuring into her shoulder.

'Well, all that matters is you're here now. Come on, let's get you sorted out.'

'That is definitely not all that matters,' Andre grumbles next to her. 'Two people are dead now. We don't know who killed either of them, and Oren's still got all our passports.'

'What?' Lola stumbles as she hobbles alongside Sam out on to the perimeter road.

'He came to get them all last night,' Sam explains hurriedly. 'Paperwork, apparently. Never mind the fact we're all trapped until we get them back. I had no choice, I had to give him yours too. I had no idea where you were. We've all been frantic...'

'I'm sorry,' Lola mutters again. 'I just had to get away.'

'So you hid in the caves?' Sam whispers. 'Of all places?'

'Let's just get out of the sun, come on.' Lola stiffens as Tom interrupts, hand closing around her other arm. She flinches, only for his grip to tighten.

'And where the hell is Dave,' Andre mutters as they reach the shade of their shared courtyard. But Tom replies as if Lola's the one who's asked, fingers digging into her flesh.

'Still out looking for you, huh. Another man you've apparently got under your spell. Last I checked, he seemed to have some idea where you were.'

Sam bridles next to her. 'Leave it, would you, Tom? We've all had more than enough for one day.' She leads Lola up the stairs to their room. Tom's clutch mercifully falls away.

Lola props herself against the closed door while Sam rummages in a cupboard for a clean pair of shorts. Worry is still creased all over her face as she hands them to Lola, ushering her into the bathroom, turning the shower on full. Lola lets the cold water thunder, soak her filthy clothes, bite right to her bones.

'Take it all off, come on.' Sam drapes a towel over the lip of the sink. 'It happens to the best of us. You think I haven't seen it all before?'

Lola gulps, shivering, motioning that Sam should close the door.

Sam replies with a frown. 'Fine, but I'll be just outside, OK?'

The door clicks closed with a tinny rattle. Finally Lola is able to unbuckle her shorts. Only then does she realise what is missing from her pocket.

Panic seizes Lola all over again, coursing with the cold water. She squats, digging around in the soaking fabric with a wet hand.

Did Moti's medical case fall out inside the caves? Could it still be somewhere in the scrub on top of the cliff – just sitting there, waiting to be found? Perhaps it plummeted down into the banana plants skirting the edge of the path, surely no one will ever find it there?

Her nails scrape cracked tile as Lola rewinds to the moment she took it, willing it back into Moti's bloodstained pocket, insisting to herself that its personalised contents could never help her. She thinks about the sea filling the holes inside the cliff, picturing every tunnel submerging as if that will somehow get rid of the evidence itself, willing it to be as simple as the water swilling away into the drain – no longer rust-red and pink, finally transparent and clear.

Sam knocks on the door. 'Everything alright in there?'

'Fine, fine.' Lola squeaks the tap closed, head spinning. 'Do you mind passing me a pad? It's a heavy month, in case that wasn't already obvious.'

The door cracks open to reveal a cellophane-wrapped sanitary towel. Lola pushes it closed again to dress, trying not to move too much. Sam is still hovering just outside the door when she finally opens it.

'So what happened?' Sam asks again. 'Am I going to like the answer?'

'I just went...' Lola sits on her cot, stops herself from saying the banana fields. 'I just went to clear my head, is all. Farid—'

Sam snorts, getting up and walking over to the kettle in the far corner.

'There's a spot on the beach Farid showed me once. I went there. I don't know why. I guess because it made me feel close to him.'

There's a hiss as the water begins to heat up. 'You thought

sleeping on the beach was a good idea after everything that's happened?'

Lola shifts on her cot. 'Not exactly. Rami was down there too.'

'The night watchman?'

Lola nods. 'I lost track of time, and before I knew it, it was dark. He knew a way out through the cliffs.'

'Those caves, you mean?' Sam pours boiling water into two mugs before adding tea bags.

'Yes. It turns out he sleeps in them.'

'What? Why?'

Finally Lola is able to meet Sam's gaze as she hands her a steaming mug.

'It's complicated, but you'd understand it all better than most people, I think.'

A beat passes between them, no need to say any more about the cloak of disgrace Sam knows all too well. Lola blows on the surface of her tea, toys with a frond of steam.

Sam cradles her mug. 'Still, it's horrific. Sleeping in a cave?' She shivers. 'I'd never have even gone inside if I wasn't dumb with shock. The sight of the body will stay with me forever. We only went down there to look for you. Dave thought of it at the last minute. And then we found Moti.'

Sam groans, screwing her eyes shut. The memories move in for the kill, but Lola battles back. She thinks about Dave, about dead women and children, about how no one ever really knows anyone.

'I can still see it, you know. He was totally carpeted. Like a giant slug. Covered in blood – although it was black. What else could it have been? I suppose it could have been banana sap—'

Their door flies open with a bang. Sam leaps to her feet, mugs clattering to the floor. Through the window, Lola sees Tom frozen on the spot in the courtyard beyond. She stands up just in time to feel the tremor in the earth below.

Sam cocks her head to the sky, as if the siren will follow her lead.

And then Lola hears it.

The unmistakable rumble of rock, groaning as it rips apart.

Chapter Forty

Jonny's almost up and over the edge of the cliff when the rocks start to shake, his fingers slipping from the final notch before the top. He cries out, scrabbling with the other hand, digging a fingertip on to a sharp edge as if it will physically pin him to the side of the cliff. The mountain itself feels like it's swaying now, the hardscrabble clatter of scree rattling in his ears. He twists round to find nothing but bright-blue sea, the white-hot glare of the sun blinding him to anything else.

Shouts turn Jonny back to the cliff face only to find sunspots blacking out the face leaning over the edge, an arm fluttering just beyond his reach. His free hand mercifully finds purchase inside the top notch, and he is able to plaster himself to the cliff face just as the stone itself seems to wail, an unearthly cracking sound reverberating from deep inside the rock. Something coarse swats the side of his face – a coil of rope, flopping down alongside his body.

More exhortations from the top of the cliff. He can't bring himself to move an inch, the rock is shaking now, it's as if the whole cliff is protesting, the water has been pounding it for hundreds and thousands of years, and now it's being attacked from the inside as well.

But Jonny feels pinned not least by the weight of his own history. How can he clamber to safety knowing everything he's been so desperately searching for is about to die inside this cliff for the rest of time? His hands slip again as he realises he is clinging to a tomb, with more bodies buried inside than he may ever realise.

'Grab the rope, man!'

Jonny reflexively looks up before he can catch himself, the face hovering at the edge of the cliff crystallising for a second. He's seen it before – one of the volunteers. They've made it out of the caves in time, but has anyone else? Panic seizes Jonny as the face disappears, just enough for him to let go of the notch and take hold of the rope glancing off his arm. He pulls on it, barely testing its weight before propelling himself up and over the last few feet of rock face on to the tufty grass just inside the barbed-wire fence at the top.

The ground still feels like it's moving as Jonny flops, face down, fitting his body on to the narrow path between the back of the chicken house and the high wire fence. He's got nothing left, not even a speck of energy or will to move a single inch further, much less get up off the ground. Below him, buried deep inside the cliff, are the only two people that could possibly compel him to do anything again. The tears come as hot as they are sudden, steaming as they soak into the dirt under his cheek, as he thinks about how the only things able to take ownership of anything around here are the elements.

'Come on, it's OK.' That voice again, urging him on from beyond the gap in the fence. 'Everything has stopped shaking now.'

Except Jonny can still feel the tremors. His heart was already broken, and now it's shattering into tiny pieces.

'Hey, take my hand...'

Something clammy and warm lands on his shoulder. Jonny has to wipe soil from his eyes, only able to prop up his head with his chin. The volunteer, as thin as he is tall, is bent over him in an almost perfect fold. Jonny coughs grit out of his mouth with his thanks.

'No bother, man, but can you at least move away from the edge? You don't have to do anything else other than that.'

'Jo!' Jonny tenses as someone else shouts from behind the warehouse. 'What the fuck are you doing up here?'

The sun hits Jonny again as the man moves away, quivering. Another vaguely familiar face peers around the side of the warehouse, brightening as its owner realises who it is still lying almost face down in the dirt.

'Don't tell me,' Jonny mumbles, pushing himself to his knees. 'You're another one of the volunteers.'

'What's it to you?' Still, the man takes a step back, allowing Jonny to totter to his feet, and away from the edge of the cliff. He leans against the slatted wall almost as soon as he hits the shade.

The smaller man turns on Jo. 'Have you been talking to him? Spilling your guts as usual?'

The taller man quivers. 'No, man, are you crazy? I came to look for Dave. I had to. No sooner do we find Lola than we lose Dave. And people are going down all over the place. He's not in the *refet*, Andre. He must still be—'

'Shit.' The two men turn to look back through the gap in the fence.

'Hey, did you come up that way?' The smaller man – Andre – addresses Jonny directly, making him start. 'Well? Is he still down there or what?'

'I'm s-sorry,' Jonny stutters, trying to buy time. 'Who do you mean?'

'He doesn't know him.' Jo puts his hand on Andre's shoulder. 'Why would he?'

'Well, he's a journalist.' Andre folds his arms as he stares at Jonny. 'They always know a whole lot more than they are willing to let on.'

'That hardly matters now.'

'Ya, of course it does.' The smaller man shrugs off Jo, keeps staring at Jonny. 'What's a journalist doing digging around here, anyway? Two dead bodies: what a story, huh? Sniffing around hoping it gets even better?'

Jonny watches Andre's eyes darting ... where? The hairs on the back of his neck stand free of sweat as he realises the gap in the fence is still only a step or so behind him. Suddenly the smaller man is right in Jonny's face.

'Lucky for you it was Jo that found you up here, hey,' he hisses, undercurrent of alcohol raw on his breath. 'I might not have thrown you a rope if I'd got here first.'

'Andre...' Jo tries and fails to pull him back.

'Now if I were you, I wouldn't ferret around this place much longer.' Andre is so close now the alcohol is unmistakable – cheap vodka, practically stronger than white spirit. 'Can't you tell it already stinks? You don't need to be inside a chicken house to know that.'

Reflexively, Jonny takes a step backward, only to find the precipice at his back again.

'I'd be really careful, hey. Really fucking careful—'

Suddenly the air crystallises into something unmistakably solid, moving with such velocity that all three men are thrown back down into the alley between the warehouses, landing in a tangle of limbs, sweat and earth.

Jonny hears it before he can fully understand it – Hebrew, then Arabic, then Hebrew followed by an embrace so tight it chokes the air from his lungs. The Hebrew continues, words he's only ever dreamt of hearing again: 'My boy, my son, my love.'

'Oren? Is Dave with you?'

But Jonny barely registers the tremor in Jo's voice, so enveloped in the pure, solid truth he's been searching for his entire life.

Oren said he'd come back for him, and he has.

Oren is his grandfather. Finally someone hasn't let him down.

There's a scuffle as the men all separate themselves, Jonny still clinging to Oren. He feels like he may never be able to let go.

'Oren?' Johan asks again, quivering on his feet. 'We found Lola. She's alright, but no one can find Dave.'

'What the fuck is going on, old man?' A waft of vodka from Andre again, so strong it cuts even through chickenshit.

'Nothing you need to concern yourself with, Andre,' Oren replies crisply, keeping his arms folded tightly around Jonny.

'Hah! Well, I'll have my passport back then, hey.'

'Of course you can have your passports back. There's nothing sinister going on here, Andre...'

'There are two bodies on the ground, old man! And sure as shit we have a journalist here sniffing around in the dirt where he belongs.'

Jonny's breath catches as the smaller man sways on his feet. The sun is at Andre's back, it's impossible to see his face clearly.

'I think he's got what he came for.' Oren squeezes Jonny's arm. 'I'm not sure this is the place to have that conversation, though.'

Andre lets out an unpleasant laugh. Jo reaches for him again.

'For fuck's sake, man!' Andre stumbles as he throws his arms above his head. 'I know you still need all the looking-after you can get, Jo, but I don't, hey—'

'But I'm—'

'Just fucking stop touching me—'

Jonny panics as Oren drops him, stepping forward just a beat too late. Time slows as the two men tussle, stumble, and finally scream, damned by a predictably toxic combination of determination, alcohol, and ultimately, gravity. They reel backward through the gap in the fence as one, banana plants crackling as they plunge off the cliff.

Chapter Forty-One

'What is this?' Sam cowers on their grimy bedroom floor. 'An earthquake? A fucking earthquake?'

The cot Lola's lying on sways gently from side to side.

'No,' she murmurs, curiously lulled by its rhythm. She knows there are fault lines all over the place up here. But she knows just as well this is no earthquake.

The open door creaks as it bangs closed again. Lola squints at the shapes pixelated through the mosquito net at the window, tries to work out which is moving.

'I think it's stopped.' Sam rolls on to her knees, hunching reflexively. 'Hasn't it?'

Lola rubs her face against the rough cotton sheets. She thinks about all the fault lines that her beloved geography lessons miss, as if the shape of the land is only ever a simple matter of plate tectonics.

Sam stands, walking the few paces to the door. 'Hang on...'

And Tom is inside almost as soon as Sam opens it.

Lola shrinks into her sheet, willing that the walls start moving again. This room is already crowded with so much. Can it handle the extra weight of Tom's emotional baggage? He pauses, hovering just past the doorway. It's as if he's wondering the exact same thing.

'Everyone alright?'

'I think so.' Sam peers past him into the courtyard. 'What the hell was that? The walls were shaking, I swear. And the floor. The ground, I mean. Was it another rocket?'

'Can't have been,' he replies. 'We'd have heard whistling. I was outside. There were these weird creaks and rumbles, the ground sort of shook, but then it all just stopped.'

Sam pushes past him, shouting for Andre and Johan.

'Where's everyone gone?' she calls back to Tom through the window.

He looks at Lola as he shrugs. 'Search me.'

Sam's back in the room almost immediately, mumbling to herself, picking up one of the mugs that's rolled into the corner.

'Amazing, huh?' Tom is still hovering in the doorway. 'Those things never shatter. They can't be made of real glass.'

'I suppose you're going to tell me you could use a cup of tea now, too.' Sam flicks the kettle back on without waiting for him to answer.

Tom's wry laugh rings hollow as Lola turns away, tracing a finger along the wall above her cot. She pictures the shiny squares plastered all over the same spot on Sam's side of the room, snapshots of smiles hiding the lies underneath. The slow boil of their ancient electric kettle bubbles into the silence.

'Do you think we're all just supposed to go back to work?' The water hisses as Sam busies herself with their tea things.

'I really have no idea.' Tom sighs. 'But I'm grateful as hell that I wasn't standing under glass just now.'

'Maybe that's where the boys are,' Sam murmurs.

Tom snorts. 'Miracles do happen, I guess.'

More murmurs move back and forth as Sam passes him a tea. Lola feels his eyes on her back.

'Are you sure you're alright, Lola?'

'Of course she isn't.' Sam sits down next to her with an audible huff. 'None of us are. I've never experienced anything like that before in my life.'

'Neither have I,' he replies. 'And I hope I don't ever experience anything like it again.'

Lola closes her eyes, just for a moment, only for the inanimate object sprawled in the dirt to take its name again in the dark.

It will always have a name, Lola thinks, little crescents of light dancing inside her eyelids. Even if she manages to ignore it while she's awake, it will be lying in wait in her sleep. Nightmares are only ever a version of reality. And now she's even got an earthquake pointing out how her world will never be as stable as she hopes.

'I just...' Sam trails off. Lola opens her eyes to find tears leaking out of Sam's. 'It's all ending, isn't it? I can't bear it.'

'What is?' Tom asks.

'This.' Sam gestures around the room with her free hand. 'It'll make the international papers, how can it not? Rockets, two dead bodies and now a fucking earthquake. It doesn't matter who killed either of them. My folks will have me loaded on the first plane out. And I just don't want it to end.' Sam's crying now, big snotty sobs out of nowhere. 'But it already has, hasn't it? I can't bear it, how can you? It was all so simple up here, so perfect...'

Tom snorts. 'Nothing that simple could ever be real.' His mug hits a side table with a clunk. 'It's the same story for the whole of Australia. The miracle of our vast and beautiful land, except it's built on one great lie. That's why I had to leave. Anyone who never does just starts believing it's true.'

Suddenly Lola is able to sit up, look him in the eye. Except Tom's head is still bowed, fingers tangling with each other in his lap.

'People out here go through more in a year than most of us will ever experience in a lifetime.' Tom's voice takes on a sharper edge. 'That's the reality of the place. That's why people like us need to experience it. Otherwise we'd never really understand anything.'

'What do you mean?' Lola hears someone ask, stunned to find it's her.

'I think you know exactly what I mean,' he replies softly, reaching out towards her, the object dangling between his fingers so familiar Lola feels lost without it, yet so alien in its current position she can't believe it's actually there.

'I only came in to give you this. You're not safe without it, right?'

The bracelet, the one that Lola can never take off, the reinforced silver chain coiled with knotted red string either side of a metal identity plate embossed with her name and life-saving medical information, swings between his fingers.

'Lola!' Sam gasps, yanking it from Tom's hand. 'Oh, my God...'

'You must have lost it at work sometime.' Even as he wipes an eye, Tom's gaze never leaves hers. 'I found it in the banana fields, this morning. Couldn't believe it myself, but sure enough. I guess that's why they make them in red, huh.'

He pauses, Lola's breath coming in little gasps as she stares back at him.

'And besides. I've never met anyone else who's allergic to penicillin.'

'Fucking hell...' Sam continues swearing as she forces the bracelet over Lola's grazed knuckles. 'If I'd ended up having to jab you with the yellow pen after everything that's happened in the last two days...'

'But how...' The rest of the question is choked out of her throat as Lola realises there is only one possible reason her allergy bracelet can have come loose in the only possible place Tom can have found it. She'd been so busy taking Moti's medical pack in some misguided attempt to further protect herself that she hadn't noticed losing something even more incriminating.

'It's physical work down there, huh? Fighting with those plants.' His eyes bore into hers. 'You should wear more than one. If it's honestly so dangerous for you to take it accidentally...'

'Of course it is!' Sam exclaims. 'She could die. I've still got the scar from where I fell down legging it for the yellow pen once—'

'Like I say,' Tom cuts her off, lifting his hands only to drop them again. 'Banana plants can be aggressive little fuckers.'

Chapter Forty-Two

Jonny's legs wipe out from under him; it's as if he hasn't been standing at all. There's a howl coming from somewhere, keening with the thousands of chickens teeming on the other side of the slatted wall. Oren is on the ground too, flat on his belly, his boots in Jonny's face as he peers through the gap in the fence over the edge of the cliff.

Jonny wills that his hand reach out and grasp Oren's ankle instead of remaining stubbornly curled into the foetal position. Not a single part of his body will obey instructions. Oren could plunge back over the side too and Jonny can't even make his arms twitch, he can't even get words out of his mouth because there's shit in his face now, of course there is, it's all over the ground, there isn't a single square inch of earth under his body that isn't covered in some sort of excrement. It's foul, it's coating his nose and mouth, he can hardly breathe until he finally vomits out every last speck of his insides.

A shadow falls over him, Oren, back from the literal edge, moaning as he tries and fails to lift Jonny out of the bile soaking into the dirt.

'What the fuck do we do now?' Jonny coughs into the mud. 'Are they dead too? Is that just what happens around here? Everybody dies? And nobody gives a shit?'

Oren leans back against the wall of the warehouse. There's a clamour on the other side as the chickens scatter.

'You couldn't stop her, could you?' Jonny lifts his head only to drop into the mud again the second he sees the stricken expression on Oren's face. 'Of course you couldn't.' He digs and scrapes at the earth below his fingers, so solid for something that was most definitely moving only a few short minutes ago.

Oren lets out a long, deep sigh. 'No, Jonny. I couldn't. But—' His breath catches before he can continue.

Finally Jonny is able to push himself out of the mud. He leans against the opposite wall, hanging his arms on top of his knees.

'What about Rami and Dave?'

'I don't know, Jonny.'

'What do you mean, you don't know? How many of these tunnels are there?'

'Enough that I couldn't try to find them if I wanted to make it out myself.'

'How many bodies are buried inside this fucking mountain? Do you people even know?'

'I suppose we don't.' Oren hangs his head.

'And you don't care either?'

'Of course we do—'

'Don't lie to me!' Jonny yells. 'It doesn't matter anymore, does it? Because the tunnels are gone. The land is safe. The empire is intact. So who gives a shit?'

'Listen to me...' Oren shakes him, gripping his shoulders tight. 'Of course I care. Every death is a waste. Every single one. Moti...' His voice catches.

A sound escapes from Jonny, so evil and twisted he can hardly believe it came from him.

'Well, I suppose there's a murder that matters,' Jonny spits bitterly. 'A founder member of the kibbutz, cut down with his own machete.'

Oren lets out a cry. Jonny looks out to sea, unable to see anything but sky, a uniform expanse of flame blue.

'I can't believe it,' the older man mumbles after a moment. 'I can't believe he would be so short-sighted not to see what Farid was really doing. Or even ask. How can you be sure—'

'I am sure. Moti killed Farid. Rami as good as told me.' Jonny peers at the sky.

'Rami? When?' Oren straightens against the warehouse wall. 'But you'd never even met Moti. How did you come upon his medical case?'

Another howl rises and falls in the background. Relief suddenly cascades with the sweat down Jonny's back as he realises where it is coming from.

'I found it in the caves,' he replies shortly.

'I don't understand,' Oren mumbles, rubbing his head. 'Where?'

But Jonny is saved from saying anything else as the dog, its lonely little bloodhound nose working overtime, comes miraculously skittering down the alley from her spot opposite chicken house number one to launch herself squarely at Oren, finally finding a hint of a scent she can trust.

For of course traces of Farid are still all over Oren. He found his dead body.

Jonny reaches out with a shaky hand, lets it quiver in the air even though he knows the hound won't touch it. This is a dog that's only after her master. She literally clambered through rocks to keep trying. The fact she also found his trace all over another dead man's medical case told Jonny the last thing left that he needed to know. There must have been one hell of a scuffle between the two of them, that's for sure. Jonny looks away, mind suddenly filling with grotesque explanations as to why the bloodstained girl he'd found hiding inside the caves might have come to have that same case in her possession too.

'Look at me, Jonny.'

His mother's face, as Jonny turns, is suddenly clearer than it's ever been – her smile, her laugh, Jonny's skin tingling as it recalls the depth of her squeeze, the one she used to give him every night as she tucked him into bed, whispering how much she loved him even through her ever-present tears. And in spite of everything, hope, that most capricious and damning emotion of all, starts to bud from deep within the void in Jonny's chest.

'Is Safta … is she really gone?'

'She must be.' Oren hangs his head, face fighting to maintain its shape. 'She was only carrying a small charge, but she will have needed to detonate it with precision accuracy to collapse the only tunnel that mattered without making a material difference to the mountain.'

Jonny has to look away once more as Oren's hazel eyes swim. To watch those eyes run with tears is to watch his mother die all over again. And he hasn't even told his grandparents this final agonising truth yet either.

'All she ever did was fall in love,' Jonny murmurs. 'How can that ever be so terrible? So terrible that her own parents would cut her off?'

'You look so like her, you know.' Oren's hazel eyes – his own, Jonny realises – appraise him through the tears. 'I always wondered if you did. Or whether, as the boy, you'd have grown up to have looked more like him.'

'My father, you mean?'

Oren nods. 'I was always able to blame him as well as her. But your grandmother, she could never get past what your mother did. It went against everything she felt as a mother herself. It was the only thing that could break that bond.'

Jonny opens his mouth again, finds a sob there, swallows it. He stares into the sky, thinks about its infinite depths.

'Your grandmother chose to forget it rather than try to understand it. It was easier for her that way. I was able to do the same, for a time. Until it soured her so much she couldn't even look at me. I reminded her of everything she had lost. I became complicit, just for looking like her. That's why I came back here. At least this way I could feel closer to her. To my daughter. And now…'

Oren has to pause, so Jonny finishes the sentence for him.

'...They're both gone.'

'Yes. But I've found you.'

This time Jonny is able to hold Oren's gaze, even swimming with tears, so intoxicatingly familiar he feels the heat start to bloom in his chest. He thinks about how everything comes into play in a community like this. The ghosts of the past haunt every step in a place this interconnected.

'She sent me up here, you know – Safta did. She must have wanted me to find you too. It can't just have been about the tunnel.'

Oren nods, a small smile turning the corners of his mouth.

'Is that how you figured it out?' Jonny asks.

'I suspected. This is information people like us take to our graves. It is beyond treason to spill it. Especially to a junior reporter at the *International Tribune*. Then I found out who your editor was.'

Jonny blinks at him. 'Allen?'

'Rivka, you mean. Rivka Allen. Your mother met her in the air force. They served their whole stint together. At least Rivka was her given name before she disappeared off to America, where no one could spell it.'

Jonny rubs at his head, this latest revelation almost painful.

'Why didn't she tell me?' he asks himself, as much as Oren.

'Rivka won't have known who you were. I don't know how closely they kept in touch – we didn't have air mail back then. America may as well have been the moon. But Rivka had an inkling of what both of us did, back in the day. I'm pretty sure she figured out that we were in the intelligence services. And still are now, I suppose I should say. Perhaps it lodged in her subconscious when you told her about your tip.'

Oren has to stop again, take a breath. His eyes are full of fresh tears as Jonny meets them.

'But I knew your name. I had that much to go on. When I saw you I couldn't allow myself to believe it until it was real. It's like when I saw her, too. Now I know it really is. I'm looking at it with my own eyes. Now I finally have all the pieces.'

Jonny shakes his head as a smile breaks out over Oren's face, perfect teeth flashing shiny white against the mud and dirt all over it.

'Pieces of what? Of the family you broke yourselves? You punished her just because she fell in love with the wrong man. You drove her to do everything she did—'

'No.' Oren holds up a grimy hand. 'What she did was unforgivable. You are right that by then, we couldn't have stopped her. We were the enemy. I'll never forgive myself for that. If we hadn't pushed her away so quickly, would she have listened to us when we tried to intervene? We could never have stopped her falling in love, but we could have stopped her ripping her own family apart if she still trusted us enough to listen.'

Jonny props a shaking hand against the slatted wall. The dog barks as he wobbles to his feet. He hasn't come this far to have it all thrown back in his face again. No. He opens his mouth to reply, finds himself yelling all over again.

'She didn't rip it apart. You did! You disowned her while she was still living under your nose. I've seen the apartment even if I'll never remember living in it. You must have had to look through her, literally stare straight past her, and me, hundreds of times. Nahariyya isn't exactly a heaving beach town. She even had the grace not to try and stay on the kibbutz, even though she'd have been perfectly within her rights to. Instead she followed you to Nahariyya, gave you every opportunity to change your minds. And when you didn't, what did you expect her to do other than move away, try and start again with her new family? You treated her worse than you treat the animals around here!'

Rami's words come back to haunt Jonny then. Unless it's an

olive, a chicken or a banana, no one wants to know. Because they occupy the land far more effectively than humans or animals ever could. Their only loyalty is to the hand that feeds them.

'You were both so young,' Oren says softly, eyes fixed somewhere firmly back in the past. 'You won't remember everything we tried to do to stop her. Afterwards it was all I could do to come back here, feel her presence in the community around me...'

'You make me sick.' Jonny glares at Oren. 'This whole place does. It's a cult, not a community. There's no room for tolerance, or difference. It's just about blind faith.'

'Isn't that all family ever is? Blind faith? I have to believe that's the only reason she did it—'

'I can't believe all I've ever wanted to do was find you.' Jonny has to bite back more tears, suddenly overwhelmed by a cocktail of exhaustion, frustration and disappointment. 'I thought if I could just come here, make sense of where they met, how it all happened, try and live it for myself, it would somehow fix everything, that finally it would all make sense.'

'You have to actually have lived our whole experience, Jonny. You have to have endured the losses, made the decisions we've all had to make, again and again in the heat of battle. No one can understand it until they've done it themselves.'

'And that's why you can justify disowning us forevermore? Making her feel like she was worth less than the chickenshit all over your shoes? All because she betrayed you for a Catholic? You're right, by the way, because it turned out he wasn't worth even a second of her time – all the more stupid, really, because if there's ever going to be any outsiders that get your "lived experience" it's most definitely the Irish.'

'No, Jonny.' The dog whimpers as Oren suddenly stands, gathering Jonny's flailing hands into his in one fluid motion. 'That's not why.'

'Well then...'

'You don't know, do you?'

Jonny tries to wrench his hands free. 'Know what? What the hell are you talking about?'

'There was a sister, Jonny. There was a sister. And your mother gave her up. She let her go.'

Chapter Forty-Three

Lola's fingers are laced into her bracelet so tight with shock that when the door flies open again, the tips are white. And this time there are two other people framed on the threshold.

'What the hell is going on, boss?' Tom's voice quavers, Oren looming from the doorframe. But it's Jonny who answers, shouldering past to plant himself opposite them.

'Where are you from?'

'Melbourne.' Tom rocks back on his heels. 'Ivanhoe, to be precise. What's it to you?'

No one replies. Jonny only seems to have eyes for Lola.

Acid rises in her throat. They're coming for her. They must be. There's no other explanation. This is where Lola's choices narrow down to one. Instead of shaking, their bedroom's four walls seem to solidify around her.

'What's this about?' Sam now, a few feet away.

Oren steps forward, physically blocking her out. 'Answer him, Lola, come on now. Where are you from?'

But there's a plug in her throat – guilt, the only emotion Lola's got left, and it's choking her.

'Who are you?' Tom squares up to the other two men. 'Why does a journalist care about where we're from?

'It's alright.' Oren holds up his hands. 'It's just—'

Suddenly Jonny is in front of her, taking her hand, cradling it in his own.

'I carried you out of that cave,' he murmurs. 'You'd never have made it otherwise. I promise you, I'm not trying to catch you out.

I just want to know where you're from.'

Lola's hand drifts to her elbow, assesses the evidence. Ridges roll beneath her fingers – livid scratches, pockmarked rocks. She relives the moment she stepped inside the cave, when all she saw was a stone cell locked inside a mountain. And how it was Jonny who stopped her being trapped inside.

The plug loosens, if only for a second. Jonny nods back at her as Lola meets his eye.

'Just outside...' She has to stop, clear her throat. 'Just outside London.'

'What about your parents? Are they English, too?'

Lola hesitates.

'Caroline,' she says softly, as that is what her mum would want her to say, because only Holly calls her Mum, and Lola is far too grown-up to call her anything but Caroline, so Lola does, because one day it might feel right, except all it ever feels is anything but.

'Caroline? That's your mother's name? Caroline—?'

'What are you after, a family tree?' Tom interrupts.

'As it happens, yes.' Jonny's eyes are still trained on hers as he answers. 'What about your dad? Where's he from?'

She shrugs. 'My step-dad's English. I never really knew my biological father.'

'Why?' Jonny's eyes widen rather than narrow.

Lola looks away. 'Caroline didn't like to talk about him much.'

'Because...?'

'He left when I was tiny. She remarried. They had another baby. The usual story.'

'Why does any of this matter to you?' Sam's walking over only to pull up short as Oren takes something out of his pocket. Lola's breath stills in her throat.

'Caroline,' Jonny murmurs, reaching out with his free hand to take the small, oblong leather booklet from Oren – a passport.

Hers? She tries to loosen her hand from his grip but the movement just seems to makes him hang on tighter.

'What are you doing with all our passports?' Tom asks, but Jonny still only has eyes for Lola.

'You've got a curious middle name.' He pins the passport open with his fingers – hers, it must be. 'Murphy,' he muses, almost to himself. 'Did Caroline ever tell you where it came from?'

'It's her dad's,' Sam scoffs. 'Making sure they all had the same last names was one less question for that daft cow to answer when she got married again.'

But it's as though Sam hasn't spoken at all, Jonny's eyes just flicking between Lola's face, her passport, and then back again. Someone else is literally holding her identity in their hands, and even now Lola doesn't want to claim it as her own. She thinks of all the times Caroline's face closed over whenever she asked. How she would turn to Holly at every available opportunity. How she would shut down Lola's worries about Richard lest they threaten the new family she'd worked so hard to build – for them *all*, Caroline would say, pointedly staring back at her until Lola had to look away. And now Lola is having to do it all over again. Gazing around the squalid room, at her fetid little slice of real estate, the truth is hitting her squarely in the face: sometimes people will tell themselves anything if it makes them feel like they belong.

'It's a stupid name,' she eventually replies, blinking back a single tear. 'I hate it.'

Jonny is still gripping her hand as he turns to Oren. 'Are you kidding me? That's all you've been going on? Her middle name and the fact we share a birthday? Have you completely lost your mind?'

'I told you, Jonny. There's a simple enough way to settle this. Call your mother. Ask her outright.'

Lola knows they are still talking, but all she can hear is buzzing, keening louder and louder in her ears. There's no way back, she thinks. Not after what she's done. Lola threatened her so-called family that she might never come back, and now she'll return in handcuffs, with no pity from the people she wants it from the most.

And Caroline will have the loudest last laugh of all. She'll finally be able to justify her behaviour because of what Lola has done.

Because she's a murderer. That's what she is. Lola killed a man. The fact she had to doesn't change the most inescapable fact of all.

'Just ask her, Jonny.' Oren's shout pierces in.

Is it safer to confess when the police are actually here? Lola's knuckles start to crunch and roll together as Jonny keeps squeezing her hand.

'I can't,' he tells Oren dully. 'No one can. Because she's dead.'

Chapter Forty-Four

Jonny runs a thumb over the leather, over this small oblong booklet allegedly hiding a sister in its pages, the very same sister he never knew he had apparently cowering before him, heat of shame spread all over her face. He flips it open again, traces out the numbers of his own birthday with a fingertip.

Is it possible that where he only ever sees one, there are actually supposed to be two?

Two highchairs, two cots, two buckets and spades in that dusty hallway in Nahariyya?

Two voices, babbling nonsensically, only silencing when one is curled into the other?

Two halves of a whole? Two sides of a coin? Much like the passport he's got in one hand, a match only to the clammy palm still clasped in his other?

Jonny taps the edge of the passport to his temple as if he can physically show it to the figure inside: his mother, her constant presence, as always, both comfort and shadow. Is it possible that she could have sanctioned this? Actually decided to separate her own twins? To let his father leave with Jonny's sister, only so he would leave them in peace for good?

Who could do that? What mother could ever do that? What mother could ever *choose*, even on pain of death?

Somewhere behind him, Jonny hears the cry of an animal, a sound that by rights should be alien, except to him is only ever nauseatingly familiar, and in that moment he realises it's coming from Oren. It's the animal sound of grief, the primal wail of despair.

It's a sound he knows all too well. The realisation breaks out over Jonny in a sickening rush of adrenaline.

For this is what really killed Jonny's mother. This is why she made those same sounds, over and over again until she died. She couldn't go on living with what she'd done. No one ever recovers from the loss of a child.

Jonny squints at the girl, at the mute incomprehension painted all over her face. Is he supposed to believe that this is what his father looked like? The legendary Patrick Murphy? There's nothing familiar about this girl, nothing at all. They share the same colouring, Jonny supposes, but don't millions of other white people, with their forgettable hair, all various shades of mousy brown?

'Lola, right?'

The girl looks directly at Jonny then, blue eyes heavily rimmed in red. She shrugs as the Australian tries to rest an arm around her shoulders.

Jonny searches those blue eyes – not even hazel, he notes – willing that he find something he recognises. Willing that this absurd fantasy be right, at the same time as wishing it wrong. He should feel *something*, he's sure he should. He should feel something other than numb. But his stomach only twists, suddenly and emphatically, as Jonny remembers the single thing he knows for sure about this girl in front him. The leather medical case still stashed in his pocket suddenly weighs heavy as lead.

'What happened?' Oren's cries find words from somewhere behind him. 'How did she die?'

'They told me she took her own life,' Jonny says, trying to hold on to Lola's eyes. 'I was nine. They had to tell me she killed herself before I understood.'

He turns to the older man, curled into a shell of himself against the wall.

'I guess it's only now that I finally do,' he adds softly.

'But I wrote to her,' Oren cries. 'After she wrote to us, told us what she'd done – your grandmother burned the letter, but not before I had the address. She said he was making her life hell and it was the only hope she had of living in peace.'

'He? You mean my dad?'

But Oren just wails all over again at the thought. 'I told you. It's unthinkable. We could never forgive her.'

'If you had the address, why didn't you come? Why didn't you try and stop her?' And why didn't you come and find me? Jonny wants to add.

'We did – I did, I mean,' Oren says. 'But you'd already gone. She warned us we would never find her. She knew she had to keep moving, she said. Or he'd kill her.'

'Stop it.' Jonny drops Lola's hand to put his own over his ears. 'Stop making excuses for your own behaviour.'

'People do unspeakable things in the name of peace, Jonny,' Oren whispers. 'Every time I thought I'd seen it all, something else would come along that was worse...'

So why was his mother's decision any different? Jonny wants to counter. His default setting is still stuck on defending her to the end.

Except he can't even get a whisper out. His body knows, even if his mind won't comply, that there's no defence left. Suddenly he becomes aware of the two others still in the room, moving closer to Lola's either side.

'You're a journalist?' she asks as if no one else is speaking.

Jonny nods, parroting back the only words he's got left. 'I'm from the *International Tribune*.'

Time slows as they stare at each other, two equally lost, shocked and disbelieving expressions. It's all coming together in a picture Jonny doesn't want to see.

Can he believe this? Does he want to? To accept that he has a twin sister is also to accept that his mother, the one person he has spent his life trying to find reflections of, could have willingly allowed them to be separated – worse, could have colluded in this separation for so long that she took it to her grave?

Even if Oren's story is true – the acid rises just at the thought, Jonny has to swallow it back down. Even if it is true, surely the so-called evidence that this long-lost twin sister is sitting here right in front of him is no more than a couple of coincidences? Lola – it's not even the given name in her passport, nor a Jewish or Israeli one at that. If Oren couldn't even find Jonny with one address to go on, how can he plausibly have established this girl's connection to him other than via total fiction? They're dealing with common names here. There are multiple different Murphy clans. And birthdays are shared by literally millions of people. Jonny can accept that a desperate father might clutch at flimsy, ridiculous straws, but not Jonny, oh no. He's a journalist. He deals in facts. He doesn't deal in emotion. Jonny stopped dealing in emotion light years ago. He had to. He wouldn't have survived otherwise.

But with that the most inconvertible fact of all lands with a sickening thud.

Jonny realises he's been concentrating on the wrong question because he can't face up to its only conceivable answer.

For what father would make it up?

What father would conjure a story about his daughter willingly separating her twin children for any reason other than the truth? The only question left is whether he really has found everything he has been searching for all along.

There's a whisper in Jonny's ear now, an echo from the past. What had his mother said to him the night before she never woke up? Even though she whispered it in Hebrew, he's sure she told him he would find a piece of himself here if he ever came back to look.

Is this what she meant? How could she possibly have known? Finally Jonny sees them for what they are, all the images he'd conjured for himself of Beit Liora playing through his mind, these fanciful imaginings of the place where he might find himself, where he might finally understand, where in actual fact, he's found himself on top of most twisted truth of all, and it's only happened by accident. And where, in actual fact, his long-lost grandfather has become so desperate he has tricked himself into the most deluded conclusion of all.

The girl cowering on the floor before Jonny comes slowly back into focus, as obviously unrelated to him as it is obvious too that somewhere out there, who the hell knows where, is another girl who is. Another girl who Jonny is now going to spend the rest of his life searching for, too.

But before he can ask his last and final question, the door opens into a collective gasp, a wiry shadow falling into the room.

Jonny's heart kicks at his chest.

For the next words he hears arrive in a language that he will forever understand.

Chapter Forty-Five

Tom steps forward, hands out. Lola gasps. There's an old woman standing in the doorframe, scuffed military-issue boots, army fatigues stained and torn, huge rips in the fabric around her waist. Rapid-fire Hebrew ricochets around the room, Jonny and Oren waving and shouting as they barrel towards the door. Behind the old woman appear the quivering figures of a shirtless and scratched Andre and a filthy, crazed Jo, shuffling past the commotion towards them.

'What the hell happened to you?' Tom asks.

'She saved us,' Jo stutters, wobbling on his feet as he jerks his head at the tiny woman, still gesticulating and shouting in Hebrew. 'She did. We slipped, and—'

'Where?' Sam exclaims.

'Up by the chicken houses,' Jo gabbles. 'We went back to look for Dave.'

The dead women and children are back in Lola's mind, surrounded by smoking canisters of gunpowder, twisted together by copper wire.

'Slipped? What do you mean, slipped?' Tom continues.

'Over the edge,' Andre mutters.

'I caught him,' Jo explains, fighting the smile threatening at the corners of his mouth. 'I did. I just reached out and grabbed everything I could – good job too as I might have thrown myself off the cliff behind him if I hadn't, hey. After that it was all we could do to just hang on and hope.'

'And what about Dave? Did you find him?' Sam's hand twitches towards Andre.

Jo's eyes fill with tears, spilling cartoonishly down his cheeks.

'She said he didn't make it out...' he whispers, jerking his head at the old woman. 'That he was still trapped inside when the rocks cracked. It was the first thing I asked when she pulled us back up – thought she must have seen him somewhere down there too if she'd found us, hey. We need to go back and try again, pronto...'

His whisper fades out as the woman steps forward, speaking in broken, heavily accented English. Lola flinches at the sound of her voice, raspy and deep, aggressive without having to try.

'This is her?' A bony finger waves in Lola's direction.

'Yes,' Oren replies eagerly, eyes shining. 'It is.'

The woman advances, an unreadable expression across her heavily lined face.

'What do you want with Lola?' Sam asks.

Tom's hand lands heavy on her shoulder. And the words suddenly come pouring out, with no resolve left to hold them back.

For Tom knows what she did. He's going to tell everyone anyway.

So she needs to instead. Fast.

'He-he just ... he just came at me,' she gibbers, pulling and yanking at the bracelet on her wrist. 'There was no one else around. We were in the furthest banana field. There's nothing else down there but the sea. There was no other way to protect myself.'

'What are you talking about?' Sam kneels next to her, eyes filling with horror.

'He wouldn't stop. I had to make it stop!'

Lola's screaming now, she's trying to keep calm, to make her case, but it's just a wall of sound, every last detail pouring out of her – the disgust, the shame, the terror, the desperation.

The defence.

Her only defence.

The questions that come next are so heavy with unspeakable pain and disbelief that she has to cover her ears. But the voice she hears is so unexpected her hands fall away almost immediately.

'It's true,' Tom says. 'He attacked her. Moti, that is. I saw the whole thing.'

Lola knows he's still talking but all she can hear is the crackle of banana leaves, the desolate wail of a hound, the swell and crash of an angry sea.

'Saw what?' Sam's voice rings around the room.

'A dirty old man taking what wasn't his.'

Lola gapes at Tom as he keeps talking. She can't bring herself to listen even as he blames himself for not acting, as to listen would be to relive it all, to put herself through every last second of it again.

'So get out of my way, would you, Oren? Let her do her job.' Tom nods at the old woman, still frozen on the spot in front of them. 'You're police, right? Or military?' He sighs. 'Never mind. It's all the same up here, isn't it? Whoever's side you're on, I know it's not mine.'

And the only picture Lola needs to see again comes inexorably into focus. She closes her eyes, forces herself to take in every detail.

Tom must have followed her into the banana fields and witnessed everything, only to freeze at the critical moment.

And Tom could never live with that.

Finally some warmth blooms in Lola's mind, fingers stealing back to the bracelet looped around her wrist. All those times that Tom has tried to make her see that it really is as simple as how much he cares about her.

Tom let it happen. But he's still got a chance to change the ending.

When she finally opens her eyes, all she sees is Jonny, still holding on to her passport. He steps forward, reaching out for her hand again.

'Teresa Murphy Brookes,' he murmurs, grip cool and soft.

'Everyone calls her Lola,' Sam grumbles. 'And no, before you ask, she's not a fucking showgirl.'

'What's so wrong with Teresa?' Jonny taps the edge of the passport with a finger.

'It was after my dad, too.' The leather booklet stills, gold lettering shimmering under the overhead light. 'His name was Terence. Terence Murphy. Never Terry, only Ter or Terence – he didn't even have a middle name. Caroline didn't want to hear anything like it ever again once he'd left. I don't know why she called me Lola instead. I guessed she just liked it at the time. And it was from a different enough world to his. I guess ... well, I guess I like it now, too.'

There's a sharp, gravelly cry, something between a laugh and a sob – Oren, or is it the old woman? But all Lola cares about is her passport, slipping from Jonny's fingers so freely it's as if he was never interested in it in the first place. Her hand is a different matter though; she has to wrench it free to take it back, reclaim it as her own.

There are no more questions to answer. There's finally nothing left to say. Those hazel eyes catch hers, filled with everything and nothing, all at the same time, like she's caught him waking up from a dream.

Lola looks at her passport photo, at the face she knows is hers, but appears so different now. Above, she realises Jonny's hand is still lingering, empty fingers still outstretched.

But she doesn't take it.

She doesn't have to.

She can stand up by herself now.

The rest is just fantasy, a series of stupid mistakes, buried on this strip of land that everyone thinks belongs to them.

Epilogue

Of course the chickens trusted her. It wasn't as if any old human could upend their nest, but this girl's scent had been all over their master for weeks, and he was right at the top of their pecking order. Her new friend, well, he was a harder sell – unlike humans, chickens can identify the whole spectrum between black and white, and it couldn't have been more obvious that these two weren't related at all. So what was he doing in their nest with her too?

That didn't matter either once the chickens heard the dog baying as usual from behind the fence. That damn hound only ever cried for their master. If it was whining for these two, the chickens could be sure they were on steady ground. And the noise was frankly soothing compared to the indeterminate racket they were often expected to put up with. There might be plenty of real estate on this particular clifftop, but it sure came with a conflicting soundtrack. If it wasn't the humans, it was the sea, all fighting each other for ownership of the land, when in the end, it was only ever going to be the most aggressive plants that won.

It should have been obvious.

The plants were the only ones capable of putting down actual roots.

It took a while for the chickens to realise what these two humans were doing. There was no hauling of heavy buckets, nor sprinkling of delicious pellets, nor gentle storing of warm eggs in soft baskets. The humans came into their courtyard alone, dressed in their dirty browns and greys, looking over their shoulders, hands stuffed deep in their pockets. Little wonder then, the birds supposed, that they made for chicken house number three, rather than the ever-popular house number one. Everyone usually heads in there. But these two were looking for a hiding place.

So by then the chickens knew what was going on as these two humans knelt, muddling around deep in their sawdust, burying secrets in places they thought no one else would ever think to look. For a moment, the birds muddled around too, remembering secrets are sometimes delicious, like the irregular delicacy they once found jammed next to their master, his body cooling and hardening with every desperate peck.

But this is where these humans made their mistake.

For chickens could never countenance leather anywhere in their nest, no matter how deep it was hidden, no matter how well it was concealed.

It just smelled wrong, of a different kind of animal.

They scattered as the man dug it out of his pocket, both humans still obsessively watching their backs. A bright red case, full of strange things that didn't belong with the birds either. Because by then, the chickens also knew those cases. They knew they belonged with the humans, were always stashed deep in their pockets. The chickens had been living on top of this clifftop long enough to know the differences between their various predators.

It didn't take long to unearth the secret, once the humans had gone. It didn't take long to move it out into the open, leave it there for some other human to find.

There was nothing left other than dirt.

But there are some places it can never be fully buried.

Acknowledgements

Early in my attempts to become a novelist, a wise screenwriter friend told me it was simple: 25% talent, 25% graft, 25% connections and 25% luck.

Three books later I have finally realised the flaw in that equation: the 99% due to the editor.

To that end I owe a huge debt to my painstakingly incisive and patient editor, West Camel, my forthright and courageous publisher, Karen Sullivan, and of course, my long-suffering agent, Jon Wood. I know you're itching to cut all the adjectives from the previous sentence but I'm afraid in this context you'll just have to take them on the chin. I promise, with the best will in the world, to make it easier on all of us next time!

To Andrew Carey, an editor and friend of a similarly outstanding class, thank you for everything, not least for explaining the difference between Rangoon and Yangon to a naïve and idealistic production assistant one dark overnight shift in 2002.

To my early readers and dearest friends – Michelle Jacobs, Noa Bladon and the unflappable Jamie Crichton: thank you for always being eager to read a draft of absolute drivel and still seeming positive enough about it that I never totally lost heart.

And to the class of 95/96 – you all know who you are: never has a year been more formative. You may recognise parts of Beit Liora and its cast of characters, but this story is, thankfully, a complete work of fiction. Except for the part about Doron...

Lastly to my darling Oli, Liora, Guy, Ben and Trixie. I am